,28

DOUBLESPEAK

Also by Alisa Smith

Speakeasy

DOUBLESPEAK

ALISA SMITH

St. Martin's Press
New York

DOUBLESPEAK. Copyright © 2019 by Alisa Smith. All rights reserved. Printed in the United States of America. For information, address St. Martin's Press, 175 Fifth Avenue, New York, N.Y. 10010.

www.stmartins.com

Designed by Mary White

The Library of Congress Cataloging-in-Publication Data is available upon request.

ISBN 978-1-250-09785-9 (hardcover)
ISBN 978-1-250-09786-6 (ebook)

Our books may be purchased in bulk for promotional, educational, or business use. Please contact your local bookseller or the Macmillan Corporate and Premium Sales Department at 1-800-221-7945, extension 5442, or by email at MacmillanSpecialMarkets@macmillan.com.

First published in Canada by Douglas and McIntyre (2013) Ltd

First U.S. Edition: April 2019

10 9 8 7 6 5 4 3 2 1

In memory of Sheelagh

We two alone will sing like birds in the cage:
When thou dost ask me blessing, I'll kneel down,
And ask of thee forgiveness: so we'll live,
And pray, and sing, and tell old tales, and laugh
At gilded butterflies, and hear poor rogues
Talk of court news; and we'll talk with them too,
Who loses and who wins; who's in, who's out;
And take upon's the mystery of things,
As if we were God's spies.

—Shakespeare, King Lear

NOVEMBER 28, 1945

CHAPTER ONE

THE NEXT WAR

I FOLLOWED THE cairns one by one to the edge of the island, grey waves crashing against black rocks, until I could forget there was ever colour anywhere. In my heavy military parka with the wolf fur snugged around my face, all I saw were swirling snow and fog muffling me inside this isolated place—four miles long and two miles wide. If it weren't for the cairns, I wouldn't be able to navigate in this weather, but their shapes were familiar and I knew where I needed to go.

The pistol inside my jacket wouldn't freeze up before I needed it.

I paused where I could go no further unless I would swim. I couldn't see it today but I knew ice rimed the shore. My breath hung in the fog and then disappeared. I took off one moosehide glove, lined with grey-white fur, to look at my own flesh, and it was grey-white too. Ghostly. I told myself: I am becoming invisible.

I screwed on the silencer and cocked the weapon, a bolt-action Welrod 9 mm. Unmarked in case captured. Best for close, quick work, because I wouldn't have much time.

Cold seeped into my hand, the wind biting. My arm grew tired as I waited for the mists to part so that I could see my target. But my arm never shook, and the gun was comfortable in my grip. I'd done this many times before.

The noise when I fired was little more than a door slamming shut. It signalled a casual death, unnotable, the way life could be too. That was fitting.

I walked over to the target to assess how I'd done. The red was shocking in the grey world.

I smiled as I pulled the paper from the clips attached to the frame I had built. Dead centre, a perfect shot. Maybe I'd finally redeemed myself.

I wasn't always good at this. I had been excited when, last year, I was sent for field training at Camp X. After a military transport plane left me in Prince Rupert, I rode the CN railway across British Columbia, Alberta, Saskatchewan, Manitoba—three days to Ontario. From the station in Oshawa, a bumpy truck ride over dirt roads took me to the shores of Lake Ontario where there was an old farm estate, with white buildings laid out in vast fields bordered by maple forests. An old man wearing tweed rushed out of a brick house to shake my hand. "Terrence Bottomley, my dear. And you are?"

"Agent 342," I said.

"Very good," he said in his crisp English accent, and handed me a pistol.

I smiled at him, and thought that finally, I might be sent to Russia. Miss Maggie must want me to be ready.

My first class that afternoon was held in an old dairy barn, with eight men and one other woman. Lock picking—I did exceptionally well. Of course, they could not know I had considerable experience observing this craft in my past. From the shifty looks of the man who taught the class, who was only referred to as Agent 49, I guessed him to be a past thief himself. I had heard rumours that criminals of top ability were being released from prison in exchange for training the secret service. For the three weeks I was there, I was careful never to speak to him directly, in case he should sense the same thievery in me that I saw in him.

After that, things went downhill. I failed at target shooting. That's why I practised out on the tundra by myself every day it was possible to see through the fog. When it was not, I sweet-talked a set of keys to the indoor range from the Sergeant. I didn't want the men to see me do it, because the mocking and catcalls would be unbearable. I went after 9 p.m. when it was closed, and only once had to fend off the Sergeant's advances, though tactfully enough that he would not revoke my keys.

I was also mortified to learn that I was afraid of heights. I had not known until standing near the lip of an open aeroplane door high above Camp X. I couldn't seem to make my fingers let go of the ceiling strap until I retreated instead of leaping. I was supposed to be third, but soon everyone else had jumped, including the one other woman. When the green light went on again, I counted to three in my head and said *go*, and I went, feeling like I would throw up. I prayed never to have to do it again.

Wait, Miss Maggie said, wait. That was easy enough for her to say—time passes more quickly for those caught up in the power struggles of Washington. Those, I understood, occurred mostly at dinner parties. She claimed to find these tiresome. Miss Maggie was the top woman in the Office of Strategic Services, or the OSS—the innocuous name for the wartime spy agency of the United States. She had personally advised the President, but everyone still called her Miss Maggie. She was in espionage well before the war, and her old civilian moniker stuck to her. She probably liked it because it gave nothing away. What was her last name, rank, or function? No one knew, but everyone did know it was she who figured out the wiring for the Japanese Purple Machine. That was how the Allies cracked the code and defeated Japan in the Pacific. She plucked me from the Canadian navy, where she supervised me through OP-20-G, the US Navy's intelligence operation for the Pacific defence. There were a lot of rules in OP-20-G, and paper trails were required, even if classified. So she decamped and took me with her.

Three years later, I was still on Shemya, among the western-most of Alaska's Aleutian Islands, where the williwaw howled eternally and the airmen hurried to leave once their orders had expired. Only one skeleton air squadron, the radio operators and decryption remained. The base was being dismantled piece by piece. The soldier's war was over, but the war I was fighting was just beginning. I could see it would be lonely, at least for a while. Miss Maggie's predictions about the Soviet threat were not widely shared. I began spying on our allies the Russians the day I arrived, while others concerned themselves with the Germans and the Japanese. When Miss Maggie offered me this transfer, she prom-ised a promotion to second in command of my unit. But it wasn't long before my crew of twelve shrank to four, which was not a satis-fying sphere of influence.

There was still no sign I would be assigned to Russian field-work, as Miss Maggie had once hinted. This was a source of bitterness, since I had the perfect cover. Before the war, I did grad-uate work in Canada with the prominent linguist Dr. Phipps. He believed the Tlinkit tongue of Alaska was derived from Siberia, and was applying for permission from the Soviet government to study its tribal peoples. My language research was something I enjoyed for its own sake, and if I was involved in a major discovery, even a woman could hope for a professorship. Since women got the vote when I was a girl, we had made great strides in the universities. But Dr. Phipps had most likely chosen another protégé by now, amongst all the men returning from the service.

This hope for advancement was why I accepted the posting to Shemya. That and my shame at what I did to Link—as though by fleeing the location of a betrayal, my guilt could be closed up like an old house and left behind. Not so. Guilt is terribly portable, I have learned. It is not the house, but the suitcase you bring with you.

When I arrived on Shemya and buttoned up the crisp new uniform with the extra stripe, I clung to Miss Maggie's reassur-ance: I was serving my country. She said Canada, as well as the US, could not afford to be blindsided by the actions of our Russian allies, and I saw the wisdom in this. After V-E Day, there were an increasing number of disturbing cables from Berlin. There may have been something improper about my assignment that required it to remain so deeply concealed. Shemya's commander, Brigadier General Goodman, had never learned the true nature of my decryptions. On the other hand, if my work was so important that it was only meant for the highest levels of government to see, that suited me. My ambition also proved to be portable. I always wanted to make a name for myself somehow. When I was younger I admit I made some bad choices in pursuit of that aim, which put me on the wrong side of the law. Of course, Miss Maggie knew something about that also. She seemed to know most things.

I told myself to have patience, since the war had only been over for three months. I might yet get to Russia with Dr. Phipps, I thought. I could practically see it from here, and the Aleutian Islands reached toward it like a beckoning finger.

On the base there was a Quonset hut that passed for a library. The books were jammed tightly together on two jerry-rigged shelves, and I often revisited the natural history of the Aleutians. I did not need the author, Mr. McGillicuddy, to tell me about the rocky cliffs that surrounded Shemya like some Alcatraz, twenty-five feet high in the south and almost three hundred feet above sea level in the north, nor the shifting sand dunes like some misplaced corner of the Empty Quarter, nor the standing swamps of the short summer. There was not a single tree, nor hardly anything you could call a flower. From this book I learned about Shemya's invisible character. The Aleutian chain was formed by volcanoes, still considered active, which explained the steep mountains of the other islands that I flew over when I came here. The Aleutians were born in a sudden hot rage. But Shemya, sheared flat, was unique among them. It rose from the sea, levered up by the Pacific tectonic plate. Shemya continues to rise an inch or two each year. The island is a piece of the sea floor that was hidden for millennia and surfaced in one jarring moment.

I felt a certain sympathy for the place. I hated the idea of sudden exposure.

In this posting, at least I had a window to stare out, unlike the Royal Navy bunker in Victoria. But there, when I stepped outside, the world was always fresh and green and growing. The seasons were marked by a progression of buds unfurling: delicate snowdrops, extravagant rhododendrons, decadent roses. I felt in tune with that world, perhaps in part because I looked on these things with the same eyes as everyone around me while we fought a common enemy, the Japanese. Here, when I raised my head from decoding the Russian radio messages, all I saw outside the Quonset hut were swirling snow and grey light. I felt utterly alone.

My unit commander, Colonel Topping, was a grey-haired veteran of subterfuges that must have gone awry to dump him in this exile also. Then there was another woman under me, Marguerite—of course they would not have me lead men if they could help it. The one who was left, Sergeant Hall, was bitter about his position. I was his lieutenant. He slouched at his desk, surly, waiting desperately no doubt for his own orders to leave. Marguerite said she felt lucky to be deployed still, since the Forces made great efforts to pack up the other ladies as soon as hostilities ended. The men who were demobbed in September darted a surprised glance at us when the orders were announced and did not include our names. But they seemed happy enough to leave Shemya. They must have had something to go home to.

Sometimes I woke in the middle of the night and wondered what it was like to *feel*. Where did happiness go, where was love, exhilaration, or even rage? In social settings I had to tell my face to smile, because it was no longer natural to me. I looked tired all the time though I went to bed at 10 p.m. each night. I often woke up in a cold sweat. I was careful not to look at the clock so that I didn't fuss about how long I had been awake. My mind was not easy about Link.

Was he alive?

I found Link on the list of MIAs not long after I arrived in Alaska's frozen wasteland. Corporal Link Hughes, Royal Corps of Signals, Chindits Special Force, Burma Campaign: Missing in Action.

Would an outside observer think this was my fault? I had

played a role in his Burma posting, but surely a rational mind would blame Miss Maggie. She had forced me to report on my colleagues in Victoria, and I noted that Link, then a lieutenant in my decryption unit, had spoken with the Spanish Consul. I thought little of it at the time, since Spain remained neutral throughout the war. I had even met the Consul myself a year earlier at a party hosted by the Lieutenant-Governor. But I should have known nothing was innocent in war: neither what Link did, nor what Miss Maggie asked me to do. She knew that the Consul was providing intelligence to the Japanese. That made Link the traitor she'd been looking for, and she punished him with a hopeless mission behind the front lines, busted down to corporal. Less responsibility, more danger, all to serve her message: she could do as she wanted with him.

The best I could hope for was that Link was a prisoner of war. Yet that was not a thing to wish on anyone. Many Allied prisoners were being found on Pacific islands where they had been held by the Japanese. Emaciation, disease, interrogation, and torture. They were mainly broken. This the public was not told about, of course, since it would dampen our triumph at winning the war. But I knew. I saw the intelligence in its raw form. It was the only time I hated knowing more than other people.

I still kept an article I had clipped out about the USS *Yorktown* after the Midway battle. Our sigint, or signals intelligence, could not prevent all disasters at sea, and when the Japanese announced that they sank the ship, I broke down and left my post. It was Link that brought me the news of its survival. The Japanese planes had left the battlefield before the sinking was complete. All our men had lived. The *Yorktown* was my proof that resurrection was possible. The article was tacked above my bunk, as it had been on the base in Victoria, though the paper had become brittle.

There was a map of Burma above my bed also. During sleepless nights I memorized the names of rivers and towns. I circled the places where prisoners were found. But if Link was alive, I knew he could be anywhere. The Japanese shipped their prisoners throughout Asia to wherever they needed slave labour. Now that the POWs were being brought home, I watched the repatriation lists, but Link's name was never on them.

Link was the second of my two badly chosen men. One dead, and the other exiled.

I had opened my heart to Link, something very rare for me. Miss Maggie understood that and I knew she would always doubt my loyalty. I assumed that Colonel Topping was watching me, reporting my actions, my words, maybe even my facial expressions back to Miss Maggie. After all, he had plenty of free time, since he did no decryptions himself but relied on our summaries. Sometimes my hand shook at awkward times, and I would shove it in my pocket. Except when I was decrypting, which I still got lost in, my thoughts darted everywhere, never settling. She had me secured in a petri dish and it was not possible to stray. We lived in group dormitories. Every outsider who visited Shemya had to come by ship or aeroplane, and each name was recorded on a manifest. From the time I arrived, I had only left the base for short leaves to Anchorage or Skagway, and always with others from my unit. I was never unobserved. I had been dependable for three years, doing her bidding.

But Miss Maggie's promises turned out to be hollow.

I pushed my finger through the hole in the centre of the target, a perfect bull's eye. I was good at this now. I was tempted to mail my paper targets to Miss Maggie so she would know it.

I retraced my steps back to the barracks, the williwaw blowing the fog away suddenly, like it had never been, and I loosened my hood. It was not winter quite yet. It only felt like it most of the time on Shemya. The Aleutians are the frontier where the North Pacific meets the Bering Sea. Siberia didn't scare me. I was already living it. The tundra felt bouncy under my boots. The earth shivered. I was walking over the peat bog, which was saturated with water, and the ground itself rippled away from me like waves. It was not a good feeling, but I'd passed over this spot many times without mishap.

Goddamn it, why did I care what Miss Maggie thought of me?

I could imagine her caustic words already. "A target is a bit of paper," she would say. "It's quite another thing to kill a man."

CHAPTER TWO

DECEMBER 7, 1945—MORNING

I STARED OUT the porthole, cupping my hand against the glare, soaking up the golden towers and pagodas that gleamed above the trees. Bangkok was like a magical kingdom, different from anything I'd ever known. Until I met Bill Bagley, I'd never ventured from Seattle except to go to the lake with my mother when I was a boy. Bill's Clockwork Gang took me a few hundred miles north over the Canadian border, but that was the extent of my previous travels. So I was annoyed that Shively wouldn't even let me stand on deck. Keep a low profile, he said. What a stick in the mud. But his authority came from Bill, so I listened. I'd been forced to listen to Shively ever since he arrived out of the blue last month with Bill's message at my saloon in Sequim, Washington. I had been both shocked and flattered to be summoned by a man I had thought dead for three years.

Shively could hustle despite a game leg, and he poked me in the ribs to hurry me off the ship. Wincing, I did my best to stare about me. The busy port was lined with warehouses with huge logs piled outside for loading, and elephants stood nearby. One picked up a log easily in its curled trunk, and I felt a boyish excitement that I was going to live in this real-life circus. The air was hot and sticky, and I caught a glimpse of palm trees beyond the warehouses. A man bicycled by, two dead chickens swinging from his handlebars. He rang his bell and I jumped out of the way. Barefoot children slurped tea from abandoned cups on outdoor tables and a shopkeeper shook his fist in rage. Women wrapped in bright fabric thronged the side streets, with heavy rows of silver baubles covering their chests, brightly embroidered purses slung across their shoulders, and large baskets carried with ease on their heads. One woman had a long neck ringed with brass. She must belong to some remote tribe. It was better than any picture book, but Shively did not slow his pace. Rather, he shoved me into a waiting automobile, twenty years out of date but with the chrome polished to a high shine.

"I'd like to get a look around," I grumbled. The man hadn't let me out of his sight during the entire two-week journey from Seattle, and I was tired of his bossiness. He hadn't a shred of conversation in him, and he scarcely let me talk to anyone else. His only outburst had been a boast. His boss—he was always coy on this point, stating no name—lived like a king, he said. Yet Shively had booked us in second class. He happily admitted he wasn't fit for the formal dining room, and if he couldn't go, I couldn't either. He planned to stick to me "like a limpet," he said. This he certainly did. Really, we should have travelled steerage for him to fit in properly, but I was glad he hadn't dragged us down that far. I pretended to myself that he was my servant and prayed he would keep his mouth shut so the other passengers wouldn't hear him ordering me around instead.

"You'll soon have plenty of time to stare about like an imbecile," was all he said, climbing in beside me and slamming the door.

As the car inched through the crowds of dark men in sarongs, I wondered if this foreign place would ever feel like home. Once we left the docks, the nest of streets had no clear plan, weaving between thatch-roofed houses crammed tight together. Men stood at the corners with large, hand-cranked machines, festooned with bells that jangled faintly as the giant gears turned. I lowered the window and stuck my head out to get a better look at what they were doing, but it was clear from the general smell that there was no modern sewer system. I spun the handle up fast.

"Satisfied?" Shively said. "That's Bangkok."

He was a master of the obvious.

I was glad when the crazed warren of streets opened to a boulevard lined with stately stone buildings in a familiar European style. I could have imagined I was in Paris, if I ignored the occasional strange glimpse of a golden tower. The shine was such that I knew the gold had to be real, and I wondered at the wealth of this country.

"Weren't they touched by the war?" I asked.

"Use your eyes," Shively said in his usual informative way. After a pause he relented. "Collaborators," he said. "Knew where their bread was buttered."

"Do you think they'll be punished in the peace treaties?"

He shrugged. "They did a switcheroo before the war ended." As we pulled up in front of the station, Shively gave a sigh. "Here at last."

The Hua Lamphong Railway Station was not what I had expected from the name. With the magisterial white columns out front, it looked Italian rather than Oriental, which led me to hope that Bill did not have a symbolic turn of mind. Italians had a long history of revenge, from the Inquisition to the mafia. My palms were sweaty, I realized. I unclenched my hands.

Bill was the one that wanted to see me, I reminded myself. If he had vengeance on his mind, why go to the bother and expense of dragging me around the world?

Because he is supposed to be dead in America and cannot show his face there, my doubting mind replied. Because no one knows I am here and my disappearance would not be remarked upon.

I told myself to buck up. I had been prepared to die that day in Washington with Bill when the cops, armed to the teeth, had us surrounded. Of course it wasn't a purely noble sentiment. The only alternative to death was capture, and I would be sentenced to life in jail with the man I hated for what he did to Lena, the gutsiest beauty I had ever known. While my hate had burned a long time, my bravery was unfortunately of shorter duration and, when not used that day, had expired. I was just cowardly me again. Once I raced out the back door away from the cops, I was free of Bill and that was suddenly the best thing I could imagine. Plus, I was rather more attached to this life than I had realized. I suppose that must be a persistent impulse or we would all off ourselves when the loneliness lasted too long.

So why was I going back to Bill when once my strongest desire was to be free of him?

I had questioned myself closely on this point on the long voyage over, when I had nothing to do but stare out to sea. Bill would never be a saint, I knew that, but if he was off the drugs, his genius would return. He was the criminal equivalent of an Olympic athlete. Only Bill could defeat the hangman and set himself up as a kingpin in Siam like it was the most natural thing in the world. I wanted to be part of his adventures once more.

"You done your lollygagging?" Shively asked. "We got no time to waste. We ain't there, he'll leave, and it'll be another month till we can come again."

"You don't know where he goes in the meantime?"

Shively didn't answer. Smugly, I thought to myself that he did not know. I jumped out of the car to follow him as he weaved through the crowd, bobbing and limping. He hurried through the main hall where tickets were sold under a high curved roof, and we passed little shops with the strange curlicues of the Siamese language adorning everything. It hit me that I was totally dependent on Shively. And on Bill. This put me at a serious disadvantage. What if Bill was crazy?

True, he was always crazy. Could he be even crazier than when I last saw him?

Too late to worry now that I was seven thousand miles from home. I was in it up to the neck.

Before I could make sense of the chaos inside the station, Shively deposited me on the platform where the trains pulled in. There were some old steam engines on the tracks, hissing and sighing. The destination signs were in English, which was a relief, even though the place names didn't mean a thing to me. We stopped beside a sign that said Chiang Mai and a clock intoned the twelve strokes of noon.

I found myself pulled into a fierce bear hug. I tensed up, waiting for my bones to be crushed.

"By God, you're here at last," Bill said.

Tears came to my eyes. Damn them. But he called me by the name I had not heard for thirteen years. *By God.* Like I was capable of surprising people with my actions. Byron Godfrey would never surprise anyone.

"A good chance to see the world on someone else's dime," I said, recovering myself. I smiled and stepped back to inspect him. He was tanned and wore a white linen suit like he'd stepped from a photograph of the British Raj. He had been ashen when I last saw him, dishevelled and undone. Now he was buttoned down too tight, maybe. But only he knew what he needed to do to hold himself together. It would have taken immense willpower to escape his fierce addiction, but willpower was something he had in spades.

"I look good, don't I," he grinned.

Already, I was remembering his flaws—Bill Bagley was not a humble man.

"I better tell you," he said, "I go by William Yardley now. Think you can remember that?" He laughed so hard that he wiped the tears from his eyes. It was a ridiculous alias and I guess he knew it. "You can still call me Bill."

"That's good. I can't imagine you any other way." I wondered why on earth he bothered with such a flimsy ruse, but I guess some evasion on official documents was necessary. Bill Bagley was supposed to be dead, while no one had such expectations of William Yardley.

"Let's get out of this fishbowl and I'll show you my place." He took my elbow and I realized that Shively had melted away. Well good riddance, I thought, as we walked across the platform and back into the main hall.

"We're not taking a train?"

"My place in Bangkok is more comfortable. You can get settled before we think of trips. We'll make some plans together, just like old times."

I wanted to ask him, was he not angry at me? But he seemed so far from it, I didn't want to spoil things. I supposed he could still murder me when we got somewhere private, but he had a childlike delight on his face that made this seem impossible. Unless the thought of murder could delight him? No, don't be a fool, Byron.

"I have a few questions," I said cautiously. Like how the hell did he get out of prison? I mean, I knew from the papers he had escaped numerous times after I last saw him thirteen years ago, so I guess he had honed that skill. Still, you would think security on death row would be tighter. But Bill understood that the greatest weakness in every system was human weakness, and he always knew how to exploit that.

"We'll have a drink and catch up. At my palazzo." He looked at me sideways to judge my reaction to this news.

"You have a palazzo?"

"Yep."

"What's a palazzo?" I said, and he laughed.

IT WAS A mansion on the river. The Chao Phraya, he told me, acting the tour guide as we stepped onto a large boat that must have been his because there was nobody on it but us and the tillerman. All the other boats leaving the busy pier were packed. His boat was long and skinny and low, painted with gold patterns, and had an ornate wood roof that served as shelter from the sun. Mats of green plants floated downriver slowly, and a white bird with long legs perched on its patch. It was undisturbed as our boat passed nearby. It found peace in chaos, somehow. Bill pointed out a spot on the opposite bank just north from where we set off.

"Palazzo is an Italian word?" I hazarded as we moved smoothly through the brown water toward it, and he nodded. I had to admit I was impressed. The mansion had two curving staircases leading to immense front doors, and it overlooked the river with a commanding air. The grounds were large, and untamed trees mingled with severe shrubberies. "Was Siam an Italian colony?"

"No," he said. I expected to be mocked for my mistake, but Bill carried on. He must have developed more sympathy for fools like me in his second life. "It was never colonized, which they're proud of. The Japs let them choose a quiet takeover during the war in the spirit of Asian brotherhood. Burma was British and had the hell pounded out of it. It's a mess. That's why I take my rest here."

"You've been in Burma, too?" I wished I'd paid it more mind. I had stared many hours at an atlas aboard the ship, but I had focused on Siam, the place I was headed, as though by tracing the country's circuitous outline I could understand what might happen once I was inside it. I had not imagined this, so I supposed, as Shively had happily pointed out, I was wasting my time. All I had made out was the shape of an elephant's head, with a long trunk hanging down. Burma crowded the elephant's forehead and China kissed the top of it, while French Indo-China was under its ear. All those places sounded exotic to this Washington boy.

"That's where my profit comes from. I'll explain later." We stepped off the boat at his dock, and native servants materialized to take our bags while he touched my elbow to guide me up the smooth gravel path. I marvelled at this new Bill, the genteel host. We sat down on rattan chairs under a shade umbrella, and a servant deposited a tray of cocktails onto a curiously carved table. After he bowed and departed, Bill passed me a martini and raised his glass to me.

"I'm about to start some new adventures, and I don't want them to be lost," Bill said. "So I'm glad to have my chronicler back."

"What do you mean?" I stared at him wildly.

"All your scribblings. Very entertaining."

Holy Jesus. The journal that I had lost after I ran away from our last heist—did he have it? The note where I said farewell and I love you to his own girl, Lena? And those loose-leaf pages where I declared I hated him? Where I said he was crazy after I witnessed him murder a helpless old man? Where I admitted I left a clue for the police to find us?

I dropped my glass onto the paving stones and ran.

I made it as far as the dock hanging over the murky brown river. I had torn off my blazer and kicked off my shoes, ready to jump in and swim away as fast as the current would take me, but I found myself in a cobra squeeze.

"Be still, sahib," a man whispered in my ear.

I could not see him because he had grabbed me from behind. I kept kicking but ineffectually as a child. Well, this was humiliating. He was evidently very tall, enough so to hold me off the ground. Then he dropped me and wrenched one of my arms behind my back and I groaned with the pain. There was a singing of metal, dagger from scabbard, and with his free hand he held a blade at my throat. I stopped struggling.

"The river is full of cholera," Bill said as he reached the dock at a saunter. "Dass is only thinking of your safety."

"He has a funny way of showing it."

Bill waved his hand and Dass put down the blade. I realized I had been holding my breath and exhaled. Dass busied himself tying my ankles with rope loose enough that I could walk—but not run again. Bill handed me another cocktail.

"Come on, let's talk this out." He laughed as we headed up the path from the river for the second time today. "No wonder you got away from the cops. You're damn fast."

"Did they follow me?"

"No. They were happy to get Bill Bagley."

"Jesus, Bill, you can't know how sorry I've been all these years." I slumped down in the seat of the lawn chair.

"Water under the bridge."

I swatted a biting insect on my ankle. Tsetse fly? I wondered. Everything tropical and deadly I had ever read about in *National Geographic* as a boy was coming back to haunt me.

"It wasn't on account of you I got nabbed," he said. "I talked to Detective Brooke a day and a night when he tried to get my confession, and I got his story too. He never found that note you left. He lost us before the cabin in Chilliwack. Was over a month till that old man was found. Not much was left of him. A bear got there first and there was no discovery of human harm." Bill's shoulders twitched and he looked away. "I shouldn't have killed him. I wasn't in my right mind and I don't remember much from those days. I was disturbed when I first read it in your diary. I think this next part of my life won't be so dark. But will you see it my way? I'll have to wait and see. You're a hard judge of a man."

I pressed the cold glass against my forehead. He was really rubbing my nose in it, showing me he could sniff out any secret I had. That damn lawyer must have betrayed me. How else would Bill get the key to the safety deposit box where I kept my journal? It was only to be opened on my death and given to Lena. Then she would know she did right to leave Bill, when she read the evil he'd done. I guess he knew that now.

"I've changed too. I wasn't objective back then."

"For damn sure. You only had one objective in your eye. My Lena. But I know I fucked that up myself. I was high as a kite the whole time on death row. But tell me, who wants to look at the world straight when he's just ticking down the clock till he gets a noose round his neck? Now that I made it out, I regret my state when Lena came."

"She visited you?" I thrummed my fingers on the arms of the chair. What did she do that for? Surely she was through with Bill after he hit her that last time and she ran away. I supposed anybody would respond to a dying man's request.

"Yes, By God." He stared into the distance, not speaking for a minute. "I was not at my best. I'd like her to know me now. God, quitting was hard. But whenever I felt tempted by the drugs, I

29

read again what you wrote and it stayed my arm. I didn't want to be out of control like that. I'll kill a man who means to harm me, but someone who never hurt a fly—well, that's not right. I'm clean for good."

I finished my cocktail and placed it back on the table, and the fellow Dass who had trussed me up like a pig silently brought another pitcher and set it down as though our encounter had never happened. This was a strange country, I thought. I waited for Dass to retreat before I asked my next question, though I finally gave up as he lurked awaiting orders in the middle distance. If he could hear us, I guessed Bill must trust him, so I had no choice in the matter. Once you were in his circle he did not hold back. I was unnerved to think Dass might know everything about me, while I knew nothing of him. I was at a disadvantage, as usual.

"So if it wasn't my note, how did we get found?" I asked.

"Those damn people at the café. Remember where we had our last coffee before the shootout? I'd thought they were okay. That's another reason to stay clean—I lost my judgment. There was a reward and they called us in. That's why the Whatcom County cops came instead of federal men. That really pissed off old Detective Brooke," Bill smirked. "Him and his scientific methods. Those hicks made him look a fool."

A wild throaty call came from the trees, and my eye fixed on a blue bird with a tail over a foot long sitting on a hooked branch above us, bobbing slightly. "What's that?"

"Some drongo thingumabob." He raised his voice. "Dass?"

The Indian walked up to us and looked where Bill pointed. "Greater Racket-Tailed Drongo."

"You need any animal name or its habits and Dass is your man. He keeps me alive in the jungles. You want to try a monkey curry?"

"It's made from actual monkey meat?"

"Yep."

"No thanks." I felt uneasy at the thought of wandering through jungles. Would there be tigers? I'd seen them at the Seattle zoo, and they had evil in their eyes when they stared at me, hypnotically, from behind the bars of their cage. They had no use for mercy. I would not want to meet one in the wild.

"Dass, could you get us some sandwiches?"

Dass nodded and walked up to the house. He was a strangely elegant sight in his billowy trousers, white jacket, and pink turban.

I felt somehow lighter with his hovering presence gone. I had a thousand questions to ask Bill, like the nature of what he did here that made him so rich. But this was a new curiosity, and I would satisfy the older ones first. I had all the time in the world, apparently, since I was roped up to stay awhile.

"How did you get out of New Westminster jail? It was never reported, even though it was your biggest escape."

"Not mine. I have a *benefactor.*" He spit out the word. His face had a dark and frightening look which revealed the old Bill was still in there, even off the coke. "Which turns out to be the worst thing that could happen to a man. It's slavery."

"Not so bad as that, surely. You were sentenced to death and instead you have all this." I swept my outstretched arm to take in the grounds and ended by pointing my hand, palm up like a vaudeville host, at the mansion.

"I'll grant you that." He smiled now. He poured more liquid from the pitcher for me, and I realized I was getting pretty drunk. "I like this place. It was built by a wealthy Siamese businessman who fell in love with a handmaiden at the royal court. He wanted this mansion to woo her, and it worked. They lived here until they died within a year of each other, not long before the war."

"So who's your benefactor?"

Bill sat there silently, though he downed the rest of his drink and refilled his glass to the brim. The breeze through the palm trees made them rustle like dry husks. "This stuff packs a punch," he said. "You like it?"

I supposed I shouldn't have asked about the benefactor. Anybody that could hold power over Bill must be pretty fearsome. It was probably in my best interest to steer clear of him.

"Yes." We'd moved on from martinis to gin and tonic, which

made me think of quinine, and then malaria. Could you get malaria here? I thought so. I'd wanted to ask my doctor about it before I left but my destination was supposed to be a secret. I drew circles on the condensation left on the glass surface of the table, following the intricate patterns of the dark wood carving visible underneath. "That stuff I wrote about Lena. I thought I was going to die or I wouldn't have said it."

"Anybody would be crazy *not* to want her. She was one hell of a gal. But only one man got her and that's Bill Bagley. Since you laid it all out there I saw that *she* never cheated. That's all I care about."

I could not help glaring at him. I was over her. Time saw to that. If we do not die of something, we will heal. But he didn't have to point out that she never gave a sweet damn about me. He put his feet up on a stool and leaned back, his hands cupped behind his head, utterly comfortable and in control, like the old Bill had always been. I was sweating like a dog in this unfamiliar heat, even in the shade, but Bill looked cool as the Canadian fall. I should get a Panama hat like his, I reckoned.

"Look, if you want me to write your chronicles, here are my conditions. I need to be free to write how I want. That means I'll hide my journal, and I'll do a better job of it this time. So don't even bother trying to find it."

"I don't want no one to find it. I'll take it out of your hide if they do. You got to learn to be more suspicious. This country is full of snakes. Don't trust no one except me. Deal?"

He held out his hand to me, and after a moment's hesitation, I shook it.

"We're partners again, By God."

"Partners," I said, raising my glass to him and smiling.

Partners in what? It struck me that I didn't know. Guess I already helped him rob banks back in the day, so it couldn't be worse than that. Could it? I thought, uneasily, as I looked at his palazzo and its grand archways. Maybe riches came cheaper here.

"So," Bill said, pressing a cool glass to his cheek. "To complete the mending of my past mistakes, I'm inviting Lena here to join us."

"Lena?" I repeated. The thought of seeing her again set off an alarm clock in my soul, and it was a call I did not want to hear. I'd been head over heels, but for her it was all Bill, Bill, Bill. Getting over her had taken a long time, and it had made me look too critically on all the other women I had met since. She'd done me no good. A thousand objections to Bill's scheme came to mind, but I landed on the safest one.

"She thinks you're dead."

"That's fixed easily enough. You thought I was dead too." He smiled. "Have I ever looked more alive to you?"

Glumly, I thought he looked pretty much as good as when I first met him, even if more than ten years had passed. You could read it in his features, those years, but he had kept his resemblance to Clark Gable, when he smiled. I studied him from the corner of my eye. He'd already stopped smiling and looked nervous instead. Bringing her here seemed to be a big deal for him. I didn't want him to get Lena back. He'd done her too many wrongs. My back felt stiff in the rattan chair and I shifted uncomfortably.

"Why would she come? Been a long time."

Bill took my blunt statement without blinking, his blue eyes cold and unreadable. "I consider every possibility, By God. That's why I succeeded at robbing banks. I have some bait to bring her here."

I wondered if that bait was me and my heart leapt. Would she come for me? I told myself quickly not to be stupid. Bill was staring into the distance, through me. I was not it. I was never it. The drongo bird squawked again from the tree and I thought its voice ugly now. I swatted the mosquitos plaguing my ankles through my thin socks, then made myself fold my hands together in my lap, calmly.

I sat and waited for him to tell me who or what was so interesting, when I was not.

CHAPTER THREE

AMERICA'S NAZIS

WHEN THE WAR was still on, the airmen on Shemya assumed, quite naturally, that my radio unit was listening to Japanese communications. But that duty was left to the team on Adak Island. We simply forwarded the Japanese news from them to maintain our cover, because my unit, the 1085th Signals Service Company, was attached to the wartime Office of Strategic Services. I was designated the Canadian liaison, which gave me an ambiguous status that Miss Maggie found useful. In fact, I reported only to her.

I had started to share her paranoia about the Soviets. Even during the war, when the lines were more clearly drawn and our countries were united against Nazi Germany, Russia remained neutral to our other enemy, Japan. From the Shemya airfield, we sometimes ran bombing missions to Paramushiro, a Japanese island base, and the Russians let us fly over Kamchatka on the way. But due to their pact with Japan, they interned any American pilots who went down over Russian terrain. After confiscating their winter gear for Soviet soldiers to wear on the Eastern Front, they shipped the Americans to Siberian camps. They were freezing in their replacement rags and always short of rations. It was not much better than how enemy soldiers were treated.

One lost B-25 stood out in my mind. I did not normally pay attention to the comings and goings of the bombers, since it happened so often. But that night I could not sleep because, for once, there was no fog muffling the base. A distant noise woke me up, a man yelling on the runway, clear as though he was just outside my hut. The dawn blued the dorm windows just after 4 a.m., since it was June. I went for a walk in the unfamiliar brightness and watched them arming the bombers. One man I noticed in particular because he looked nervous—the seasoned pilots had learned to swagger to hide their natural fear of death. This man must have been a civilian in a non-combat specialty because he was carrying photographic equipment. I had the sudden thought that this B-25 was on an aerial reconnaissance of Russia, and the Japanese mission was merely a pretext. The rest of the squadron returned, but not that plane. It was shot down by the Japanese, they said. A crew went out later, searching, and located the plane on the ice at Petropavlovsk. The men were not in it, no sign of blood, but they never answered their portable radio. They were the only downed pilots in Kamchatka that had never been found alive or dead. Around that time, Russian cables arrived that I was not able to decipher. They had changed their coding system. I was sure they had captured our pilots, and that was when I realized Miss Maggie was right: the Russians were the enemy for the coming days.

I had to admit I enjoyed the Russian work. I was in my element. I was fluent in Russian, while my Japanese had only ever been tolerable after six months of training, so that I depended on the language specialists when I was stationed in Victoria. I was not alone in that. Most of the cryptanalysts had not been fluent speakers—the government had not trusted the naturalized Japanese in North America. We had been chosen for our skills in cracking puzzles and our ability to pick up language quickly. Some of the girls were Oxford mathematicians and I was intimidated by them. But I had studied Russian for five years before the war, and now the other cryptanalysts came to me. Well, not all of them. Some of the men had not wanted me over them as lieutenant. I knew that. The blue braid on my sleeve would always be a reminder that they need not treat me equally. The men of my rank wore gold.

I paused my pencil over my decoding sheet. It was a cable to Moscow from a Soviet agent in Germany. After the surrender, every Allied nation carved out its piece of Berlin, and the Nazis were being interrogated. Americans, British, French, and Russians all had their teams on the ground, hunting them down. There was a trial underway at Nuremberg about the death camps. It would be a new era of justice, where war crimes would be punished not by mob mentality but by rule of law. Ruthless acts would be banished forever from mankind.

That was the theory, anyway.

I put down my pencil and wiped my hands over my face. Since the surrender, the Soviets had been massing their armies and spies in Eastern Europe, and I was convinced they had dreams of empire. Meanwhile, in their coded cables, they claimed that the Americans were trying to recruit Nazi secret service agents. I hadn't believed it, at first. It ran counter to the directives of the brass in US army intelligence, who wanted to round up every single Nazi for trial. I had told myself it was just Russian paranoia, but now the details were getting too specific to brush aside. Army intelligence was a different creature than the OSS had been. I read the cable over once more.

BERLIN—Accelerate operation POLE CAT. *Agent 37 recruited von Roth, an* SS *officer with access to Politburo files during occupation of Ukraine. Urgent to retrieve him from American sector.*

I picked up the sheet of paper scrawled with my decryption and walked across the room to Marguerite's desk. Sergeant Hall was not here, which was good, because he did not have clearance for the Berlin cables. He only worked on Romania, which chafed him because it was less important and he knew it.

"It's about POLE CAT," I said.

She stared at the sheet of paper until I got tired of holding it and put it on top of her cluttered desk.

"Agent 37. That is one of ours in Berlin," she said finally.

I slumped into the chair beside her desk. "The whole point of this damn war was to destroy the Nazis." I pulled at my lapel to look at the new silver bar above my pocket. "Aleutian Islands Campaign" was embossed on the metal along with a lightning bolt. I had felt a surge of pride when I pinned it on the month before—I had served my country as well as any man. Our unit had gotten a letter from President Truman too, though the service we were congratulated for was left vague. We were the secret service, after all. "And now we're recruiting them?"

It seemed beyond belief. The war was barely over, and already the Allies were enlisting Nazis for their own spy agencies. Fighting over them, in fact, such that at least one ss officer, though stationed in faraway Berlin, was already my colleague. From my front-row seat in decryption, I knew that allegiances were shifting by the hour. The war was moving from the battlefield to the backrooms. No nation, or person, was permanently classed as friend or enemy. I had come to terms with this. But to make allies of ranking Nazis from the notorious ss was too much for me. They had embraced a doctrine of pure evil, which made systematic torture and murder a norm. They had crossed over to a dark place and I did not believe they could return. I pulled off my campaign medal and shoved it in my pocket. If this was what my work had been for, I had no pride in wearing it.

"The Soviets could be lying," Marguerite said. "If they show a paper trail that we recruited the Nazis first, then they can use them too, while making us look like the bad guys." I was grateful to her for trying to find some better explanation. But I didn't believe it, and I didn't think she did either. Shortly after we got our medal, there was an executive order disbanding the oss—officially, at least. Those of us in decryption and espionage were left in a holding pattern, transferred to the War Department under a smaller division now called the Strategic Services Unit. It was a fight to survive. Who was still relevant?

Marguerite tipped a cigarette pack and pulled one out, leaning back in her chair as she lit it. She squinted against the smoke. I noticed for the first time that her eyes looked hard. She was not the same naïve French girl I had met on the navy base in Victoria four years ago.

"*Merde,*" she said. "Everything is different now."

I DIDN'T FEEL any better for having slept on the news. Winter had returned, and mornings in the Quonset hut were hard to take. Not just cold, but lonelier now. Marguerite and I had a dorm to ourselves since the other women who served on Shemya went home the month before, to become wives and mothers again. For some of them, I thought, that existence would feel pale against the urgency of their wartime mission. I dipped a facecloth in the can of water I'd put on the oil stove last night to warm, so I wouldn't have to shock myself awake. Cold air poured through the cracks of the wood-panel floor and into the soles of my slippers. It was ironic that much of the timber for the Alaska bases came from Russia. Alaskan mills had not been able to supply wood at the pace demanded. Russia's economy had been decimated by the war on the German front and they would take anything they could get. So now their wood became houses for the people who would spy on them.

"Has Miss M said anything about that cable?" Marguerite asked as she brushed her hair. She must have been thinking about it all night, as I was.

"Yes." I had received a message from her in our private code, for which we each had matching one-time pads.

"And?" she paused her brush, and the engraved silver shone in the flickering light from the drum stove.

"She said not to tell Colonel Topping about it yet. We should just keep monitoring the situation." Sometimes I wondered what Colonel Topping's purpose was, since I never reported anything of interest to him. I supposed he had to be there so there was not a woman in charge—like me.

I whipped off my pajamas and changed as quickly as possible into my uniform to keep the freezing air off my skin. First thick wool tights, then the double-serge skirt. I buttoned up the collar shirt and knotted the tie. I had requested casual khakis like the men's, though I tailored my skirts shorter than regulation length after they arrived. These were the small advantages of my obscure posting. Since women officers had never before served as Canadian liaisons in the American forces, I could invent my own uniform. At my request, Miss Maggie had sent it from New York, along with one for Marguerite. She included a sarcastic note about couture garments not being part of the budget, but I knew that her budget grew as the war grew.

It did not matter your nationality or branch of service: mountains were quietly moved. We were pulled from the army, navy, and air force; from America, Britain, Canada, New Zealand, and Australia. Valuable civilians were made officers overnight. Marguerite said there were six thousand OSS personnel working stateside, mostly out of Washington and New York, and eight thousand more served overseas. I had no idea who Miss Maggie herself reported to, but the head of the OSS, General Donovan, reported only to the President. We were a shadow army.

"Do you think that means she's okay with it?" Marguerite asked.

Neither of us could bring ourselves to say the word Nazi out loud. Of course, we had developed a natural circumspection after years in secret work, but there was something particularly ominous about all this. If it was true that Nazis were being recruited, the person who ran the operation was cold beyond anything we had ever seen. Millions of murders were nothing to this spymaster. But the more I thought about it, the more I believed it. No one knew the Soviets better than the Nazi intelligence service, since they had occupied parts of the USSR for almost three years. The Western allies were watching Communist Russia with growing suspicion, and no one was more anti-Communist than a fascist. It was a grim logic.

"Who ever knows what she's thinking?" I said.

I did not mention that Miss Maggie had opened a new private channel of communication with me for anything about the Nazi development. That did not tell me, though, whether she was for or against it.

"You going to the runway?" Marguerite asked as she shimmied into her tights.

"Of course. I'll meet you there when I hear the plane." I knew she had the day off, while my shift was starting in ten minutes. But everyone dropped what they were doing when the transport arrived, even though it was often random what supplies were on it and how much time had passed since they were ordered. We didn't care. It was our only connection to the outside world.

I walked across the base. The Quonsets were scattered like overturned oil drums, many unoccupied, adding to the sense that my existence was a sort of rubbish. Now that the war was over, I wondered, where would the money come from to continue our work? The Russian cables were stepping up. Every country they liberated in Europe they considered fair game as wartime spoils. The Soviets were rounding up ethnic Germans and shipping them to Siberian work camps in retaliation for the invasion of Russia. Here on Shemya, I was closer to Siberia than I was to my home in Victoria. This nearness to the gulags made the future feel grim and grey.

As I entered the empty "L" Hut, the sad remnant of my decryption unit, I wondered if they would ship all the extra desks back to the Lower 48, or if it wasn't worth the bother and one day soon we'd just pile them in a heap and burn them. I guess the Japanese work I did before was something anyone could be proud of, since we won the war against them. But really, was that not the result of dropping atom bombs? All my cleverness was just so much fancy dancing. Sitting down at my desk, I drew flowers idly in the corner of my decryption sheet, and I sighed. Since President Truman shut down the oss and demoted us to the Strategic Services Unit, or ssu, no one knew exactly what we were supposed to do. Well, maybe Miss Maggie did, but she wasn't telling.

From the corner of my desk I grabbed the day's cables, which I'd retrieved from a locked cabinet on my way in. The process we had to reverse had three steps. First, the Soviet agent would consult his master codebook, where each word had a four-digit number assigned to it. Then, he would pick a page out of a second book of randomized four-digit numbers, called the additive keys, and match each master number of the message with this new number, going by sequence on the page. Finally, he would add together these two numbers, dropping any extra digit, in a technique called modulo zero. In this world, eight plus four equalled two. In that way, each word's code remained four digits long. These random four-digit sequences were supposed to be unbreakable if you didn't have the matching book of additive keys, but luckily for us, the Soviets sometimes used the same page twice. A new book could not always be obtained in war conditions, or people just made mistakes. We found the reuse by painstaking searches for common openings and closings, like "To Moscow" or "Part 2 of 2." That gave us depth, so if we could find common four-digit numerals between two messages, we could determine the underlying code for those words. Then, we might wrestle out a few more based on context. We had quite a few listed in the master codebook we were constructing, which would one day mirror the Soviet's entirely. Probably they would change encryption methods before then, but one could dream. It was my pride to fill in another page, though this might take weeks or even months of work. Sometimes we received solved batches from a unit in Berlin. A woman there was very good, and I felt competitive with her from afar. Did she also tally the number of words she unscrambled compared to me?

I was distracted by a young corporal from HQ standing in the doorway, clearing his throat.

"Ma'am?" he said, clutching his cap at his stomach, like a shield. When had I become so terrifying?

"Yes?" I stared up at him. His face was pink. It wasn't so bad to make people uncomfortable. They knew who was boss.

"Telegram for you."

"Leave it there." I waved at the corner of my desk.

He approached cautiously, dropped the envelope on top of a heap of papers, and hurried off.

A telegram. No one liked personal telegrams in the war. It always meant bad news—loved ones dead and gone forever. But I had no loved ones. I ripped open the envelope to see that the note inside was handwritten.

Honeylamb.

That was the first word, and my eyes froze there. Only one person had ever called me that, and he was dead. Hung as a criminal three years ago. Bill Bagley, the only man I'd ever truly loved. The only man I'd ever truly hated, too. He turned out to be violent and crazy. He'd have killed me, I think, if I hadn't left him when I did. Young girls don't know how to spot these things until it's too late. I steeled myself to read on.

"Honeylamb. I have changed. No longer on the drugs. So you should not be surprised I got out of that place in the nick of time. Made a perfect plan and did it. I can tell you about it when you come see me. In the Far East. Get to the Honolulu docks and a man will take you here. Is your mind hesitating? Reconsider. I found someone else you will want to see. You worked with him at Esquimalt until he got shipped out. He was in your line of work. Captured by the Japs but I freed him. Keeping him safe until you arrive. Couple Russkies want to speak to him but I won't let them. Don't like their looks. He is not well. Hurry."

Only Bill could have written such a message. He was alive.

Where had this letter come from? I went to the door, looking for the corporal, but he was nowhere to be seen. Who was he, anyway? I returned to the desk in a daze, reminding myself the letter had been sealed. And if it wasn't, surely it would be meaningless to anyone else. Wouldn't it? Damn it, Bill was putting me at risk again. The room felt hot and I removed my cap. There were too many shocks in this message. I didn't know if I would cry from happiness or frustration or fear. It sounded like Link was alive, too. A burden of guilt lifted from my shoulders. My report to Miss

Maggie had not meant Link's death. Not yet, at least. Bill said he was not well. The paper was damp against my fingertips. What exactly did the Russians say to Bill? What did he say to them?

Bill was meddling, of course. That's what he did.

Somehow Bill knew about Link, and they were in the same place. This was alarming. I read the message through again, and there was no one else he could mean by it. How much did Bill know about what I'd done? I did not like to think of them together. Bill could get a stone to confide in him.

I crushed the letter into a ball.

Bill made it sound like an offer of help, but the last time I heard from him he had wished me dead. I had not managed a pardon for his case, despite his blackmail. He had threatened to unravel the respectable life I'd made for myself in the military. He'd been the trap Miss Maggie used to make me spy on my colleagues—on Link. If it wasn't for Bill, I'd never have written the report that got Link in trouble in the first place.

Now it turned out Bill hadn't even needed my help. He'd found someone else to free him. I wanted to scream.

Was this his elaborate plan to ruin me, by having me caught going AWOL? Or might he dangle Link in front of me and then throw him to the wolves, these Russians he spoke of, in some sadistic game?

I knew Bill valued loyalty above all, and I had failed him in that. He could still hate me despite his freedom.

I did not cry, but I could not trust my face. My lip was quivering, I could feel it, and I bit it lightly to still it. Luckily no one else was in the room, since most of the soldiers had been shipped out. I had to be composed, though, in case someone arrived and observed me.

How did Bill escape from jail? I supposed he had done it at least a couple of times before. It was hard to know how much to believe of his embroideries, but it was in the newspaper how he'd broken out of Walla Walla with a weapon he had made, and exited San Quentin with a fake gun waved at a guard he'd conveniently bribed to believe in it. Well, that last part was left out of the news-paper accounts. They did not like the public to know the rot was from within. Probably Bill bribed somebody at New Westminster, too, and the humiliation of losing a death-row prisoner made them suppress the news of his escape. He must have quit the coke not long after I last saw him, shaking and jittering in the New Westminster jail's visiting room. He was not humble, but what he said in the message was true. The old Bill would have had no trouble concocting an escape plan. He'd been the mastermind of the Clockwork Gang, after all. The Dunsmuir mine payroll heist from the Royal Bank was the biggest robbery in the history of the Pacific Northwest.

I remembered the old Bill. When we met, he rescued me, in a way. I was a teller in the bank when the gang struck. I was poor and struggling, with a lecherous boss determined to bed me or fire me. When Bill left the bank with the loot, I went with him. At first, Bill took pains to learn everything about me. When he discovered my father had been a postman who lost his job in the Depression, because no one could afford to send mail any longer, it had broken Bill's heart. He was funny that way, sentimental for the troubles of regular folk. In the month leading up to my twenty-first birthday, to show his solidarity with the postman, he sent me a letter by express every day even though we were living together. He'd stand over my shoulder as I tore open the envelope stuffed with little scraps of paper that spilled out like confetti, each one printed in his boxy unschooled hand: *I love you.* Then he would hug me tightly. But that was not the Bill I fled thirteen years ago.

The "Russkies," Bill said. His slang made them sound harm-less, like ice hockey players on a field trip. Did Bill understand how dangerous they were? Whatever they wanted with Link, it was bad news. From the cables, I'd seen how they operated in Germany. There were only three possibilities: They wanted to interrogate him. They wanted to recruit him. They wanted to kill him.

I was stuck in Alaska, half a world away. I had to get to Honolulu. Could Bill really be off the drugs? What would it be like to see him again? I stood up, smoothed my skirt, and fetched a glass of cool water. Finishing it, I set it on a coaster with a picture of a duckling. How had this ridiculous piece of whimsy made it into the room? It wasn't mine. I was not sentimental. I didn't want to see Bill—but I had to help Link. That was a matter of honour. I was the reason he'd been a prisoner of war, even if my missteps were ones anyone might have made. When I had reported his meeting with the Spanish Consul to Miss Maggie, I little believed that simple thing was really "spying."

It had seemed a dirty word, then. Now I spied on our allies, the Russians, for a living. My adopted country of America was recruiting Nazi agents to be my colleagues in this enterprise. What was the meaning of anything?

All I knew was that if Link died, it would be my fault. I could not leave him to the Russians, or to Bill for that matter. I knew too much about both.

I resolved to be on that transport the next day.

CHAPTER FOUR

DECEMBER 7, 1945—AFTERNOON

COCKTAIL HOUR WENT on and on, just like at my bar back in Sequim. The chamber of commerce had convinced me to delay opening until 12:01 p.m., so they could truthfully say no bars opened in the morning in our upstanding town. Of course, after the Ponderosa locked its doors at night, I let anybody stay in and drink past sunrise if they wanted, leaving the bar in business most of the twenty-four hours in a day. It was a technicality but it kept every-body happy.

"So there's this fellow called Lieutenant Link Hughes." Bill said the name with no great relish while he patted the table dry with a napkin. He'd spilled some of his drink. "Let me back up a bit."

I sighed a little to myself. Bill had taken to speaking in frag-ments. This was not like the old Bill who was chatty and confiding with his friends. Perhaps he did not trust me yet. After all that happened back in Washington State, I understood that I might have to prove myself again.

As I waited for Bill to explain, Dass made the long approach across the lawn carrying a silver tray that seared my eyes with the midday sun reflecting off it. Bill watched him as though it was the most interesting thing in the world right now. I was pretty hungry, I realized. It had been a long trip and a strange day. At least I was rid of that Shively fellow. I wondered where he hid himself while in Bangkok if he did not live with Bill. I imagined there was no shortage of dens of iniquity here.

Dass put the tray down beside us and Bill gestured at me to take a sandwich. I thought it tasted a little gamey but did not say so.

"How do you like it? It's water buffalo," he said, and I almost spit it out. But on second thought, when I recalled the monkey he mentioned earlier, this didn't seem so bad. I wasn't entirely sure what a water buffalo was anyway.

"Great," I said, giving him a thumbs up.

"I've had to adjust myself to the strange ways of this country," he said, taking a sandwich for himself. "But it's better than Europe during the war. Couldn't get meat of any kind."

"Were you a soldier?"

Bill ate all the crusts off first, which was not something I remembered him ever doing before. He seemed to have grown more particular. "Not exactly," he said. He chewed for a very long time, longer than even the stringy meat would warrant. I took it the subject was closed.

"I arrived here a few weeks after the Japs surrendered," Bill said, brushing some crumbs off his pants. "In August."

From where he came or why he did not say. In any case, he had imported jeeps and covered trucks for his business, and the ownership of these vehicles had thrown him in with the British against his will.

When the British liberated Siam they learned about the prisoner of war camps along the Burma–Siam railway, which the Japanese had built to shorten their supply lines. Around twenty thousand Allied prisoners had been conscripted at appalling loss of life. The British had the job of finding the remaining camps and recording as many of the graves along the way as they could. Long story short, Bill said, was that there weren't many vehicles in the country that could handle rough roads, so they requisitioned all of his.

"I travelled with the Limeys because I wanted to keep an eye on my jeeps. But I wish I'd never seen what I seen. Prisoners still alive were just sacks of bones. The dead ones, some were piled in pits, others the Japs just let rot where they fell." He slumped in his chair and pulled the brim of his Panama hat down lower. "Don't think I'll ever get used to the sun here," he said.

He had followed the British convoys to a field hospital at Nakom Paton, just outside Bangkok, where the British sent the prisoners for treatment. He talked to some of the men—those who were at least capable of speech. There he met a Canadian who said he had served at the Esquimalt naval base before being transferred overseas. "That word Esquimalt is a strange one, sticks in your head. As soon as he said that, I thought to myself, does he know Lena somehow?"

"She was there?"

"Yes."

"How'd you find her?"

Bill held up a finger for silence, and I followed his gaze to a man on the riverside path just outside the palazzo's iron fence. Bill had told me he'd like to block it off, but such a move would incite outrage because it was part of a public access route along the river from ancient times, and as a foreigner in Siam he could not afford bad feelings. Somehow the grumblings would get back to the chief of police, whom he needed to keep jolly. In any case, the man walking by looked harmless, a bare-chested local in a faded blue sarong. He led a goat on a string, which shook its grey and white head, a bronze bell jangling.

"Shively came across her," Bill said, once the man had disappeared. "He has his uses, hey? He was an old ship hand, so he volunteered for the navy in the war. They took him on at Esquimalt to free up the young ones to fight. Anyhoo, Lena was there. Shively saw her sometimes talking to a lieutenant. Link Hughes." He took another slug of his drink. "Lena thought I was never gonna get out of jail."

I felt sorry for Bill, and tried not to look at him. It would just make him mad. Even after all these years, Lena was still in the front of his mind. It seemed more like a fixation than love, but maybe those were nearly the same thing.

The drongo cackled from its perch. "Shut the fuck up," Bill yelled. He was certainly drunk now. He wiped the sweat from his brow with a silk handkerchief.

"She wasn't the only one who had people wanting them," he said. "I got outfoxed by a mountain girl when I was up in Burma."

"A mountain girl?"

"They're wild ones. Ride a horse like nobody's business. Anyhoo, her parents made a ruckus about her soiled honour. They saw I was rich and made me pay her bride price." He looked at me sidewise. "We're not really married. No paper, no priest. But I don't have the heart to throw her out of my house in Kengtung. It would ruin her." He kicked his feet against the chair legs, an angry drumbeat.

"The family doesn't bother you when you're away?"

"Men can go off as they please."

I guess I couldn't expect him to live like a priest all the time he waited for Lena, though it made me wonder if he loved her enough. I stared up at the clouds, frail things being frizzled up by the white hot sun. Of course Bill's problem was getting rid of a girl. Maybe I should go to Burma, I thought, and see if one might latch onto me.

"By the boo, if Lena hears about this, I'll know who told her," he said, leaning forward to poke me in the chest.

"Don't worry," I said, smiling in what I hoped was a trustworthy way. It made me nervous to hear him use that cute expression because he used to talk like that when he was at his most crazy.

"Dass, we need some more goddamn ice," he bellowed. He sat brooding until Dass returned from the pool house, the glass bowl he set down frosted with the blessed coolness.

"Back to business," Bill said, dropping some cubes into our empty glasses. "The British made lists of these POWs we found, and Lieutenant Hughes's name was on it."

I stared at Bill, uncomprehending.

"You're making this a goddamn trial." He took a deep breath and poured us each another drink from the side table. He gazed at the pale blue water in the pool, which earlier had been smooth and taut as a sheet. Now the rising wind mussed the surface. "Lena will want to see him. I'm not the only one who needs to do a patch job. And that's when I make my case," he said. "She'll see how I've changed. She thought well of you, By God. So you'll be there to greet her when she gets to Siam. To smooth things over."

"Me?" I kept my voice even, but did not trust myself to say more. The ice clattered in my glass and I saw my hand was shaking. Carefully, I put my drink down on the table. I wanted to be the first one to see her, very much. And wouldn't she be glad to see an old friend? I didn't have to follow Bill's instructions to the letter. I'd be on my own, at first. I could say whatever I wanted.

As always, he appeared to know my thoughts and cocked an eyebrow at me. "I trust you," he said, making me ashamed of my internal treacheries. "Anyways, that won't be the hard part. First we got to extract this Link Hughes from a certain situation. The Russians know where he is, and they'll move on him soon, most likely."

"Russians? Aren't they our allies?"

"Six months ago they hated Hitler as much as we did, but that's about it. Now that the war is over, the whole world's a chessboard. Except the game's gone underground."

This sounded far more dangerous than robbing banks. "I don't know this Link Hughes from Adam. Why do we have to play chess with the world?"

Bill laughed and laughed, until I became concerned he might choke, and then he wiped the tears from his eyes. "That's a fucking good question. Turns out it's good fun though."

Dass must have heard his cue, because he approached to hand Bill a scroll. Bill smoothed it out on the table, using our glasses to hold down two corners. It was a map with hatches of railway lines leading out of Bangkok. Bill drew a finger to the west. "That's Nakom Paton. It's not far." He tapped the spot with a satisfied air. He'd always loved maps, whether the close-up of a vault's innards or the byways of Washington State. The boys in the gang used to say he had every road in the Pacific Northwest stored in his brain.

He leaned back and smiled. "This is going to be easy-peasy. I got some friends in high places who can keep everybody occupied while we get Hughes. The police, no less."

He saw my doubtful look and laughed. "Don't worry, all the police are crooked. You just got to pay the right price. Why do you think I love Siam so much?" He handed me my glass, and the map rolled itself up with a thwap and fell on the paving stones. Dass picked it up silently and tucked it under his arm. "Your ice is melting already," Bill said. "Drink up before it gets warm. Enjoy life. Tomorrow we'll have work to do. You're going to help me capture Lieutenant Hughes."

"Capture?"

"Let's call it a rescue. Except the man being rescued maybe won't come willingly."

CHAPTER FIVE

FOGS AND WILLIWAWS

THE HUM OF the propellers grew louder, and I pushed my seat back from my desk. I knew it was the transport with its low deep rumble. The bombers were smaller and revved at a higher pitch. I took the pencil from my mouth, staring at the marks I'd chewed into the yellow paint, revealing bare wood underneath, and shoved it in my drawer. I grabbed my parka off the hook by the door and zipped it up. There was something about crazed winds and the roar of propellers that made me want to run, so I did, though the transport was still at the far end of the runway. It hulked over the fighter planes as it rolled past them, fat and slow with its load. It was three days late, since the weather paid its schedule no heed. Experienced pilots said that Shemya had the worst weather in the world. The arctic and temperate air masses constantly collided there, causing the fierce williwaws. This also created strange fogs. The fighter pilots spoke with more dread about the weather than being shot down by the Japanese. The nearby islands had large mountains that pilots crashed into when fog descended. There were more weather graves than war graves in the Aleutians.

When I got to the plane, Marguerite was already waiting at the open door to the hold. "There's a crate for you. It must be your champagne."

"About time," I said. I had ordered bubbly, the real stuff, in August when they announced the surrender of the Japanese. *The war was over.* We'd all run out onto the airstrip to listen to the loudspeakers, and I'd hugged Marguerite. Unknown pilots hugged us both. Then we retreated to our dorm. There were not many women so we were careful to stay away from any excitement.

The airman knew I always came for the Canadian newspaper, so he passed me *The Globe and Mail.* I looked for news of Link, as I always did. After the Japanese surrender, there were stories of men returning home who had been reported missing in action—their wives believed them dead but then they were not. They had been sheltered by the local resistance when their planes went down, or they swam to shore from sinking boats. These Lazarus soldiers returned home to great fanfare: the town would put up bunting and a band would play.

Link was one of these miracles, but there would be nothing in the paper about him. His existence was still secret, and it would be up to me to go to him. Why was I even imagining he would forgive me? I supposed unreasonable hopes were like wet wood fires: stuttering and small at the beginning, but once they take hold, raging hot until even falling rain evaporates in the heat, and they are unquenchable.

"Here's your crate, Miss," the airman called down from the lip of the hold.

I folded shut my paper and sighed. I had given up on making the men address me by rank. Most of them didn't mean anything by it, they were just flummoxed. Their brains could not conceive I was anything important. And mostly in this war, women weren't. I had heard of oss women being sent home from the field if their parents got worried and demanded it, as though they were still children. Married women were denied overseas postings because separation was an affront to the husband's authority. I was lucky, I supposed, to have neither parent nor husband holding me back. I was free to make my own reckless decisions. I was owed a one-month leave for my past service, and I thought it would be possible to make it to Siam. Getting back on time was another story.

"You need help with that?"

"No thanks." I smiled to myself, thinking he was so obliging because he knew champagne was inside my crate. I grabbed the heavy box off the ledge and rested it against my hip. I'd ordered twelve bottles. Well, I could cellar it. Is that not what one did with fine vintages? If I didn't come back, Marguerite could toast my memory.

"When are you leaving?" I asked him.

"Tomorrow morning at 0700. Weather permitting. But I have no plans for tonight."

He called out those last words as I was walking away.

ALONE IN THE dormitory, the champagne safely locked in my steamer trunk, I straightened the artificial flowers in the vase by Marguerite's bed. They were red silk carnations she had bought at ridiculous expense in Anchorage. I myself kept no such frivolous objects, but their prettiness pleased me anyway. I wished they needed watering so that I could contribute to their existence. I was as useless as these fake flowers. Even less useful, in fact. No one needed me, and I gave no joy to anyone.

I picked up the broom in the corner by the door and swept up the sand the wind had blown into the Quonset. This was an eternal job, the wind constant and the sand infinite. I shook the dustpan out the door, and a little blew back inside. I should have stepped further out the door, but it had felt so cold.

My hands clasped behind my back, I stared out the window at the brown airstrip, the dead flat island, the grey clouds. The loose edges of the aeroplanes' canvas shelters flapped in the williwaw. The makeshift structures only covered the noses, because there was not enough lumber available to build a full hangar. The mechanics huddled under the canvas, trying to stay out of the icy gusts as they worked on the engines. I didn't know why they bothered. The planes rarely flew since the war ended.

I turned the globe on my bedside table. Halfway between Alaska and Siam was Hawaii. A convenient stepping stone, and a destination that no one would think twice about for a leave. I put my coat on and marched across the base to Colonel Topping's office. Standing outside his door, I composed my face into what I hoped was innocent eagerness to make my request.

My knock went unanswered, but that was not uncommon. Colonel Topping was often napping. "Sir, may I come in?" I asked, and opened the door a crack to peek inside.

Sitting at his desk was a woman with a severe grey bun, steel-rimmed spectacles, and ramrod posture. Instinctively I took a step back from the door.

It was Miss Maggie. I had not seen her in person since she sent me here, three years ago. Her orders simply arrived by cable, as through by the hand of God.

"Please do," she said in her booming voice, which I had witnessed unsettling even an admiral.

I had forgotten how horrible the damage to the left side of her face was. There was a white scar running from her left cheek to her chin, and that side of her face sagged like a curtain missing hooks. The rumour mill said it was from a car accident when she was young. But the one thing she had confided in me, for reasons of her own, was that the man she loved had beaten her severely. It was not the first time. She chose not to get surgery so her own face would remind her every day not to trust anyone.

I looked at the wall beside Colonel Topping's desk, where a map of the South Pacific was still covered in white and red pins. These had been meant to make our unit look busy with the war on Japan, and nothing had changed since the surrender. The space inside the Soviet border, where we really focused our efforts, was left unmarked.

Miss Maggie followed my gaze and smiled coldly.

"That old fool has the subterfuge of a toddler, hiding his head under a blanket and believing he's disappeared," she said. I laughed, mostly from relief that she was not tearing into me immediately.

"By next year, if I have my way, the Russian sector will be the one full of pins, with all hands on deck," she said. "That is the coming war."

"Yes, I see that in the cables. They want to take Eastern Europe."

"In Washington, there are only a few believers so far."

I clasped my hands, but realized this looked nervous. I dropped my arms to my side. Why hadn't Marguerite warned me Miss Maggie was here? She must have come off the transport before I got to the runway.

I didn't know how old Miss Maggie was, but she looked no different from three years ago. Lithe and strong, like a shaman who could be dumped in the middle of the desert and walk for a hundred days unscathed, through trials that would kill lesser people.

"Tell me about this Nazi business," she said, leaning her elbows on the Colonel's oak desk. "Leave nothing out."

I had already reported everything to her through our private channel, but I went through it again, keeping my tone neutral since I didn't know where she stood. From my decryption, I knew at least one cell of the former OSS was trying to recruit Nazi secret service officers, especially those who had served behind the Soviet border during the occupation. Agent 37, whoever he was, had got hold of a Nazi known as von Roth.

"What do you make of it?" she asked.

"I took off my pin." The words came out of my mouth unconsidered—I had been too long away from the presence of any real authority figure.

She laughed.

Was her laughter approving or scornful? I could not tell. This was her genius, I supposed. I felt my admiration for her returning, along with my uncomfortable desire to please her. She was the most formidable woman that decryption had ever seen.

"Why did you come to see the Colonel?" she asked, staring at me over the top of her spectacles.

It was just like jumping into a Canadian lake, I told myself. A shock and then it's over.

"I was going to ask for my leave," I said. "I have a month owed. But I had no idea you'd come to Shemya."

"That's a long time," she said. She studied me even more closely. "Where would you go?"

"Hawaii. I'd like some heat after this place."

"No doubt," she said, and to my surprise she stood up and went over to the steel-green filing cabinet, her starched A-line skirt immobile above her legs as she walked. She rifled through a drawer. "He needs to work on his filing," she muttered to herself. "Ah, here it is."

She sat down again and pulled a gleaming black fountain pen from her jacket pocket. She placed a blank leave pass on the desk and leaned over it. "And when would you go?"

"The transport is leaving tomorrow, and they don't come often, with the weather. So I thought, why not tomorrow? But I didn't know you'd be here."

"Enjoy yourself," she said, pushing the signed pass across the desk.

"There's a path that goes around the island, near the sea," I blurted. "Just follow the rock piles. You can't get lost. There's no forest or anything."

"Sounds delightful," she said, ironically. "You may go."

Why did I always say silly things around her? Feeling like a child released from detention, I clutched my leave pass to my chest as I hurried out the door and down the hall. Outside, the williwaw nearly snatched my pass away. I jammed the paper into my pocket, keeping my hand there to feel it, to keep it safe. The wind swirled my hair about in tendrils and I figured I must look like a madwoman. I didn't care. I thought: I'm really leaving.

Back in the empty dorm, I put my suitcase on the bed. I'd bought it last year in Anchorage. It was expensive but not stylish, like everything in the North. I wasn't certain whether to feel rewarded or stung by Miss Maggie's actions. How long would she stay on Shemya? What had she come here to do? I hadn't seen her in three years, and she didn't even care if I left. She didn't need me. I shoved my clothes into my bag without bothering to fold them. To hell with military discipline. To hell with Miss Maggie. The idea of escaping Shemya was pure relief.

I snapped shut the first clasp, but my hand stilled over the second. What if I went all the way to Bangkok and Link would not see me? What if he hated me and blamed me for whatever terrible things happened in Burma? He must be seriously injured if they weren't sending him home yet. Based on the reports I'd seen, everyone fit to travel had left. I couldn't stand it if he were to die before I had a chance to fix what I had done.

Of course, I also wanted to know why Link had betrayed *me* and, even worse, the Captain. The Japs learned the location of our sigint operation through Link, when he tipped off the Spanish Consul in the record shop. As a result, the Japanese bombed the Esquimalt radio tower and killed the Captain, the sweetest man I'd ever known.

I still couldn't believe Link had intended for the Captain to die. Even if he was indifferent to national loyalties, he had cared about the Captain, too, I was sure of it. Maybe the Spanish Consul had deceived Link. And I wanted to know if Link had used me coldly, or if he had really felt something for me. I could not go so far as to say love, because love belonged to knowing a person. Unless you believed in love at first sight. Did I? I didn't think I loved Link when I first saw him. Maybe Bill, I had.

Bill. Thinking of him would do me no good. He had strangled my love in a thousand ways when we were together. I was not born a thief—but he was. I had just been a silly romantic who saw Robin Hood where there had only been a vicious thug. So why, despite everything, did I sometimes imagine a world in which there was a happy ending for us?

Fairy tales have lives of their own.

I DUCKED MY head to keep out of the propeller's range as I boarded the Liberator at 0700. I strapped myself into one of the four seats in the hold—this was not a passenger craft, so the trip would be cold and noisy. I looked out the hatch at the Quonset huts spread across the desolate sand flats and the tundra beyond, where the cliffs dropped away to the sea. Marguerite had come to the runway to see me off, and I pressed my palm against the plane's metal skin in a gesture of farewell. Startled at the chill, I drew my hand away. I was leaving the perpetual winter of the Aleutians, but not quite yet. I tucked my scarf into the edge of my collar and put my gloves back on for the flight.

The two other men in the hold seemed little inclined to talk. That suited me. One was reading the newspaper, and the other guzzled from a large bottle of bourbon. While the postings on Shemya were as random as anything else in the war—men raised in sweltering Texas were sent here, and men from snowy Colorado went to the tropics—it seemed to attract a particular breed of solitary eccentric. Or maybe Shemya just made them that way if they stayed too long. Like me.

Their presence made me wonder if Miss Maggie would tail me. Why would she need to do that, when she herself had granted my leave to Hawaii? She knew exactly where I was going, or at least she thought she did. Maybe she wanted to make sure. Miss Maggie's strength was in trusting no one and learning everything. She had had me followed to great effect before, since it led to her discovery of my criminal life with Bill. This was the source of her power over me. I looked uneasily at the men in the hold and wished I knew more about them. Directly across was a young base mechanic whose name I could not recall. His cap was askew from tipping his head back to drink the bourbon. He looked convincingly celebratory. Maybe his tour of duty was over. I could see the backs of the pilot and co-pilot where they sat in the cockpit, which was open to the body of the plane. They had their headphones on and fiddled with the dials in front of them, readying the plane for take-off. They would have a hard time paying much attention to me. The second passenger, an officer from HQ whom I recalled was named Tex, wore a ratty wool sweater and had a cigarette hanging from his lips as he read the newspaper, a week old. Who was more likely to be a spy: a man who feigned inattention or a man who pretended drunkenness? Either, I supposed. It would depend on the man's personality. I committed both their looks to memory. Tex had brown hair worn long and in a tuft across his brow, rather dashing. He had a manly face with a broad nose. I studied the mechanic next, who actually appeared weirdly similar to Tex. His hair was the same shade of brown, worn longer and wavy also, but it was as if the same man had been made goofy instead of serious. His hair was pushed back underneath his cap, which was barely clinging to his head now. One of these two could be Miss Maggie's agent. Well, there was only one way to leave Shemya, so I would just have to keep my eyes open.

The co-pilot closed the hatch, and the plane sped up the runway and lifted into the sky. My stomach lurched a moment before I settled into the lightness of flight. There were no windows in the hold, and I briefly wished I could see Shemya disappear beneath me as I left it, perhaps for the last time.

CHAPTER SIX

DECEMBER 12, 1945

ON THE TRAIN to Nakom Paton, I shared a first-class compartment with Bill, so he could "make sure nothing happened" to me, which I didn't like the sound of. What was he imagining? He had boarded the train ten minutes before me. His alarming associate Smile Chang was in a separate compartment, disguised in a monk's orange robes. There was apparently a large temple in the town, so this would help him blend in. But he was the toughest-looking holy man I'd ever seen. As I settled in, Bill adjusted the worn red velvet curtains so there was not a single crack of light. "Protection from the heat, and prying eyes," he said. "No one will remark on it, because everyone shuts the curtains in the tropics." Bill then sank into silence. Was it possible he had doubts about this job? I couldn't let myself believe it. He'd always been the still centre of every tornado.

The track was in ill repair from the war, and the train travelled fitfully across the countryside. I wished I could see it, since this was my first time outside of Bangkok. Just once, I pushed the curtain forward an inch and Bill broke from his reverie. "I got to tell you twice? Close that," he said, and I did, resentful. Who could possibly be out there, in the middle of nowhere beside a moving train?

I wondered why I could not stand up to Bill. In our years apart, I'd proved I could make a success of something, with my saloon in Sequim. But that was the sort of thing any schmuck could do. Bill was in another league. The best I could hope for was to be his faithful lieutenant and experience adventures at his side. If I angered Bill or let him down, he could send me away, I supposed, and I wouldn't even have that much. But I was pretty sure, much as I admired him, I didn't want to be him. His success didn't seem to make him any happier than I was. All he wanted after all these years was Lena, it seemed, and he didn't have her. The curtains didn't matter. Let him keep them closed.

"You know it was called the Death Railway?" Bill asked.

"No," I said, wondering why we were travelling upon its rails, then. It did not sound safe.

"Because so many POWs died building it. Twelve thousand dead, they say." He jittered his knee. "And Link Hughes wasn't one of them."

"A lucky bastard," I said.

"Yes. Well, at least he'll be useful to me."

When we arrived at the station, there would be a separate automobile for each of us, while Smile would walk as befit a monk, Bill explained. Then he pulled his Panama hat down over his eyes and slept, or at least pretended to. His breathing did not sound easy.

After a few hours of jolting and shuddering, the train slowed to a full stop. The station was a small wooden building through which we hurried toward the waiting cars. Looking around quickly, I saw a monstrous gold structure like an inverted bell, which was the temple rising above the trees. Though it looked substantial, the inside would just be hollow, I reflected. People flowed toward it with the eternal hope of seekers, yet they would never know until they were dead if their faith had been of any use. The street was unpaved, and in the opposite direction from the temple, there were more stray cats than people. The town itself felt abandoned. Maybe the prison hospital was bad luck.

I climbed into my car. The Siamese driver had beefy shoulders, and I supposed he was one of the corrupt policemen Bill had enlisted. The man did not speak. The rear windows were curtained, limousine style, so there was not much to see, either. My thoughts turned inward to the night before.

AS WE'D FINISHED the last of too many drinks, Bill still had not answered my question about how he would know when Lena arrived. It did not sound like she had responded to his invitation. He just said "I'll know it" and fell silent. I felt impatient in the unfamiliar heat. It was heavy as a wet cloth against a fever patient's brow. Maybe he had Shively staking out the ports. As usual, I was at Bill's whim, and all I could do was wait to find out. I decided to change the subject for the sake of pepping up our reunion. Bill would no doubt enjoy talking about his success in this country.

"In your telegram you said you needed a numbers man," I said, "so what business did you bring me here for?" Besides writing his biography and smoothing the way with Lena, I thought with annoyance.

"It's legitimate. I'm quite proper now," he said, his mood brightening, just as I'd hoped. He hooked his thumbs through his belt loops as though asking me to take in the cut of his linen suit, which was admittedly fine. But such outward measures did not signify. As a thief he had worn nice suits at times, and we had reposed a while in a mansion on Capitol Hill, which was Seattle's swankiest district. I raised my eyebrows.

"It's an agricultural product," he said. "Guess what it is."

"Rice?"

"That's not so profitable. It's the opium poppy."

"That's what you call legitimate?"

It was legal to sell in Siam, he said, though it was only grown in the remote mountains of Burma, and that's where his crops were. Now I understood how he'd got entangled with that mountain girl. Bangkok was by far the best market, Bill said, since the Siamese government ran licenced opium dens. This was a peculiar country, I thought.

"Isn't it hard being in this business with your old drug habit?" I asked, my caution gone at least three drinks back.

"When I decide something, it's done. Quit is quit. Anyhow, there's a world of difference, By God, between coke and this monkey business. You ever seen someone in an opium stupor?"

"I did it once. All I remember is my head floating off by itself." I hoped he would not ask me the circumstance, since it was after the cops shot me running away, when Bill was caught. I remembered staggering through the forests of Washington State, clutching my wounded arm, on fire with pain. I made my way to Chinatown in Bellingham because of its reputation for opium dens; I thought it would be a good place to hide while I recovered. I supposed others in the den must have been equally pie-eyed but I was in no condition to know it.

"That's just it," Bill said. "While you thought your head was floating, you were laid out flat doing nothing. Cocaine at least keeps a man busy. You're ready to take on the world."

"You're never tempted to try your new product?"

"That's what my quality control associate, Smile Chang, is for. He has a naturally vicious and active nature that seems to benefit from opium's calming effect. His knowledge of the drug can't be matched. When he grades the batches I know exactly what I should pay."

Smile was connected to the Chinese Nationalists through his family, Bill added. They, in turn, were friends with an important general whose army was garrisoned in Burma—safe, but also convenient to the battle with the Communists in Yunan. The general's main funding came from the opium business. To operate in Burma Bill had to give him a cut, and he'd protect the shipment until it reached the border with Siam. There, Bill's other connection—the Siamese chief of police, called Phao—took over the racket. He was trying to position himself as a military force, Bill said, and might have designs for a coup.

"This sounds an uncomfortably political business," I said.

"More than you know, but the chief's going to help us get Hughes. We'll go tomorrow on the nine o'clock train."

The sky had closed in since I arrived in the garden and it had grown hotter, though it seemed the hour had turned late. Bill stood up and put his face to some exotic white flowers the size of teacups that were planted in a large ceramic urn alongside the pool deck. "Come look at this, By God," he said. I got up, a little unsteady, and peered at the flowers. They were big and sweet enough that each one had five bees in it, lazy and stumbling. "This is Siam," Bill said, and laughed a hard, barking laugh of pure delight.

As we sat down again, he said he had filled a closet upstairs with clothes for me, figuring I would not be prepared for the tropics or the ways of his new crowd. It was not like America. Here, everyone dressed for dinner, and he announced it was time to get ready for ours.

"My size has changed since we last met," I said, patting my stomach. Though in truth I was only one size larger than in my youth, and in pretty good shape if I did say so myself. I waited in vain for Bill to disagree.

"Shively telegraphed me your measurements," he said instead.

I suddenly imagined filthy Shively, on our trans-Pacific journey, creeping into my cabin at night to measure me like a corpse. His exacting nature would encourage such sneaking, rather than simply reading the labels of my clothes. I suspected I wasn't imagining it at all, and it just might have been a memory. Unsettled, I followed Bill inside to dress.

Dinner was a peculiar affair. The table would have seated twenty, but there were only three of us: me, Bill, and Smile. Bill, of course, sat at the head of the table and arrayed us on his left and right. Smile had the build of a speakeasy bouncer. His fists were the size of softballs, disproportionately large and meaty. His head was shaved bald, and my own brown waves seemed a little poncey in comparison. I thought it best not to be seen observing him, and I averted my eyes. Smile's handle must have been born of sarcasm. He hadn't so much as twitched his mouth so far.

There was a mural on the wall behind Bill, with some nasty-looking naked baby angels flitting around a reclining naked woman. This all seemed unfitting should there be lady guests, but perhaps it was classified as "art." Bill caught me gawping at it all, and explained his luck in snagging the mansion. It had become available with the tasteful purging of some Japanese collaborators who had used the palazzo during the war, to satisfy the Allies that Siam had not, in fact, been an enemy nation.

"Though they bloody well were. Now they're friends with the Americans. And the British," Bill said, chewing on his food. I had taken the roast to be a ham but did not ask in case it turned out to be another switcheroo for a foreign creature, which would dampen my enjoyment of it. "Smile knows them well, which is useful." Smile had gone to a colonial school in Burma and learned the Queen's English, Bill related, while Smile remained silent. I noted that Smile had an identical tuxedo to my own, right down to the red pocket square, which made my blood boil. Was I just some kind of bookend to Bill?

"Smile here is equally suited to fine dining or fisticuffs," Bill said, possibly noticing my interest in his apparel, and I lowered my eyes. "He'll come with us tomorrow, just in case. A moment, gentlemen." Bill laid his white napkin on the tablecloth and walked out of the room.

Was I some kind of weak flank? I felt a little touchy. Bill hadn't even asked me yet what I'd done all these years. In that regard he had not changed. He was only interested in himself and his own schemes. I supposed I could not expect that being yanked from the brink of death had changed him entirely, as though he was rebuilt top to bottom like some Frankenstein.

With Bill out of the room, I tried to seize on anything to talk to this Smile fellow about, since it was clear I would have to make the first effort. He sat staring straight ahead. Certainly Bill chose his associate wisely in that he was no rattletrap, and no secrets were going to escape from him. His eyes shone like the gaping windows around us, black with the night outside, reflecting me back to myself, tiny and marooned.

"What does your family do in Burma?" I asked.

"Run an opium den," he said, his voice surprising me, sounding British and upper crust. I wondered what such a criminal upbringing would be like, as opposed to my own gentle mothering. But my father had been a Wall Streeter—some considered that a criminal pastime after the stock market crash.

Bill returned grinning and carrying a small canvas sack that looked unaccountably heavy for its small size. He thumped it on the table beside my dinner so that the china rattled. "Take a look."

I untied the bag to see gold pieces stamped with foreign scroll-work. "Jesus," I said. "Are you King Midas now?" I held up a coin to the light and it glinted, beyond beauty, a sight that had corrupted men's souls for time untold.

"This is what I need you for. What's the value of the gold I pay out to the cops versus what I make from my business? Then I get paid in guns or gems. What are they actually worth when finally, down the line, I get some hard currency? Right now I got stashes everywhere like some fucking squirrel. I need an accounting of it all."

"The war's over. Who do you sell your guns to?"

"By God, don't ask questions when you won't like the answers," he said, spearing an escargot. Or at least I hoped it was nothing worse than French snails. "Let's talk about tomorrow."

I would go into the hospital alone, Bill said, posing as a cousin of Link Hughes to sign him out. Bill could not go himself because some of the British officers knew him from his work liberating the prison camps, and he did not want them noticing his interest in the man. I wasn't sure why this would be a problem, and Bill did not explain. Smile would wait outside to ensure that nobody troublesome got through Chief Phao's net. I wondered if this plan came from Bill's perfectionistic nature, or from a distrust of Chief Phao.

Alone, Bill had said. I was nervous about that, but at least he had faith in me.

THE CAR SLOWED and I craned forward to see through the front windshield. There was a gap in a long wall where a metal gate had been wrenched off its hinges, twisted back like the lid on a sardine can. We drove through unchallenged. Passing row after row of wooden buildings on the vast hospital grounds, I felt a growing dread. Not just for the job I had to do, but at what the war had done. I'd been remote from it until now. The place was desolate. There was only pounded dust, and not a single tree. How many thousands of wounded had there been, to fill these buildings? With their roofs of slatted bamboo, they were hardly better than huts. I could still see the faint outline of Japanese writing on a post that had been painted over. These outer structures, which the Japanese forced the prisoners to build, would be empty, Bill told me, and only the old headquarters building, solid pre-war masonry, was being used to house the last patients. The car approached its entrance, two half-hearted columns surrounding a heavy wooden door. The hospital was a two-story rectangle painted beige like the dusty earth, and its roof was covered in terracotta tiles the colour of dried blood.

There was a single soldier posted outside with a rifle. British, I thought from his uniform, which I'd seen in news trailers during the war. He looked battle-hardened and I hoped I wouldn't need to tangle with him. At least there was only one of him.

"I wait," was all the driver said as I got out of the car. It felt equally threatening as helpful.

All the curtains were drawn in the hospital windows, giving the place a reclusive air. I detected a flash of motion on the second floor, as though someone had been peering out a crack and let the curtain fall again. Somebody curious, as I had been on the train. I walked past the soldier, who did not challenge me, and continued through the hospital doors, wishing I had eyes in the back of my head. I would have to trust the driver, whoever he was, to watch out for me. I wondered what Russians looked like. I could only picture Cossack hats, but that was absurd. I wished I was back in Sequim, drinking a nice cold beer with farmer Joe types. I wiped my palms on my trousers. I paused at the front desk where there was a nurse stationed, wearing a crisp white uniform and cap. I opened my mouth, closed it again. Come on, By God, I told myself. Bill is depending on you.

I looked around the glaring white foyer, but it was empty of any other people. I supposed Chief Phao had done his work and cleared it out.

"I'm here for Link Hughes," I said to the nurse.

"And who are you?"

"Charlie Hughes, his cousin from Canada."

"They told me you'd be coming," she said, and I hoped "they" were Bill's men. The nurse ran her finger down a list. "Bed 247. Follow me."

She was young, barely past nineteen I guessed, and I wondered what brought her here. Had her parents supported her Florence Nightingale dream of healing in foreign lands? As we passed the moaning patients, many missing limbs or with lesions all over their skin, I looked away. This was not merely mopping sweaty brows— this was gruesome work. The men were just skin and bones. I wondered if Link Hughes would be like this, and how Lena would hold up when she saw him. Maybe she'd need me, for once, after all.

The young nurse led me upstairs, where the men looked a more normal weight. Some were walking around in their white robes. They must be getting ready to ship home. That was a relief after the scene below, though I felt an uncharitable dread that Link would be hale and heroic.

The nurse stopped in front of a bed that was empty. "Maybe he's in the bathroom," she said, and went to knock on a nearby door. There was no answer. "Link?" she said, cautiously pushing it open. She returned to the empty bed and unhooked the chart from the metal bedframe, scanning the first page. "He's not getting any tests," she said. "Let's try the common room."

As I followed her down the white hallway, there was a tall man bumping his head against the wall, over and over. It was odd. The nurse paused to speak to him softly. He stopped a moment, but as soon as we passed on, he started up again. Another fellow with hair down to his shoulders tugged at my sleeve. "Have you seen the little prince?" he asked, his dark eyes looking everywhere but at me.

"Who?" I asked.

"We'll look for him later," the nurse assured the patient. As we rounded the corner a horrible noise assailed my ears. A tuneless piano played at top volume. We entered what must be the common room. Crowded on one table, there were clay heads of extraordinary talent jumbled in with alarming lumps barely recognizable as human. All the other tables were empty, as were the chairs. There was only one person in the room: the frustrated musician at his stool. He was missing his leg below the knee and was wearing a metal contraption with a boot in its place. I assumed it wasn't Link, since I hadn't heard he was so afflicted, but I looked sidewise at the nurse to see how she reacted.

"This is strange. There's nowhere else he could be," she said. She approached the musician and put her hand over his, and the loud music, if you could call it that, stopped. The silence descended sudden and heavy as a thundercloud. "Jefferson, have you seen Link?" she asked.

He pointed at a high window, which was open. It did not look large enough for a man to squeeze through. Well, maybe this fellow Jefferson could. He was thin as a rail.

"He went out the window?" the nurse exclaimed. The man nodded, and returned to plunking his tuneless song. "Mary, mother of Joseph." She dragged a chair to the window, stood on it to reach up, and patted around the sill. She pulled in a length of clothes tied together in a sort of rope. She gave an exasperated hiss of breath.

"I don't understand," she said. "He'd been doing so much better the last few days. Or we never would have let him out of the straightjacket." She stared at my face, which must have betrayed my surprise—though thinking back on what I'd seen, I should have figured it out sooner. "You didn't know this is the mental ward?" she asked.

"No." Damn that Bill, why'd he leave that part out? I didn't know I was retrieving a madman.

"Oh, goodness. This has never happened before." The poor young nurse stepped down from her chair and picked up her metal clipboard again to make a note on it. Finished, she clutched it tightly to her chest. "This building wasn't designed as a hospital, and we never thought of them leaving through that window. It's so high up. And they're usually pretty settled when we've got them on the morphine."

She looked like she was going to cry. Back home, she'd probably never had more responsibility than soothing some kid with measles, and now she was supposed to manage hundreds of ex-prisoners, each damaged in unique and terrible ways. I reminded myself to stop wasting time on pity for this pretty young girl. I had to find Hughes.

"Maybe he's still nearby."

"Maybe," she said, and I sprinted out the door. I wondered how quickly the Russians would be after him. Or had they already got him? Bill was going to blow a gasket.

To my surprise the nurse kept pace with me as I ran. She was a game one. This was less than convenient, but I didn't have time to think of how to get rid of her. I'd take Hughes by force if need be, and I didn't want her to see that. Well, I wasn't such a tough guy. She'd probably seen worse if she worked in a mental ward, wrapping them up in straightjackets and such.

"Get the prince!" cheered the long-haired man, waving his fist in the air, as we ran down the hall.

Outside the main door, the midday heat punched the air right out of me, and I stopped to look left and right. My eye caught the flash of a bright orange robe and a gleam of metal. A man fell to the ground and a monk bent over the body. Smile, I guessed. The other man stayed unmoving. Dead, I guessed. Oh, Jesus.

"Guard!" the nurse yelled. She stared around in puzzlement. "Where'd he go?"

The dead man wasn't in uniform, so it wasn't him. Maybe the chief bought off the guard.

I didn't have time to ponder. A new guy was running at Smile, and he tackled him. The nurse screamed. I didn't know what to do. I wanted to help Smile, but I didn't want anyone to guess I was with him. Plus, I didn't want to get killed, if that was going around. Damn it. I supposed even a stranger would go help a monk. I started running toward them.

The nurse blew a whistle. Three short blasts.

The attacker knocked the gun from Smile's hand, but it skidded far out of his reach. He kept his eyes on Smile and pulled out something from his jacket. I saw the flash of a blade.

I was no fighter, but maybe I could grab the gun off the ground while they were busy. I veered toward it. Smile rolled out of the man's grip, leapt up and danced away, the man following close. He looked a regular sort of fellow in his khaki pants and blue long-sleeve shirt, but he must be one of these Russians, I thought. As far as I knew, they were the only other ones after Hughes.

From between the rows of wooden buildings two military police appeared, rifles at their chests. They trotted toward us, dust rising up in clouds from their pounding feet. I skidded to a halt. The sight of them froze everybody in a strange tableau, the brute's arm raised, Smile poised in a fighter's stance in his orange robes. A split second later, Smile and the other man scattered in different directions. Each had his own private reason for not wanting to be nabbed and questioned. The military police yelled into their radios and split up, each following one of the two fleeing men. I didn't want anything to do with those soldiers either. They had guns, and it was time to vamoose. My driver was still waiting in the car, a discreet distance away on the dirt road. Bastard could have helped out. I jogged toward the car.

Looking over my shoulder, Smile's pistol gleamed where it lay in the dirt and I wondered if it could be evidence against us. Wouldn't Bill have bought untraceable ones? Maybe even that hinted something to certain enemies. I couldn't risk it. I checked the main door and the nurse wasn't there. Now was my chance.

I ran back, scooped up the gun, and jumped in the car. We raced off, the wind in my face and the pistol grip gritty with sand in my palm, and it felt like old times in the gang, making a getaway after a bank job. The guy could really drive, I'd give him that.

Then I felt a pang as I thought of Smile out there, unaided. Well, at least the Russian went off some other way. Smile could handle himself.

Our car left by the main gate, where the Siamese police waved us through. The crooked cavalry was here. And just beside the road, a procession of hundreds of monks in orange, with yellow flags fluttering in the wind.

It was a beautiful sight. Bill had always arranged things with style.

BILL AND I met back on the train in our private compartment as planned—except for the fact that Link wasn't with me. As I had predicted, Bill was in a rage. At least it wasn't directed at me. "Hughes fucking bolted? What do I pay the chief for? We got to go see him." Bill flipped down the table to scrawl a note, and pressed the buzzer angrily for the conductor. Bill told him to send the telegram right away, before we left the station in Nakom Paton.

"Smile must have got away okay," I said, trying to soothe Bill as soon as we were alone. The train jolted and the engine sighed as it started on its way. "All those monks were pretty great, filling the road outside the hospital." I'd been surprised at the sight of them in their masses, the orange robes blazing, the men all shaved as bald as Smile. Silver bowls gleamed in their hands, leaving one to think that Smile too must only have been holding a bowl, not a silenced pistol—that Smile was just an innocent monk in the wrong place at the wrong time, lost in a crowd of his fellows.

"My idea," Bill said, looking pleased for a moment. My ploy had worked. "The chief paid them off so they'd have a procession. There's crooked monks in this country too. That don't bring Hughes back, though." Bill slumped into the worn red velvet seat and closed his eyes. After about ten minutes they flipped open, sudden as a doll with those winky eyes. It startled me. "I bet he's on his own. If the Russians had him, they wouldn't have stuck around to fight Smile."

"Agreed," I said, though I wasn't quite sure, and he closed his eyes again. I didn't believe he was sleeping, since his breathing was not even, but I let him be for the rest of the journey. No use rousing his ill feelings against me. He could use his energy for scheming how to find Hughes instead. Quietly I shuffled some cards on my flip-down table and played solitaire.

By the time we got back to the palazzo a few hours later, there was a reply telegram from the chief, or at least a dinner invitation for the next day. "He better serve us T-bone steak," Bill grumbled. "Don't say anything about this problem, By God. Leave that to me. The chief can be touchy."

CHAPTER SEVEN

AWOL IS THE BLOND

THE PLANE'S WING dipped toward the ocean as we turned, lowering in altitude. The Hawaiian Islands rose out of the blank Pacific and looked unnervingly like the Aleutians from this distance. Volcanos, accordioned mountain ridges, cliffs, and featureless green cloaking everything, wisped in clouds. Maybe it was a trick of perspective but the islands even trailed off in size, the largest closest by and the outer islands increasingly smaller, also like the Aleutians, where nearly the last and smallest had been Shemya. It gave me an eerie feeling, as though I could not escape the place. But no, as the clouds shifted and parted, I could see there was no snow on any of the peaks. Even in the height of summer, not all the snow melted in Alaska. On the north faces, in the shadows, a perpetual cold remained. Of all the islands, only Shemya lost its snow cover because it had no mountains. On Shemya everything was featureless and laid bare, and there was nowhere to hide. I would have to hope for better shelter in Hawaii.

As the plane banked lower, the green resolved into heavy jungles, a riot of life. There was a glare of white along the coast, bright and shining, desolate and pure, like the curved blade of a knife. Why did my mind always ascribe a sinister appearance to things? It was a beach, for heaven's sake, and no doubt very pleasant.

In Honolulu I would finally meet the man who would take me to the Far East, though I did not even know what country. It might be Burma, where Link disappeared, but the Japanese could have shipped him anywhere. The mystery was frustrating, but secrecy was warranted. Miss Maggie would certainly want to find him, and apparently the Russians did too. Perhaps they believed a traitor could be turned to their own purposes.

It had taken days to get this far, and I tried not to count them down against my thirty days' leave. After Anchorage, where I watched a movie at the cinema and drank a bottle of wine in my room alone, there were stopovers in Seattle and Los Angeles. I sighed to myself and twirled my thin silver bracelet. It was etched with indigenous Tlinkit designs, eyes within eyes. Being in Seattle had brought back painful memories of Bill, after all the time we spent together there. We had had wonderful nights in the So Different speakeasy and the black-tie Bergonian restaurant. Then there was the bitter year in the mansion on Capitol Hill, when everything unravelled. Even then, I had continued to love him.

At the Seattle airstrip, I had stood waiting for porters to bring my luggage, my arctic parka slung over my arm in the unaccustomed warmth of the south, though all the locals were bundled up. All around me families reunited as the military continued to shed personnel. I, of course, had no one to welcome me.

The stewardess announced Honolulu over the loudspeaker. I realized I'd been crushing my bracelet into my arm and let go of it. From my seat near the front I was one of the first to leave the aeroplane. I was finally in a place where I could start to make things right. *Sunshine*, I thought with sudden joy as I climbed down the folding metal stairs onto the runway. I'd been three years in the North—too long. The balmy air caressed my skin as I strode across the tarmac. Despite my hurry, I had to stop when a native woman stood in front of me holding loops of flower necklaces, which she put over the heads of the passengers as we walked past. I fingered the fuchsia flowers, soft as velvet, though as I did so one fell off and was crushed under my heel. Well, I was not sentimental, and in the terminal I tossed the rest of the garland in a trash can. No sense in marking myself as a new arrival when I got into town. I hailed a cab.

With its plain brick buildings, Honolulu was trying hard to act like an American town, but at the end of the main street a mountain rose up, filling the view with tropical splendour. The street was lined with shops and it seemed like every other store sold shoes. I realized that the ones I brought with me were no good for the tropics. I went into a shop called McInerney's that looked a cut above, and I bought some strappy cream sandals. When I stepped out, well pleased, I noticed a man standing against a lamppost reading a newspaper. He had been there when I entered the shop. I'd been careful in Anchorage and was sure I hadn't been followed by the men in the aeroplane from Shemya, or anyone else. In the Los Angeles terminal, I'd worried that a man in a brown business suit looked like Tex, but then I reminded myself that Tex had looked the same as the base mechanic sitting next to him on the Liberator. Generic, but that was no comfort. It would be a good quality in a spy. In the end, the man left the terminal without a backward glance. People following you never leave first—I was pretty sure about that much from Camp X.

I walked up the street half a block, paused at the window of Mercie Gordon's Beauty Salon, and looked in the reflection. The man had started walking in my direction. His shoes clicked on the pavement like Morse code, sending out a warning. I had to lose him because I was reaching the point of no return. Honolulu was where I would officially go AWOL.

I took a deep breath to calm myself. Since I was at a salon I might as well get my hair done. He could cool his heels, and it would give me time to think how to shake him. Now that I was on the last stage of my journey to the Far East, I wondered how I would look to people who hadn't seen me in years. I knew that my mouth was set more grimly than before, and there were some furrows in my brow. Passing the age of thirty brought no great joy. I needed to spruce myself up. A bell jangled as I walked in the door, and a plump woman with a formidable updo ushered me to a chair.

"Nothing with pins," I said. "Something a bit softer, like Lauren Bacall."

"Have you ever considered going blond?" she asked. "It would suit you."

I had not planned a new colour but perhaps it was time for me to stop hiding as a brunette, as I had done since I left the Clockwork Gang. As a girl I had been a natural honey blond, and had kept it up with lemon juice rinses in the sun.

"All right, do it. But not too blond-blond."

Mercie Gordon, for a name tag announced it was the proprietor herself, wheeled out a cart and painted some gloop onto my hair. The smell of bleach burned in my nose. Instead of observing my own image in the glass, which I never liked to do anyway, I watched the street behind me. There were a lot of buses.

"Which bus goes to the docks?" I asked.

"Be careful of those sailors, honey," she said, painting more strands of my hair.

"Not the navy docks. The public marina." I didn't know exactly where to go, but there was no way Bill's plan would put me under military eyes.

"There's a couple yacht clubs at Waikiki. Number 10 bus."

I watched the street in the mirror until a number 10 went by and checked the clock. It was 3:10 by the hands, which seemed strange to me after years of using the twenty-four-hour military system. I couldn't see the man lingering outside, but that didn't mean he wasn't there. I only had a limited slice of vision. Mercie put a vinyl cap on my head and left me a while as she waited for the bleach to set. She started to cut the hair of another customer.

Once I'd seen the next Waikiki bus go by at 3:20, I knew its schedule. Every ten minutes on the ten. I couldn't help but think now of the people it would carry me toward. Link, whose forgiveness I had to hopelessly seek, and Bill, whose apology I would never receive. I was sure he would try to blame me as always. How could he ever expect I'd get a pardon for him? He was a notorious criminal and no sane politician would ever give him one.

My soaked head felt cold underneath the cap and time crawled. Why was I going on this doomed mission, anyway? I suppose the same reason knights have always gone into battle. Because I had honour, and more than that, I wanted other people to know it.

Finally, Mercie told me it was time to wash out my hair. I tipped back my head and tried to enjoy the feeling of her rubbing my scalp with shampoo. Pretty scents rose from the sink, lavender and verbena, I thought, scents from before the war. Seating me again, Mercie combed my hair and set it in curlers. In the mirror I caught a glimpse of the man across the street. So he was still waiting. I marked the spot where people got on the bus, so I could run for it. Mercie escorted me to the dryer, where she lowered the huge celluloid half-sphere over my head.

A half hour later Mercie touched my elbow to retrieve me. I sat back in the chair by the mirror as she pulled the curlers from my hair and brushed it out. As she gently adjusted the ends that hit my shoulders, she told me I looked stunning. She knew where her bread was buttered. Though I did not quite believe her it lifted my mood, and I felt more elegant than I had in a long while. There had been no salon on Shemya, the place being designed for men. We few ladies had to take turns doing each other's hair and the results were sometimes a little strange.

I made small talk until the clock showed 4:19. I stepped out onto the sidewalk, which was busy with uniformed sailors despite the general demobilization. After Pearl Harbor, the US government wasn't about to close down this base. The hubbub suited me perfectly. Shouldering through a knot of men, I ran for the bus signed "Waikiki" as it was just pulling away from the curb. I waved and it lurched to a stop. I jumped aboard, the door slamming behind me. "Thanks," I breathed, and dropped a dime in the box by the driver.

Settling onto a blue vinyl seat, I glanced out the window, where the persistent newspaper reader was left behind on the sidewalk. I felt smug as the bus roared down the street. *Sayonara, sucker*, as they said in the war.

The last sight I had of him, he was walking toward a payphone. Damn. I had a brief thought that maybe he was Bill's man. Had I mucked things up? But Bill wouldn't need to have me followed, because he'd know I was going to the docks. If there was any chance he belonged to Miss Maggie, I needed to shake him.

As the bus left downtown, the view gave way to palm trees and explosions of bright flowers everywhere. Frangipani, I thought suddenly. Is that what that was? I liked the word, anyhow. It sounded fresh and new, like I wanted my life to be.

Most of the passengers were gone by the time the bus reached the Hawaii Yacht Club, where I rang the bell to get off. The boats were large and shiny, looking ready for long voyages. But the locked gangway to the dock was hung with a sign, Private, Members Only. This was no good. I needed public docks to find the lowlifes Bill had always favoured. I paused at the intersection, where there was a small grocery store, to read the signs. A motley row of bored-looking men sat on the store's porch, sipping sodas or smoking. An older Black man stood up, stubbing out his cigarette, drawing my eye. He stared at me and I stared right back at him—he looked familiar.

"Lena?" the man said, approaching me.

"Sho-nuff?"

He smiled. "I go by Frederick now."

CHAPTER EIGHT

DECEMBER 13, 1945

APPROACHING CHIEF PHAO'S mansion gave me a new perspective. Either Bill preferred to be tucked away on his own, away from his dangerous cronies, or maybe he was not quite so rich as I first thought. Bill's palazzo, though grand, was set amongst estates that had seen better days. I inspected the neighbour's property, which you could not see from inside Bill's grounds, on the boat ride across the river. The livestock in their yard had trampled it down to mud, so that Bill's garden was an oasis beside it. Apparently, those in the core of national power, like Phao, had moved away from the river and into a new neighbourhood where everything was clean and modern. There were paved streets rather than filthy canals, and smooth cement walls instead of chaotic thatching in every empty space.

Bill rang the bell and a genuine English butler swung open the door. He held a silver tray, and Bill deposited a calling card upon it. Silently, the butler led us through echoing marble hallways into the drawing room, where Chief Phao sat in velvet gloom. "Mr. Yardley and Mr. Godfrey," the servant bellowed, startling me with this sudden departure from his former quiet.

The chief of police did not stand to greet us. As I shook his cool hand, I was conscious of how sweaty my own was. He had pudgy baby cheeks that should have belonged to an innocent face. But his narrow eyes contained more darkness than Bill's ever did at his most drugged and deranged, though Bill had assured me that Phao did not confuse himself by taking opium. I sat down and the servant handed me a glass of cognac before withdrawing, bowing as he closed the double doors behind him. Having time to look about me as Bill humoured the chief with small talk, managing to raise a curled smile to the madman's lips—for such I already thought him to be—I noted that his hideaway was incongruously decorated with paintings of European ladies having picnics. Surely he did not choose these himself. He must have had a decorator to tell him the styles favoured by normal rich people.

Chief Phao launched into a story of a police hunt he had recently led, where they had caught the criminal at the river's edge. "It was unfortunate. I had to drown him myself to keep him from escaping. He was a danger to public order," he said, his large, sensual mouth suggesting an enjoyment of the taste of terror. The chief leaned over an ornate gilt table and plucked a cigar out of an inlaid ivory humidor, then invited Bill and me to do the same.

I supposed such stories were meant to reassure us that the chief could find Link, but he showed no intention of apologizing or explaining what went wrong.

"I assume you don't mean to drown Hughes," Bill said at last. "I want him alive."

"Do not worry. I will find him. The Americans promised to send me cash to recruit more men." He puffed on his cigar in satisfaction, and I wanted to ask, What Americans? I did not want to believe this could be any kind of official aid, given the unholy pleasure he had in taking the law into his own hands.

"You been talking to the Russians as well?" Bill asked.

"Not me, my friend." Chief Phao held out his arms as though offering to show us how open he was. It looked more like an invitation to be strangled.

"Don't care if you do, as long as I get what I want." Bill smiled easily.

"I cleaned up that mess Mr. Smile left behind. No trace. I look out for my friends."

"My concern is, we don't have Hughes yet," Bill persisted. He tapped the ash from his cigar into an ashtray table made of veined glassy stone.

"Chief Phao always finishes what he starts. You will still pay me now, yes?" On his pinky finger, a ruby ring glinted, as though it was the very object rage would choose to be. He was not a man to say no to—though I worried Bill might try.

Bill placed a small cloth bag containing gold coins on the table and I felt relieved. Chief Phao looked inside and silently raised one finger, and Bill took another gold coin from his jacket pocket and put it in the bag also. I was glad the social portion of this awkward visit was over. I discreetly wrote down the price in a notebook I had brought.

In the car on the way back to the dock, Bill opined, "That's one crazy fucker."

I wanted to ask, So why do you deal with him? But I knew the answer. Chief Phao controlled the Siamese police force, which numbered forty thousand and was more powerful than the military. No one else had a strong enough grip on the country to escort a drug shipment from the Burmese border to the Bangkok warehouses—or to root out one man hiding in the chaotic backstreets of the city.

"After this business, we need some relaxation. You want to see some sights?"

"Sure." It was good of him to think of me at last.

He said that tomorrow we would tour the Grand Palace, Bangkok's most famous landmark. It would be nice to forget about

Link Hughes for a while, I thought, and let the chief do the work to find him.

AFTER AN EARLY lunch at the palazzo, Bill handed me an American passport with another man's name but my own likeness. "Where'd you get the picture?" I asked.

"Shively took it."

I had no memory of him taking a picture. I scowled. The man's sneaking knew no bounds. Instead of making a comment I knew would be useless, I asked if we were leaving the country. Bill explained that we needed a tourist permit to visit the palace grounds, and he didn't want any trace left of us. I understood Bill's interest in invisibility, since he'd escaped from death row, but why did I need some fake identity to tour the palace? I supposed, since I was in an underground trade, it was probably safest not to be on record anywhere.

We crossed the river and walked through the cool archway leading from the pier to the street, where an unmarked cream limousine waited. Dass had gone ahead of us to collect it from the garage. We drove along New Road, and Bill seemed to take special interest as we crossed a canal with portions of brick wall standing twelve feet high in places. "The ancient City Moat," he said. "I like these old canals. Isn't there one nearer the palace?"

"Yes," Dass said. "Klong Talad. Even the English call these smaller canals a *klong*. Asdang Road runs beside it." The translation was obviously for my benefit, but I already knew that much Siamese. I decided I liked Smile better than Dass, because he didn't waste words condescending to me like that. I was glad Smile was safely back at the palazzo, so I didn't have to feel guilty about abandoning him at the hospital.

Smile had been frustrated that he couldn't give Bill any more information about those Russians. He had been as surprised as I was by their arrival and had no chance to talk to them, what with the bullets and the knifings. Though apparently Bill knew something about the dead one. Chief Phao had sent over some pictures of the body, and Bill nodded to himself as he flipped through them.

I leaned forward to enjoy the view out the car window. There were temples everywhere I looked, spires and towers like extravagant wedding cakes. The canal walls dropped off from the road and on the water, about eight feet below, men rowed small boats Dass said were called sampans. The poor fellows were doing their best to avoid the faster motor barges in the narrow *klong*. The barges left large wakes behind, and the waves slapped against the canal walls, rocking the small boats mercilessly.

"Let's drive around the palace walls," Bill said.

The walls were blindingly white, tall, and crenellated, with watchtowers sprinkled along the expanse. Bill counted off the entryways in a notebook, licking his pencil. Most entrances had only a single heavy door with two guards. Over the top of the walls I could see golden towers and red pagoda roofs crammed everywhere. The palace looked like a town to itself, and I was keen to get a gander inside.

As we swung around to the river side, Dass pointed out the king's royal yacht, the three-masted *Maha Chakri*, moored at a private dock. "The king often arrives by river from his country palaces. It is tradition."

"A man can't have too many palaces," Bill said.

"Your palazzo suits me well enough," I said.

"You could earn enough in our ventures to buy your own," he said, leaning across to punch me on the shoulder, too hard as always. "This is the real land of opportunity. Forget about America."

He looked a little sad as he said it, though. He could never go back there—but I still could, if I wanted. Did I? I was sometimes homesick, but it was irrational. There was nothing and no one waiting for me there. I wouldn't mind a palazzo.

Bill pulled some official-looking papers from his pocket and gave them a read, brusque now. "Hey Dass, any idea which is the Gate of Supreme Victory? What a name. That's where we're supposed to go in."

Having completed the circle, Dass pulled to the curb and retrieved a tourist map from the glove box. "This looks like the place," he said. "Good luck."

Bill presented our papers to one of the guards, uniformed in a Western style with standard black dress pants, a white jacket with epaulettes, and a leather strap across the chest. The white helmet was more fanciful, Napoleonic maybe, with a golden crest, a tall spike sticking up, and a gold strap that looked uncomfortably balanced between the guard's lower lip and chin.

Once the heavy red door was safely closed behind us, Bill muttered, "Let's make a show of looking at the gardens." We strolled up the stone-paved roadway past compounds within compounds, the roofs nearly blinding me with the reflected glare off the bright metal. "Is it real gold?" I asked.

"Supposed to be plated, anyhow. If you want to see gold, I've heard the Emerald Buddha temple will blow your brains. But my itinerary has the Chakri Palace listed first. So we'll go there like good tourists."

After we passed through an iron gate with another two guards, we had a full view of the three-story main building. It was like an Italian palace wearing a pagoda as a hat, which somehow worked. Bill took out a small book, *A Guide to Bangkok*, published by the royal state railway, which described the areas open to the public. "Fantastically pruned dwarf trees, it says." Bill rolled his eyes. "Whatever cranks your handle. Wish they had less words and more maps. There's no floor plans at all."

We walked up a long flight of stairs and yet more guards waved us inside the main doors of the Chakri Palace after a cursory look at our papers. We stood in the centre of the throne hall and stared at the ceiling, which was distant and dripping with fanciful carvings of a European type. The throne itself looked foreign with a golden carved disk behind and a tiered dome hanging over it like an umbrella. The images over the flanking doorways were elephant heads, I realized. Another exotic touch. A European court would probably use a lion.

"Doors everywhere," was all Bill said.

He looked over his shoulder and then tried the handle of one, wiggling it. "Nope."

By now it was dawning on me that Bill was not in fact giving me a chance to see the sights. He was behaving very much as though he was casing the joint. I was irritated that he couldn't have just told me we were planning some kind of job. As Bill paused to draw schematics in his book, I felt a sudden anxiety to be involved in a plot against the most formidable structure in Siam. We'd passed a lot of guards. When he was done sketching, which seemed to take forever, we backtracked to the main foyer where we'd seen two more huge rooms leading off from each side. Consulting his guide, Bill said these were the Eastern and Western Galleries: one for the kings, one for the queens. Each was ringed with portraits and black marble busts. The royal clothing throughout time was a hodgepodge of Far Eastern pointed shoes, sarongs, and European military styles. Our steps echoed across the star-patterned stone tile.

"Fewer doors, but more mirrors," he said. "Mirrors can be useful."

He casually tried these doors too, but except for the one we'd come in, they were all locked. "Time to check out the Emerald Buddha," he said. "By the boo, it's just jade, but it's still worth a fortune in Asia."

Was he planning to steal it? Oh Christ. This would be a thousand times more difficult than robbing a bank in Nanaimo, British Columbia. Bill had specifically chosen that job because of the Canadians' naïve reputation. This was a royal palace, for heaven's sake.

We descended the main palace stairs into the sun, which was now blazing. So far, we had not seen any other tourists, so I felt conspicuous in the wide-open plaza. We drooped our way through the heat to the temple complex, the gods living behind their own walls. Inside, the buildings were close together, creating shady little mazes. As we climbed steps made of swirled marble onto the porch of the main temple, I noticed a tidy row of sandals along the outside wall. "We got to take off our shoes also," Bill said. "This is a holy place to them."

"Hope my feet smell okay," I joked, trying to cover my nerves. I peeled off my socks and stuffed them in my shoes. I sniffed. "Maybe not."

The black and white stone was cool on my feet as we padded inside. While the palace had many riches, the temple blew it out of the water. There were gold statues guarding statues that guarded other gold statues, and the Buddha on the highest platform had a precious green face above its gold robes. The emerald one. About thirty monks kneeled or sat cross-legged in front of the artistic madness, praying quietly. Thankfully they paid us no mind, and did not turn their heads. To my surprise, Bill had dropped to his knees in a position like the monks', and I wondered if he thought to pray. Then I realized he was feeling along the edges of the stone tiles, looking for something. I wished he didn't have to do that. What if a monk got suspicious?

Hoping to dissociate myself from Bill, I walked along the walls of the cavernous room, which were covered in murals of endless buildings and people. I got interested in them in spite of myself. As I looked more closely, I realized they were paintings of the palace complex, over and over, depicting different episodes in its history. I almost imagined if I looked long enough, I could find a little painting of me and Bill somewhere.

I lingered over the paintings as Bill changed spots a few times, testing more tiles. When he finally straightened up, tugging on his pant legs, I followed him out the door with relief. I sat on the porch to pull on my socks and shoes. I wanted to ask him what he was looking for, but it seemed a question best saved for outside the palace walls.

"They like their gold in these parts," Bill said. "I managed to capture some from the Japs at the end of the war. You can take a gander when you're at my warehouse. Nothing like a bar of twenty-four-carat gold. Not really stealing, I think, if you steal it from thieves. Kind of undoes itself."

"Maybe it's double stealing. You could give it back," I said. I knew my argument sounded weak, since I'd helped Bill steal stuff myself. But I really didn't want to break into this walled-up, guard-infested palace complex.

"Nobody knows whose it is anymore. Except I know it's mine now." He started to walk away. "Come on, let's check out the wall from the inside."

We left the temple complex and headed to the edge of the main grounds. Bill said we should look involved in a conversation, so the guards wouldn't think much of our wanderings—we were just distracted tourists. I was distracted, all right, by the worry that the guards would clue in to us. Bill paused in front of the stables and poked at some grates which smelled not too fine, apparently being where they washed out the horse dung. After checking there were no witnesses, he even bent down and pulled hard on one of the grates, but it didn't move. We completed a full circuit of the walls, Bill casually making a note in pencil now and again on his list of sights. We followed every pathway between all the buildings until I was baked as a foil-wrapped potato. I'd used up my supply of dry handkerchiefs, which I kept stuffed in every pocket for mopping up the heat. Sweat ran down my forehead unchecked, but I dared not suggest we leave.

"I'll just lean in the shade here, if you want to look around more." Though this was a tough place to lean, with pointy-beaked heads carved everywhere.

"No need. Got all I can get today."

I had a feeling of skulking as I passed the stern-faced guards, but Bill sauntered as always. The red door snicked shut behind us, well oiled, barely making a noise despite its heavy weight.

We rendezvoused with Dass where he was waiting for us a few blocks to the east on a side street, and he pulled the car closer as he saw us coming. Once we were safely inside, I asked Bill what he had been looking for on the temple floor.

"A door to a secret tunnel," he said.

That was far more intriguing than anything I expected, and I felt my eyebrows raise up my forehead. Looking satisfied at my reaction, Bill explained there was a legend of an escape hatch in case of war to spirit away the Emerald Buddha, the nation's prize possession, along with the king.

"Tell me straight. Are you planning to steal the Buddha?" It had not been as large as I expected, and in theory could be carried, depending on its weight.

"That would be crazy," Bill said. That didn't answer the question as far as I was concerned, since he'd been known to do crazy things. "But I need that goddamn tunnel, and I couldn't find a trace of it. I'm going to have to work my source a lot harder," Bill said. "With Mr. Smile Chang to assist."

I wasn't sure if I looked glad or sad. I hated to be left out of things, but this sounded like a dirty job.

"Don't worry. I need my chronicler to record this piece of history, if it exists. You'll be coming along."

CHAPTER NINE

THE QUARLO

I HUGGED THE man I'd always known as Sho-nuff, one of Bill's loyal men from the Clockwork Gang, and stood back to study him. He had streaks of grey at his temples, and a nautical air with the jaunty captain's hat he'd adopted. He still looked strong as a longshoreman. I had a thousand questions, but could only ask one at a time. I started with the easiest. "Why Frederick?"

"Better question is, why Sho-nuff? Frederick is my God-given name. I didn't mind that minstrel talk back in the day, but times change. I joined the N double-A CP. You want to have a cold drink and catch up? I live nearby."

"I thought you'd settled in Seattle."

"Left there before the war and sailed here single-handed. It was a dream of mine."

I desperately wanted to ask him if he had known all along that Bill was alive, since he was clearly in Bill's employ now. How else would he have found me here? And how much did he know about Link Hughes? The road was empty, but it didn't seem safe to say these things aloud. The men on the store porch had certainly taken an interest in us, all of them staring like a row of scarecrows. I averted my eyes and sighed.

"We can talk when we get away from those nosy parkers. Harmless guys, though. Known them all for years," Frederick said, taking my arm. "I got a live-aboard at the harbour. The public docks. The private club don't allow coloureds. I got a petition against them. Maybe you'd sign it?"

"Sure. If I can use another name on it."

"You in trouble?"

"Could be."

Frederick and I continued arm-in-arm along the road beside the beach, which swept the edge of a mountainous bay. There were signs for a navy base nearby and service jeeps passed on the dirt road. One fellow whistled at me and I was annoyed, but also a little glad I had decided to go blond. Another jeep slowed.

"Hey nigger, keep your hands off her," a sailor called out.

"He's a friend," I said. In the driver's seat his buddy stayed silent, glaring at Frederick. I wished I was in uniform so I could order them off: they were only able seaman, the navy equivalent of a private. But since I was about to go AWOL I would not mention that I far outranked them. At least not yet, if I didn't have to. Frederick gave them a cool stare and rolled up his sleeves. His forearms were like a blacksmith's.

The driver returned his eyes to the road and shifted into gear, peeling off. I let out a breath.

"Stuff like that's why I joined the N double-A CP," he said. "Anyways, we're almost there now."

A small yacht was stranded in the shallows near shore, with only the mast sticking out above the water's surface, tilted. Frederick followed my gaze.

"Don't worry about that junk. I got a proper ship."

A blue heron stood stock still on the edge of the dock leading into the public marina, staring in the water with endless patience. I was comforted to see this familiar bird from my old home in British Columbia, halfway around the world. As we passed by, it startled and flew off, though it did not speed up its ponderous flight.

The first moored boats we passed were small and weather-beaten. Some old men shuffling on their decks gave me curious glances. Independent sailing did not seem to be a lady's game, for I did not see any. I supposed they preferred to sit on deck sipping cocktails on the luxury ships back at the yacht club.

"At least these fellows mind their beeswax, unlike those navy boys," Frederick said. "This is a decent place."

I followed Frederick until he stopped beside a ship with *Quarlo* painted on its side in gold curlicue letters. It was larger than the other boats and the brass was well polished. "It's beautiful," I said. "Where will it take me?"

"Thanks. Restored her myself," he said, ignoring the last part of my question. He took my elbow as we walked the ramp, which bobbed gently. "Anyone tailing you?"

"I shook one off downtown."

"There'll be more eyes on us soon enough—a pretty woman like you and a Black man. Let's get below deck."

I nodded and, after crossing the wooden deck, lowered my head to step down into the galley.

"Settle in," he said, bustling around his compact kitchen. "I got a full bar. Anything you want. Whisky and soda? Or I can make a Hawaii cocktail with pineapple juice and coconut."

"And vodka?"

"Goes without saying."

"Sounds lovely."

He poured the liquids into a jigger and then into a tall glass, stirring it with a swizzle stick and dropping in some ice. He set it down in front of me on the table.

"Thanks."

He made a whisky and soda for himself and sat down. "You look different. Not from time passed—you're pretty as ever. Professional, but I can't think what profession. Did you go back to studying foreign tongues?"

"For a while, yes."

"Your eyes say you have more secrets."

"I'm afraid that's true."

"You still in some criminal business?"

"No, but that might have been easier. Frederick, where are you taking me?"

He smiled. "Setting sail for Siam. And it sounds like the sooner the better."

"That's where Bill is now?"

He nodded.

"Did you know all along that he was alive?" My expression must have narrowed, because Sho-Nuff, now Frederick, put his hand to his heart.

"Swear I never knew until a telegram came last month. Could have knocked me over with a feather. But I was happy about it. And happy to be asked to help you."

"I don't know if I'd call this helping *me*," I said. "It's what *he* wants." My throat felt dry, and I took a sip of my Hawaii cocktail. The pineapple burned in my throat, too acidic.

"He goes by William now. Safe enough I guess. That's a name for any man."

"William. Typical of Bill to run as close to the line as possible."

"Like a bull fighter with a red cape," Frederick admitted.

"Do you know how he got out of jail?"

"Nope. Good on him, though. A real Houdini getaway."

Frederick downed his drink and stood again, and I sensed he was restless to get moving. My eye roamed around the galley, wishing for something to fix on. I was dreading asking about Link Hughes, in case Bill had given Frederick an idea of what I'd done. Over the doorway, there was a stern portrait of a man wearing a white robe. Being Canadian and a daughter of Empire, I immediately recognized the portly form and ducktail beard of King Edward VII, though he'd died a few years before I was born. My father had thought well of his reign. "You're a fan of royalty now?" I asked.

He laughed. "No, but *Quarlo* was built in Liverpool in 1903. Last of the age of sail. I noticed a pale spot and figured a picture had been there. Did some research and saw these English ships always had a royal portrait. So I found one in a junk shop. I think it's good luck."

"I could use some when we get to Siam." The tall Collins glass had sweated into my hands, leaving them damp. I wiped them on my dress. "Do you know anything about Link Hughes?"

"All I know is that I'm supposed to get you safe to Siam, and there's people out there could mean you harm. I got the last supplies I needed at the store while I waited for you. Best we leave right away."

The boat was rocking a little in the harbour, and I felt the beginning of nausea. So it seemed like I might really see both Bill and Link again—talk about a reckoning.

"The minute we leave Hawaii, I'll be AWOL," I said. "All because of Bill 'helping' me. Some help." Not only AWOL from the military, but from Miss Maggie. She was the greater threat, if she had a mind to find me. I looked around the small cabin, which had little decoration besides the picture. The teak woodwork shone sparely and the cupboards were closed tight. "Do you have a radio?"

"It's in the wheelhouse."

"Turn it off, completely off, and never use it."

"That's crazy. I won't hear about storms or nothing."

"A radio signal is a dead giveaway. They can triangulate where you are."

His expression looked doubtful.

"I was a radio operator in the war."

"Okay." Frederick walked up the little stairway. "Preferred being a bank robber," he said over his shoulder, before shutting the hatch behind him.

WHAT WAS WRONG with me? I'd been on boats before. Large ferries when I lived on the coast of British Columbia and speedboats on sheltered inland seas. Apparently, these were not the real test. A small craft on the open Pacific—that was the meaning of hell. It had only taken me a few hours to find this out. "Oh God," I moaned, grabbing the rail as the boat lurched yet again.

I bent in half and vomited into the ocean. I wiped my hand across my mouth and stood up from the railing. My throat burned and my thoughts were sickly also. First, I discovered during my war training that I was afraid of heights. Now I learned that I had no sea legs. Was I only competent on solid ground, in a single dimension?

I was supposed to be on watch for a few hours later in the night while Frederick slept. Of course, I had no idea what I would do if something was wrong with our course. Wake him up, I guessed.

The sky glowed red in the west, and the sun was sucked under the horizon. In these southern latitudes, there was little coy preamble to the sunset. In Alaska it had been all preamble, the twilight lasting forever, until suddenly it was time for the sun to rise again.

I had offered to make dinner for Frederick in the happy innocence of the harbour, before I felt seasick. I had too much pride to take back my offer now. I told him I was heading down to the galley. He examined the instruments, adjusted the tiller and retied it, preparing to leave the ship to steer itself while we ate. Well, while he ate. I would not even try. I grabbed the brass handrail as I walked down the steep wooden steps. I had already laid the groundwork for my terrible cooking, and he had accepted the idea of an omelet for dinner with good grace when I promised him lots of bacon on the side. An omelet was one of only three things I knew how to make, and I told him it was normal for dinner in France, at least.

I started up the propane burner with a hiss and flare, heated up the iron skillet, and cracked three eggs into it. I tried not to retch as the smell rose from the pan. Frederick had baked bread this morning in the little gas oven, and I sawed a couple slices off the loaf. Crooked, as usual. I'd always been hopeless at this. Frederick came downstairs and sat at the table, which was only a few feet away from where I stood at the counter. "You feeling alright? It's a little rough."

"I'm fine," I said, putting his plate on the table. He did not comment that I left my placemat bare. The coffee started to wail in the Italian pot on the stove, and I rushed over to grab it, pouring it into a cup. I'd need it to stay awake tonight. I had already mixed up some powdered milk, and it sat on the table with the sugar in matching porcelain containers, chipped Royal Doulton. I thought this an amusingly feminine touch for Frederick's solitary male existence, though perhaps there had once been a lady friend to please. He asked if I'd like milk, and I shook my head no. He held up the jug and inspected the chip in the lip before dumping some in his own coffee. "Never should've bought fine china for a sailing ship. I knew it was a folly."

He held up a piece of the toast to stare at it also, and I groaned.

"It's not that bad, is it?" I asked.

"However you've been filling your time, it wasn't in cooking, nor carpentry neither. Don't let this lady near a saw."

"I told you, I was a radio operator. When would I learn to cook? In university, I lived in a boarding house where they made the meals. In the military, they served us slop, but I was glad I didn't have to make it. Basically, I'm completely non-domesticated."

He smiled at me, but then looked away. "You've always been your own woman. Are you sure you want to do this?"

"Why wouldn't I?" I sipped the hot coffee, and it sat bitter in my stomach.

"You said you were followed. By who? How would the military know you were going AWOL before it happened?"

I sighed. "My life is not normal."

"Aren't you tired of danger? I'm glad, myself, to be a reformed character. Good for the appetite." He patted his belly. "You're too skinny."

"I'm not a thief anymore. I just live—beyond the law, I guess."

"That's what Bill Bagley thought. It's easy to go too far. He was nearly killed for it." He stared down at his plate and shoved some egg onto his toast with his knife, then raised it to his mouth.

"Bill's nothing but a crook and a junkie. He wasted his life." I felt tears hot in the corners of my eyes, though I knew they would not fall. I had not cried about Bill since the day I thought he was hanged. It had been one of the worst days of my life. For years before that, a part of me had hoped he would reform and come back to me the way he used to be. But in the end it was drugs he loved the most.

"That's a harsh judgment," Frederick said, shaking me from my thoughts. "I never met anybody smarter than him."

"He tried to blackmail me before he escaped. About the gang."

"He did that?" Frederick turned the red flowered cup around and around on the saucer.

"Yes. And he let slip enough to put me under somebody else's control for the rest of my life."

"Who's lording it over you?"

I shrugged. "All I can say is that the war's over, but bad things are still going to happen. I don't want to be responsible. That's partly why I left."

Frederick stood up and looked out the porthole, his back to me. "We could just turn around, head back to Hawaii. I can protect you on my turf. Nobody asks questions at the docks. Probably they all got something to hide, or something they're running from. It's the nature of sailors." He rooted around in the cupboard and pulled out a duster made of ostrich feathers. He stood on tiptoe and brushed the portrait of King Edward.

I wondered for a moment if Frederick was inviting me to live with him. He had never shown a speck of interest in me over the years—I was Bill's girl and everybody knew it. Well, that didn't stop Byron, but Byron was a fool. Frederick had always been sensible, like an older brother, but why was he avoiding looking at me now? There was no dust on that print.

"I have to see Link Hughes. Without meaning to, I had a hand in what happened to him. I need to know if he can forgive me."

"Or if you can forgive Bill?" He stared at the king a while longer and then put the duster away, sitting down beside me on the bench when I did not answer. "Every morning is a chance to start over," he said, patting my hand. "The past is past. It don't own you."

CHAPTER TEN

DECEMBER 15, 1945

SMILE CHANG WAS going to put the squeeze on a palace guard that Bill had personally selected. I learned this in the longtail boat on the way to the man's house, which was in one of the old districts that still had no roads. It turned out that Bill and his network had researched the background of as many guards as possible to find the weak link. The man he settled on had a sickly son, and Bill paid for a European doctor to cure him. "He owes me. Plus, the man has the spine of a hunk of cheese. Surprised he made the cut for palace guard. But his father and his father's father and so on did the same job, and that means something here. Bonus for me is he learned all the old stories." If the tunnel was real, this man would know where to find it.

For this mission, Bill left the tillerman at home and drove the boat himself. Smile sat silently, cracking his knuckles. He weighed down his side of the boat so that we tilted in the water. The sun had been down for a couple of hours and the water was black, reflecting only the dark, cloudy sky. Here and there a lantern shone on the river from the little fishing sampans. I thrummed my fingers against the gunwales, but stopped as soon as I noticed I was doing it. Nerves. I'd never forgiven myself for the time I failed to prevent Bill and the boys from pummelling an old pawnshop owner. If things went too far tonight, I vowed to stop it. I looked sidewise at Smile and his mass of solid muscle. I wondered how bad he'd beat on me if I stood in Bill's way.

"By the boo, he knows me as Mr. Noland, so don't look surprised if he says it," Bill said.

I was curious how many aliases Bill had, but I kept my trap shut because we had arrived. Bill slowed the boat and turned it to rest against a dock in front of a squat house with fanciful Victorian scrollwork. Smile leapt out and grabbed the rope Bill threw him to tie up the boat. A square of light came from inside the open door of the house. It was the only light on shore. Most neighbourhoods had no electricity, and fuel was scarce since the war. Light was usually saved for pursuits that made money, such as the fishing we'd seen in the distance.

I suddenly realized a man was sitting silently on the dark verandah, which startled me but should not have. Life was lived mainly outdoors in the tropics. The man on the porch, who I already knew was called Silanon, greeted us, having recognized Bill immediately. "You come to see my son, Mr. Noland?" Silanon asked. "He is getting strong now." But the look on his face betrayed that he did not think Bill had come to comfort his son.

He was thin and smooth-faced, certainly not as hefty as I'd expect a guard to be, but I supposed they carried weapons and that was enough. Most Siamese men I'd seen were smaller than me. He wore only a sarong and I thought it would be hard to conceal a weapon, though not impossible. Smile himself had managed to tuck one away in monk's robes though these were much more voluminous. Thigh holster, maybe, but I didn't see any telltale bulge.

"And who are these men? Your friends are my friends," he said, holding his arms guileless and wide, and my heart sank.

"Mr. Wong and Mr. Stonehouse," Bill said. Silanon gave us each a bow.

Bill said we were in a hurry tonight, and only had time for the errand we'd come on. Through the door I glimpsed the kid propped up on pillows on a wooden bed, reading a book under the only circle of light. Bill said the doctor had suggested another course of medicines to be certain of the recovery. Silanon should come with us now to the doctor, Bill said, to get the medicine.

"I would be happy to thank him in person," Silanon said.

A blinking set of eyes rose out of the dark water, and I shuddered. "What's that?" I asked, hoping my tone did not sound as panicked as I felt. I had a fear of hidden creatures in dark water. The thing was about three feet long, with a tail like some kind of lizard.

"It's a water monitor," Silanon said. He grabbed something from a bucket and threw it into the water. The lizard snapped its jaws and thrashed its tail. I hoped this was its way of being happy. "I feed them fish, for good luck," he explained. "You want luck?" He held out another slimy fish. "Not from a lizard," I said. Silanon shrugged and tossed over the fish. I didn't think his luck was so good tonight, fish or no fish.

The four of us climbed into the longtail. We were silent until we reached the Chao Phraya, and Bill cut the engine when we hit the lonely middle of it. We floated a little while, until finally Silanon asked if we'd run out of gas.

"Cut the crap," said Bill, his voice suddenly cold and hard. He leaned forward on his bench. "You're going to tell me where I can find that tunnel, the one that leads out of the palace."

"That is just a legend," Silanon said, clutching his hands together. "I should not have mentioned it."

"But you did, and it sounds real to me."

Smile reached into his jacket, and Silanon looked shiny now. Sweating.

"You said these were friends?" Silanon asked.

"I have lots of friends," Bill said. "I had dinner with Chief Phao the other day."

Smile pulled out a cigarette and lit it. He passed the pack silently to Silanon who took one from it, his hands shaking.

Silanon's face flared red as Smile held a match to his cigarette, then he was smothered in shadows again, with only the glowing tip remaining as a beacon of his existence. The man said nothing.

"Let me make it easy for you," said Bill. "You're sworn to protect your king, right?"

"Yes," Silanon said, sitting up straighter.

"There's a man going to try to kill the king. I plan to stop him, but I need you to show me the tunnel."

Silanon sat silently a while. At last he said, "I don't believe you."

I felt some admiration for his resistance, but it made me worry I'd have to step into this business. Come on, just tell Bill, I urged him inwardly.

"Ah!" said Bill, seeming to delight in the increased difficulty of this project. "But if you're wrong, the king dies. And the guards take the blame. You don't want the blame, do you? I've seen what happens in this country to people who get blamed."

Silanon considered this, taking long draws on his cigarette. "You could be planning to kill the king yourself," he said finally. I had to admit that I, too, had had this thought.

"Then consider this," Bill said, moving his face close to Silanon's. "You tell me where the tunnel is, or my friend here cuts your son wide open and feeds him to the lizards. Tonight. You'll watch it happen. You'll have brought your son back to life just to watch him die. And remember, Chief Phao is my good friend. There won't be anyone you can turn to." He leaned back again. "Or you can trust me when I say that your king is in danger, and I'm not the enemy."

Silanon was quiet a long time then. Bill seemed completely at ease, like a man waiting for a train. Finally, Silanon raised his eyes, though he looked out across the river instead of meeting Bill's gaze. "This story is my honour," he whispered. "Two hundred years in my family."

AFTER BREAKFAST THE next morning, Bill and I took our iced coffee in the downstairs salon, the huge teak doors open to let in the cool morning breeze. Soft light poured through the carved screens above the doors, throwing patterned shadows over Bill's face. He always preferred to be in the shadows. He did not seem excited that he got the guard to reveal where the secret tunnel was.

"What's wrong, Bill?" I asked, sipping my coffee, which was sweet and cold.

"I got a lot of irons in the fire. It weighs on a man."

Bill put down his coffee and reached into his jacket pocket. He pulled out a heavy ring of keys, both ancient and modern, and handed them to me. "I need you to understand my whole business. Guns, gems, and opium. I'm trusting you with everything."

I felt a flush of pride at these words, and was happy to be Bill's lieutenant again. I smiled at him and nodded.

"Dass will show you the ropes."

That deflated me a bit. Dass already knew this stuff.

As though reading my thoughts, Bill said that there was something only I could do. Once I understood the business inside out, he wanted me to get to know the expatriates who were starting to arrive in Siam, looking for opportunities. I would be in charge of finding new markets for his products. "We're not looking for straight arrows, but there's some real bastards washing up on these shores," he said. "Who can we trust? Report back to me before handshaking any deals."

Smile entered the room, and Bill stood to leave. He and Smile were going on an unspecified errand that I for one didn't want to know more about. Not after I saw Smile kill that fellow at the hospital. I followed them out as far as the garden and watched as they locked the iron gate behind them on the way to the dock. Bill turned back and held up his fingers in the V for Victory sign, flashing his Clark Gable grin. A few local children appeared on the pathway, running and shouting in English, "Candy, please." Tiny missiles of glittering silver flew from Bill's hand before he boarded the longtail, and the kids leaped in the air to grab them.

"Sahib," was breathed in my ear, and I jumped. Why did Dass have to sneak around like that? "We will go to the warehouse now," he said. I followed him out the palazzo gate. Bill's boat was already a tiny dot on the river, roaring south. The children, still sucking their candy, hung back a little but stared at us curiously as we walked onto the dock where a second boat waited. One sad barefoot boy approached us. "Candy, please?" His lips quivered as he held out his hand.

I patted my pockets but of course I had no candy. All I found was an American silver dime, which I pressed into his palm. "Buy candy," I said, hoping he would understand. He held up the foreign money to his eye and smiled before he dashed off to join his friends.

"You will find that an expensive hobby," Dass said over his shoulder. I scurried to keep up with him and nearly fell over, with the boat still rocking from his jump aboard. "Since the soldiers came, all the children want candy. It will rot the teeth from their heads."

"I only did it because Bill did," I said, irritated to find myself making excuses to this fellow.

"It is true, Bill does that," Dass said. I got the sense he did not approve of that either, but had enough caution not to say a word against Bill.

When we reached the other shore, Dass hailed a rickshaw. The one that stopped was shabbier than the others, but Dass did not wave him away. His chipped blue bicycle was rigged with a homemade sidecar, with two hard wooden seats arranged so the passengers sat back to back. It was not comfortable, but at least I had an excuse to ignore Dass. The driver wore a short sarong hiked past his knees but was otherwise barefoot and shirtless, and as he started pedalling, leaning against our weight, I felt sorry for his exertions under the hot sun while we rested under an awning.

The rickshaw bumped and jolted along the potholed roads. I craned my neck to stare down the mysterious side streets, and each seemed to have its own special purpose. One was crammed with men working behind foot-pedal sewing machines, while another had women rubbing plants between their palms, making rope that lay coiled up beside them. One street was decorated with a black and gold archway, and beyond it monks in orange robes crouched, creating huge patterns on the ground from coloured sand. I wondered why, but Dass was not convenient to ask, and he probably wouldn't have told me anyway.

We stopped at a brick building painted white, two stories tall. I smoothed my hair after I clambered out of the rickshaw, and we stood there until Dass reminded me I had the key. "Right," I said. I jingled through the pile, trying a few in the lock, but none worked. "Which is it?" I asked, trying to hide my embarrassment. Silently Dass touched one of the antiques. The heavy wooden door swung inward with a groan, and once we were inside, Dass slammed and bolted it behind us. The only light came from clerestory windows up high, and dust motes floated in the pale sunbeams. It took a minute for my eyes to adjust, and then I made out tall stacks of wooden crates. Dass reached into a corner and pulled out a crowbar, wrenching open the lid of a nearby box with a creak of nails. I pulled out a rifle that was nestled in straw. It reminded me of the tommy-guns we'd used in the Clockwork Gang, but that was the extent of my weaponry knowledge.

I asked how many were in the box, and if each box was the same, and were all the guns in the same condition. Dass just shrugged at each question. It felt good to be in charge of things all of a sudden, and Dass a puzzled naïf.

"We'll have to do a detailed inventory, including age and condition," I said. "Then I can get quotes in the international market. How many men do you trust to handle these and know their worth?"

"Not many. The best would be an Englishman, Jack Dodgson."

"Who are the main customers so far?"

"Burmese hill tribes mostly. We exchange guns for opium. But for cash, South America looks promising. India also. I have some connections there."

I wondered what so many people wanted guns for. Hadn't the world had enough of war? I guess it depended whether you felt like a winner or a loser.

"The gems are locked up," Dass said. "Follow me." We climbed a circular metal staircase and paused in front of a steel door on the second floor. "He brought food, cigarettes, and radios into Burma when they were in need, and he got paid in gems. It is possible they are fakes, but Bill trusts his people."

I held out the ring of keys to Dass and he touched one, which opened the door to a windowless room. Dass pulled a cord on a bare light bulb to illuminate two safes, bank quality and about five feet tall. "Nice," I said.

Approaching one of the safes, Dass turned the dial left, right, left. I felt a surge of nostalgia at the familiar sound. He pulled open the door, revealing three shelves holding canvas sacks. I picked up a sack and untied it, and inside were large chunks of translucent rock with red glitters in their secret depths.

"Rubies," Dass said. "Some raw, some roughly cut."

By the time I had opened the sacks, filled with stones sorted into red, blue, green, and white, my head was spinning. Some of the raw stones were as big as my fist. But these rocks might be worth nothing at all, I told myself, trying to remain calm in front of Dass.

He opened the second safe and inside were large gold bars. About ten of them.

"Holy Jesus," I said. I picked one up and almost dropped it. It was heavier than I expected. There was only a single mark on the gleaming rectangle: "24K."

"We ran into a Japanese convoy trying to make off with these right after the surrender order."

"In terms of valuation," I said, trying to sound blasé in the face of this haul, "gold is easy. We just need the weight. But for the gems or rocks or whatever they are, we need an appraiser."

"The royal court employs the good ones. The others are bamboozlers." I smiled that Dass would use such a Bill-like word in his otherwise lilting and formal speech.

"I know just the man in Seattle, but we'll have to bring him here."

"Tell me the message and I will send a telegram," Dass said. "He shall come."

WORKING WITH BILL again was like being handed a magician's wand. Think of a thing, and it would happen. The jeweller I wanted was arriving today from Seattle. It was a plus that Vitale Levitsky had never seen Bill's face, because I was the one who had dealt with him back in Washington. He'd been recommended by the speak-easy men, because he never cared where your money came from, and was just as incurious when asked to appraise or recut jewels of uncertain origin. I still had a hard time saying, even to myself, words like "robbery" and "criminal." It was nice that Bill's business here was legal. Well, at least the opium that stayed in Siam. I was pretty sure some of it went to the States. I also worried about the people he wanted to sell guns to. I fanned myself with the ledger. Let's face it, this whole so-called legal business was more crooked than any bank job we ever did. The police were up to their eyeballs in corruption and mysterious schemes. Chief Phao was scarier than the worst gangster I ever met in the US of A, and Bill was in tight with him.

Bill had his finger in every pie. From studying the ledgers, I knew he was also "donating" money to the democratic leader, Mr. Pridi, so I followed his activities in the *South China Morning Post*. He had gained favour with the West during the war when he built the Siamese resistance against the Japanese. Now, Pridi was agitating for a constitution that would allow full elections for the first time in the country's history. Despite that, British support was wavering under peacetime realities. Back in the thirties, Pridi had been exiled from Siam as a Communist. If this label was proven, they would probably abandon him. On the other hand, he was popular in Siam and might win an election. I supposed Bill played it safe by putting a bet on all sides.

The warehouse door opened, a shaft of light piercing the dark room as Dass entered with another gentleman. I paused in my work of recording the guns and asked Mr. Dodgson to take a break. I was tired of him. Mr. Dodgson was the gun expert, but he was no use to talk to. He had clammed up the moment he arrived in the morning and only opened his jaw to spew out the facts I required of each gun he inspected. It was probably just as well I didn't get to know him because he seemed like a lowlife. He had hooded eyes and thick eyebrows that made him look perpetually angry. When he rolled up his sleeves, he revealed a snake tattooed on his forearm, and there was a long scar on his right cheek, as if he had been in a knife fight.

"Vito, so glad you could come," I said, clapping the newcomer on the back, as I imagined Bill would do.

"Long time no see." Vitale Levitsky was short, but the ladies in Seattle had thought him attractive. His delicate features contrasted with an intense dark stare, and it probably did not hurt that he dealt in fine jewellery. Dass silently withdrew from the warehouse with Mr. Dodgson, and I suggested the two of us go upstairs to the office.

"This must be something pretty special to drag me around the world," he said, as he followed me up the steep metal staircase.

"Mr. Yardley hopes so."

I placed myself between Vito and the safe as I turned the knob so he would not see the combination. Though he was smart enough that he'd never pull anything—next thing he knew he'd be floating face down in the Chao Phraya River. Lord, what brought such a thought into my head? Maybe I had been better off as a barkeep in harmless old Sequim, where the worst thing to happen in the ten years I lived there was the time some kids egged Mrs. Spencer's door on Halloween. There was practically a manhunt over the outrage, since the cops had nothing better to do. The delinquents, though, were never found, about which I was secretly pleased.

I placed the pouches on the desk and flicked on the banker's lamp. Vito picked up the largest stone and pulled out a magnifier. He whistled as he turned it under the light. "I'm gonna need my microscope and cutting tools, but you have the real deal here." He inspected some of the gems that had been roughly cut, and looked pleased. "At a guess I'd say you're looking at over a hundred grand."

I was staggered. That was as much money as the biggest heist we'd ever pulled back in the day, and this was from legitimate business. All because Bill trusted the remote Burma traders. His instincts had always been good, at least when he was not on the drugs. Bill had told me the few British soldiers that passed through the region had scoffed at the rocks as just that, pretty rocks, and wouldn't even trade their rations for them. The Burmese were that desperate after the war.

Vito asked if I could set him up with a workshop with good ventilation, because cutting stones was dusty work. "Mr. Yardley have any preference of the style they're cut to? Any of these to be made into something for a special lady?"

"We're not sentimental. Whatever will fetch the highest price is what we want."

Dass knocked on the office door and I came out, closing it quickly behind me. I wasn't sure why I bothered to conceal these doings with Vito, given that Dass seemed to know everything that was going on. Was it wrong to want my own fiefdom?

"Telegram from Mr. Yardley," he said, holding out an envelope between thumb and finger. As soon as I took it he turned on his heel. "The boat is leaving for the palazzo. Now," he said, more like an order than a piece of information. His insolence was annoying. After that first day when he had served drinks in the garden, he had refused to behave like a servant at all. I would have to talk to Bill about him, and subtly try to get a sense of what his position was. Then again, what was mine? Talking to Vito about his commission, I realized that I didn't know the nature of my own share in Bill's business. In the bank-robbing days, he had divvied things up equally between the gang members, reserving for himself the larger portion. Here in Bangkok, I lived in luxury at no cost, but I wanted something more substantial. There was more danger in this business than anything I'd done before. In the Clockwork Gang, cops might have shot at us, but they were usually small-town bunglers. Chief Phao was a professional killer.

I ripped open the envelope.

"LENA IS ON HER WAY. STAND BY FOR DETAILS."

I stared at the message and noticed my hand was shaking. So she was really coming. Would she recognize me? It would be humiliating if she did not, yet unsurprising. She only ever had eyes for Bill back then. Would I recognize her? This much time could have changed her. I had burned in my mind forever an image from when we robbed the bank in Nanaimo: Lena had tossed her hat to a poor coalminer's daughter as we fled the scene, her beautiful face so joyful.

She would not be that girl anymore. She would be thirty-four years old, I reckoned. Old enough to know her own mind, and to have grown out of girlish attractions to dangerous men.

CHAPTER ELEVEN

THROUGH THE PORTHOLE

WE HAD ENTERED the body of water named for my destination: the Gulf of Siam. I felt excited, for arrivals are always exciting somehow—nothing has gone wrong yet in a new place. Perhaps later I would be wretched here, but for now, I couldn't keep foolish hopes from taking over.

The weeks had felt long and I would be glad to leave the *Quarlo*. While my seasickness had subsided, whenever the waves swelled too high I was ill again. Christmas had come and gone. Being single, I never expected much of the holiday, but this had been the worst. I spent the day heaving over the rails and couldn't touch the cured ham that Frederick cooked up special. Finally, we had sailed past the southern tip of French Indochina and were heading northwest through the turquoise sea. A boat travels slowly enough that one hardly notices the changes in the water or sea air, but now the scent of land wafted on the sunrise breeze, and it smelled like flowers and rot.

Small mountains rose in lumps on the horizon, indistinct in the humid air. In the grey-pink light, a V of huge white birds flew silently overhead, their wings pumping slowly, as though they were kept in the air only by great strength. Beyond them, higher and smaller, dark birds yelled *eeee* with a sound of fear. I rubbed my arms and descended the stairs to the galley.

It was still dim inside, and the kerosene lantern flickered in the small sitting room. Frederick offered me the sole easy chair. He perched on a wooden stool, looking worried. I felt my landing was all worked out between us, but I bit my tongue, because it seemed to make Frederick feel better to go over it. He traced his finger over the map.

"There's islands we can creep between on our approach and not be seen from a distance. Where we'll land, Bang Saray, looks like a small fishing village. Hopefully not too many people about when we get in after dark. There's a road marked here, and you follow it about two miles to the railway tracks. This line goes to Bangkok." Frederick shook his head as he looked up from the map. "Lena, I don't feel so good about dumping you alone in this foreign place. Can I go as far as the train with you?"

"I'll be all right. I learned way-finding and such." I turned my face away so it wouldn't betray me—I was nervous about what I had to do. I'd never been in a foreign country. Also, I was sad to be leaving my old friend. I could not tell him everything, of course, but I trusted him with my life, which was more than I could say for anyone I'd met since my time with the gang.

Through the porthole I saw the sun rising, a red orb leaping from the horizon. I had not slept well and I rubbed my eyes at the sudden brightness. I had dreamed last night of Fala, back on Shemya, and in the dream he was shot. The real life story didn't end that way, but it easily could have.

During the summer, three airmen out for a walk had found an abandoned fox pup. They bundled it in a jacket and carried it back to the base, and they connived canned milk from the cook to nurse it with. The men were bored between missions, which were not frequent in the months leading up to the Japanese surrender in August. It was touching to see the pilots, who normally swaggered like cowboys, lavishing love and attention on the little fox.

It was adorable as any tame pup: it looked like a teddy bear with its tiny ears and thick red-brown fur. They called him Fala, after FDR's dog, and he would wait devotedly outside the mess hall for the pilots who rescued him to emerge. One day I hid around the corner from the mess until all the men were inside. I approached the puppy casually and then, looking around to be sure I was alone, I picked him up and cuddled him. I did not want to be seen in this girlish weakness. I did not necessarily like my reputation as cold and distant, but this brought me whatever little respect I managed to command among the men. The puppy was warm and his little heart beat quickly though he did not struggle in my arms. He felt so vulnerable, never believing for a moment that anyone would harm him. I brushed my cheek against his soft fur. I wished for the first time in my life that I could have a dog. I had never wanted to be tied down by any creature. But after all, a dog was man's best friend for a reason. Loyalty, unconditional love. Did I not deserve it? Wasn't I capable of giving it? Why did they have to call him Fala anyway? It was too sad. Fala was a famous dog, true, and famously loyal; more so than even your average dog. When FDR died last spring, the story went, Fala howled at the funeral as he stared glumly into the grave. Afterward, at home, if he heard a motorcade approaching he perked up his ears, but of course his hopes were always dashed. FDR was dead. Was the result of love and loyalty always so tragic? I had put the little fox back on the ground and walked away.

As the summer went on and Fala got bigger, he liked to play rough wrestling games with the airmen, clamping onto their forearms and calves. That was fine when his teeth were not sharp but soon, I thought, it would get out of hand. He was a wild creature. The men carried guns and their nerves were strung tight.

In the dream, Fala bit too hard and drew blood. The man who'd saved him, who had loved him best, pulled the trigger.

Fala yelped, twitched, bled from the mouth, and was dead.

I had been covered in sweat when I woke at his last cry. Was it a warning? That those who once cared for me were the most dangerous of all?

I tried to calm my breathing. In real life, Fala had left in time. When the first frost rimed the ground, the news went around that he had vanished. He must have gone back to his kin. When out on my walks, if I saw a flash of red-brown fur, I always wondered if it was him, and I wished him well. It was better to be free than anything, I reminded myself. If Link did not forgive me, I'd still have that much.

To prepare for landing, I opened my Siamese grammar book, but nothing new would sink in. When I imagined my meeting with Link, I was scared of what condition I might find him in. The Japanese had treated their POWs worse than even the Germans. The genocide of Jews was a horror the Nazis kept in its own compartment. They followed the Geneva Convention to the letter when it came to the soldiers they captured in battle. I found this inexplicable. Evil and honour. How did the human heart hold so many contradictions?

I put the grammar book away and went into the adjoining galley to fix coffee for Frederick, who'd been up in the night sailing the ship. We were in more sheltered waters, so I was not feeling sick. I could most likely keep down some breakfast. As soon as the coffee percolated on the burner, I yelled to let Frederick know it was ready.

We sipped our coffee in silence, while Frederick examined a nautical map on the table. I scooched over to the porthole and stared out at a curving shoreline dense with forest, forbidding and dark. A small white beach made my heart glad, I suppose from memories of childhood, digging in the sand at English Bay with my father. Sand always means summer to a Canadian, but I supposed it was just ordinary life here. One would more likely hide from the sun than seek it out, as I was used to doing. In Alaska I had found a straight-backed boulder I used as a chair on the rare sunny days—it collected the heat and was sheltered from the wind. I would sit there with my eyes closed pretending it was summer when it became warm enough to take off my jacket, though I still kept on a heavy sweater. Small pleasures, there. Mostly, it felt as if I was crawling through each day as over sharp gravel on bare knees.

"That's Koh Kut Island," Frederick said.

Grey cliffs streaked with orange rose straight up from the small white beach. "It's beautiful. Don't you wish you could lose yourself here forever?"

"Hawaii's my paradise. Still part of the good old USA."

A rhythmic thumping sound came from the deck above us, and Frederick paused in the middle of slurping his coffee.

"What's that?" he asked. "Something come loose?"

"I'll go check. Just enjoy your coffee."

I went upstairs, shutting the door behind me. Everything looked in place on deck, but I was startled by the sight of a large boat pulled up behind us. We hadn't heard it coming from downstairs because it had arrived under ragged sails. It was a strange creation, stitched together like Frankenstein's monster. There were no windows in the stern and the upper cabin was made of metal scraps welded together inexpertly. Things were sticking out of a skinny rectangular window, though it was more of a gap in the patchwork. I walked to the railing to get a better look. The things were hands and feet, both. The bodies inside must be stacked up like cordwood. Were these prisoners?

An arm closed around my neck, squeezing from behind so I could hardly breathe. I felt the metal of what must be a gun pressing into my back.

"Stay quiet. Put up your hands," a man hissed in my ear.

I did what he asked, my mind paralyzed. My arms quivered.

"How many more on ship?" His accent made his words clipped.

"One."

"Truth?" he asked, tightening his grip.

"Yes." My voice rasped, like air straining through a reed. The man's arm forced my chin upward so that I stared at the sky. How could it be so blue, cloudless, portending nothing?

"You tell him, come up now. Be good or I kill you."

CHAPTER TWELVE

JANUARY 10, 1946

I LOOKED AT my watch and it was 3 p.m. I no longer had the pocket watch Bill gave me long ago as a birthday gift, inscribed with his nickname for me, BY GOD. I lost it during our final wilderness journey together back in Washington. In any case, such a thing was out of style now, with everyone wearing wristwatches. A pocket watch had been a little quaint even then, but I had liked its dandiness.

So Lena was coming. I didn't feel like working anymore and decided to cut out early. I would take one of the local ferries down the length of the Chao Phraya. It was peaceful on the water. I liked the sight of the golden temple spires, more fanciful than any church tower, rising up from the trees as I sailed by. I supposed if I did not get on the boat to the palazzo, Dass would accompany me anyhow. He never let me out of his sight, and I was starting to find him almost as annoying as that Shively. No, I would not go that far. There was something of the graveyard about Shively. Bill picked some mighty strange companions, but I guess they all had their uses. Perhaps I just needed to make more of an effort with Dass.

He was an exotic, genteel fellow and I would like to know more of his history.

Aboard the ferry, I put up my umbrella and was glad I had brought it. It was a hard thing to remember, since it had the opposite purpose as in Washington State: there it was for rainy days, here it was for sun. Not every longtail boat had an awning. In Siam, things were not designed around the frailties of the white man. We were a small minority, and the British had never ruled here to mold the country to their needs.

"Have you ever had a sunburn, Dass?"

"No."

He kept his back to me while the boat cut smoothly through the water. Well, I'd just try to enjoy the ride. It was peaceful. While the ferry was motorized, most of the boats in the river had silent oarsmen. The clatter of automobiles was like a headache I never knew I had until it was gone. It was the same with the trains that clanked into Bangkok, steam engines of a type I had not seen since I was a child. I wondered if Lena would step off one of these antiques, appearing out of the smoke like an apparition.

Standing at the edge of the ferry, I stared into the tree branches overhanging the water. Not one bird to tempt Dass into conversation. I had never seen the river so devoid of life.

Dass stood silently at my shoulder.

We approached five grey towers washed out to nearly white in the harsh sunlight. They struck me as more ancient than the gold ones, as though their outer coating had been worn off over ages. "What's that temple called?" I asked.

"Wat Arun."

"Do you know its history?"

"Not much, sahib. I am no Buddhist. But the base of the temple is from Siam's Hindu era, which is the religion of my ancestors," he said. "Arun is the god of the rising sun. He was born too early from his egg and so did not achieve the beauty of the noon sun, like his brother, who was born at the correct time. But Arun has the consolation of the paler beauty of dawn."

"I like it. Shows not everything goes to the top gun."

We stood admiring the temple as the boat slowly passed by. I shaded my eyes but it was still too bright. I should come at dawn one day to appreciate it fully. The more I thought of it, the more I liked Dass's story. I preferred the soft early light to the glare of noon myself. My eye caught a bobbing motion from a tree branch overhanging the river—a spot of pink, like a bird spun from candy floss.

"What's that?" I asked, pointing.

"Black-backed kingfisher," he said. "Nice find."

"How'd you know from this distance?"

"Bright colour, small size, large beak, and most of all, that bobbing motion. Every bird moves in a unique way. It's no trick. It's the same as how you would recognize your love, even from far away." He rotated his body as the boat moved past to keep his eyes on the bird. It shot at top speed out of the tree and low across the water, and was suddenly gone.

I was uncomfortable about his reference to love. How was my face composed when he saw me open the telegram about Lena? "How do you know so much about birds?" I asked instead.

"When I was a boy, by accident I shot a bird that was special. I had never seen one like it before. I took it to the Bombay Natural History Society to learn what it was. The president of the group took a liking to me and encouraged me to keep a journal of the birds I saw. I studied biology for a year at university but my family fell on hard times and I could not continue. Perhaps if I had been allowed to join the Society my life would have been different. But natives were not allowed."

"In America we believe in equality," I said.

"Are there not places the negro is not allowed?"

"In the south, yes," I conceded. "But a Black man was a part of my former business with Mr. Yardley."

"Did he have an equal share with the white men?"

"Yes. And the woman, too."

Dass looked pensive. I hoped I hadn't stirred up a hornet's nest. I didn't know what his arrangement was with Bill. But my own standing might be no better than Dass's, or possibly worse. So far I had mainly been a financial drain. I would prove my worth to Bill when Lena arrived. Though how I was going to smooth things over, I didn't know yet.

I got rid of Dass by telling him I had work to do on Bill's orders. I went to scope out the port, so I was familiar with its layout should Lena arrive there. I'd only seen it for a few minutes when I came to Siam, what with Shively shoving me along. Then I took a taxi to get a closer look at the train station he'd also rushed me through. Where might Lena stand waiting? I wanted to be ready.

I asked the cab driver to let me out in Chinatown, which was a short stroll from the station, and had a reputation for better restaurants than the Siamese districts. I couldn't read any signs so I picked a place that looked busy. Dead ducks hung from hooks in the window, but one had to learn to ignore such things. I managed to order a soup that I struggled with, the noodles slipping from my chopsticks. I was trying my best to learn them along with some basic words of Siamese. It helped that their word for thank-you, though difficult to say correctly, involved a prayer motion with the hands and a bob of the head, so I could always make myself understood that way. The soup lady responded with a brilliant smile as I paid my bill at the back counter. I don't know, maybe she only spoke Chinese.

I realized I'd left my umbrella on the ferry in my hurry to leave Dass and cursed under my breath. To hide from the sun, I stayed underneath the porticoes of the shops, solid Victorian buildings of wood or plaster, lining Yaowarat Road. Shop owners swept their squares of sidewalk with handmade brooms, while chickens stood glum but resigned beneath rattan cages shaped like upside-down bowls. Ceramic pots by each door held small trees and flowering shrubs, freshening up the otherwise grey street, which was paved on this main thoroughfare. There were some old billboards from before the war, in English, for Eveready and Coca-Cola, which made me feel briefly homesick. I was jolted back to the present by an ad with a ghostly Asian woman smoothing cream on her face, the only English words among the jumble of foreign characters being "Snail White." A strange beauty aim given the lowliness of mollusks. I never did understand American women—in Siam it seemed hopeless indeed.

As I carried on past a white temple perched atop a high stone staircase, I recalled how Bill told me it contained a Buddha made of five tons of gold. I'd like to see it sometime, but I had too much to do before Lena arrived, so I carried on. The street was a chaos of people milling over the tram lines, a danger to themselves and a hindrance to public transit. The traffic here was mainly three-wheeled bicycle rickshaws, and the native drivers wore an odd uniform of British pith helmets and shorts. Was this some misguided government attempt at Westernizing the people? I suppose they looked happier than the men in traditional sarongs who played the part of mules, hauling loaded wooden carts. Everywhere little tables were laid out with fruits and vegetables in front of the real shops, with skinny country vendors squatting behind each one. Were they hopeful or hopeless? How long did it take for one feeling to bleed into the other?

Reaching Hua Lamphong station, I spent a good forty-five minutes circling it and examining all its corners. Every shady niche outside held a food stall, and small sparrows pecked at the ground, thin and barely feathered in the heat. Curs hung back, bedraggled and long snouted. Inside, underneath the high curved roof, some shops sold newspapers and cigars, while others displayed lengths of silk cloth, which young Siamese women eyed wistfully. Behind a tall teak enclosure, labelled in English, "Silence: Monks Only Waiting Area," holy men in burgundy robes fanned themselves, expressionless, their empty silver bowls beside them on the benches. I thought of Smile's ruse and peered uneasily at their faces before passing on.

Looking upward, I figured the giant wall clock in the main hall was a good place to meet. Here, each minute ticked by, hugely momentous. I crossed the polished stone floor and entered the platform where the trains stopped. Glancing over my shoulder, I saw a smaller clock over the doorway, alongside a portrait of King Ananda, who was thin and delicate. The English newspapers said that he had just reached the age of majority, and had returned from his studies in Switzerland to take the throne in December. This was the king that Bill meant to protect, if what he told the guard was true. Frankly I had a tough time imagining Bill taking that on—it was so unlike anything he'd done before. Maybe somebody offered him a lot of money. Standing beneath the gold-framed portrait as the crowds parted around me, I wondered idly what it would be like to be born a king. From what I understood, in Siam a king was halfway to being a Buddha, their god.

As foreigners in all kinds of strange clothes flowed by me, I wondered what would happen if you put the world's religions in a boxing ring—if one would come out on top as the ultimate truth. Or were all religions just stories we told ourselves to find meaning in our small lives, and keep the fear of death at bay? Bill had taken a surprising interest in this Buddha business, and had told me a good deal about it. Maybe that was why he'd want to save the king. Was Bill seeking some kind of redemption?

When I thought of his fingers probing the floor tiles in the royal temple, I thought it more likely that he coveted the Buddhists' wealth. He'd told me the tops of the towers were solid gold, and sported diamonds so high up that only heavenly beings could see them. "What a goddamn waste!" he'd said, sounding more like the Bill I knew. But why would he risk stealing that Emerald Buddha, under the nose of hundreds of guards, when he had a perfectly legal method to get rich with his opium? I supposed Bill had never been happy unless he had a challenge that would crush a regular man. I sighed. I was a regular man.

I compared my watch to the clock above me and inched the hands ahead by one minute to match it. My visit here was a piece of foolishness, and I fancied a change of scene. At the Oriental Hotel, I could talk comfortably to the Americans and Englishmen who were arriving in the country, more almost by the day. The Americans were not good news for Bill. Hopefully no one would recognize him in his altered circumstances, but it was still safer for me to scope out the bar alone.

When I left the station the sun blasted me like a sucker punch. By the time I reached the curb sweat poured down my back, and with relief I stepped inside one of the few taxi cabs waiting. Even with the window open it was still sweltering inside. I removed my hat, and in the rearview mirror I saw it left a dent where the band had squashed down my hair. I turned the Panama hat to read the label inside: a Montecristi Super Fino, just like Bill's. He had left it sitting on my dresser one day as a gift. I believe he took some pleasure in forcing me to ape him—back in Seattle he had dragged me to his favourite tailor—though reluctantly I had to admit this Panama hat was the ideal protection from the tropical sun. Of course, the wealthy locals seemed not to wear hats, because they preferred to avoid being outside entirely. Only I, Bill's lackey, was left to bake outside at midday. I had the sudden urge to crumple up the hat, but smoothed it carefully instead, since there was a dress code at the Oriental.

The Oriental Hotel bar was soothing with its dark wood panelling and private nooks. It nodded to the locale with teak filigrees crowning the bar like the border to an exotic land. As I scanned the room, I wondered what an arms trader looked like. So far I hadn't met any, at least that would admit it. Whatever they were up to, the foreigners here struck me as cuckoo, because they were willing to descend into the chaos left after the war. It was no place for cozy homebodies. Like me, I thought with a sigh as I raised my hand at the bartender. Pull yourself together, *By God*, I thought, conjuring the power of Bill's name for me.

I ordered a gin and tonic, hoping to build more malarial resistance. It was not comfortable living so close to the river. The biting insects rose up in clouds every sunset, and Bill laughed at me when I took off in alarm and refused to come outside until they had settled again after dark. But Jesus, he had had malaria, and I noticed that he meandered into the palazzo not long after I closed myself in. I think even Bill feared the mosquitoes, though he'd never admit it.

"You been here long, in Siam?" asked the man on the stool to my left.

"Six weeks maybe."

"I just arrived. Name's Warner. You?" He reached over to shake my hand.

"Byron," I admitted, disliking my name whenever it was laid out like a dead fish in front of people.

He was American—East Coast money, I figured from the accent. Warner was dressed casually in a pale yellow cotton shirt. The way he carried himself was self-assured, and he spoke in hearty tones as though confident you would find him fascinating no matter what he said. He was what I imagined an Ivy League man must be like. His glasses could not conceal his craggy good looks, though I judged him to be five years older than me, in his early forties. Blond, with no trace of grey. The ladies still went for him, I guessed. A fellow who got whatever he wanted.

"What business brings you here?" I asked.

"Oh, you know, import export."

I wanted to roll my eyes at his shillyshallying, but I restrained myself. God knows, he could be on the straight and narrow. But what legal thing could be worth importing or exporting in Siam? The economy was in ruins. The government had a store of rice, but that was hardly worth the interest of a man of his station. I would have to draw him out.

"I deal in gems and other resources of the mountain tribes. Of Burma," I said. He kept his profile to me, but I could see his face fully reflected in the bar mirror, appearing as if floating between bottles of scotch.

"What's it like?"

"I haven't been there yet. My—" I was going to say boss, but Bill wasn't really that, after all, and I did not want this man to think I was nobody— "associate manages that side of things. William Yardley. He's well known in Bangkok."

"Then I'd like to meet him." He handed me his card and I studied it. Nice cream paper, raised cursive script. *Warner Knox, Jr., Resident at the Oriental Hotel, Bangkok.*

"You're staying on here?" If he could afford the Oriental for long enough to put it on his card, he certainly had the kind of money we were looking for. It was the most expensive hotel in the city.

"For now. Though I'm sick of living out of a suitcase, and looking for a house to rent. All the best places seem to be taken. Have you found something?"

"Yes, though you can only get to it by boat, and that takes getting used to. It's like being marooned on an island."

Shut up, Byron, I thought. Why did I tell him that? Bill had not ordered me to keep our location private, but he didn't exactly want it advertised in the newspaper, either.

I felt at risk of doing something wrong in this exchange. I needed to confer with Bill before I gave away more of our game. There was something about Warner's expectant silence that made me want to tell him things, and I did not trust myself. I downed my drink. "Sorry, got to run. Great meeting you. See you again soon, I hope."

He waved as I left, already turning to speak to the fellow sitting on his other side. Well, he was no wallflower.

The pier was only a minute's walk away, through the hotel garden speckled with a few solitary Englishmen in white like mushrooms in the shade. I continued down a narrow street, past the brick Catholic mission with its spread-armed Christ behind a wrought-iron fence. A group of bald monks in pink robes walked past, as though to prove whose religion really belonged to the streets. With a shock, I realized from the shape of their bodies beneath the cloth that they were women. I hung back near the fence as they passed, no doubt headed for the green and red pagoda that was just visible beyond the Oriental Hotel's perimeter wall. I was in no mood to ride a crowded local ferry, so I asked the attendant, who spoke English, to instruct a private water taxi to take me to pier thirteen, across from the palazzo. I would take Bill's long-tail from there, because he didn't like strange boats pulling up at his dock.

When I arrived, Bill was ensconced in his library, reading the *South China Morning Post*. He set it aside to hear my report, and his fingers were stained grey from the cheap newsprint. I told him I'd found a wealthy prospect at the Oriental Hotel. "An American, I think," I said.

"Did you trust him?"

"Not sure. I didn't trust myself around him. He seemed like somebody trying to find out more about you than he was willing to give away."

"You say he's rich?"

"Must be, if he's taken up residence there. Costs a mint. And he seemed interested about the gems. That's all I mentioned so far."

Bill carefully wedged the newspaper in the magazine rack beside his chair and stared into space a moment, his expression unreadable.

"This man's business is top priority. Good work." He stood up and clapped me on the shoulder, and I could feel myself grinning like a fool while he told me to book his favourite table for the three of us in the Oriental dining room, for tomorrow night. So I hadn't botched the whole thing after all.

That evening, lying down on my bed, I stared up into the swirling fan high above me on the ceiling. Bill, praising me? I wished I had it in writing, it happened so seldom. Damn it, why did it matter? I was starting to step out of Bill's shadow, I reminded myself. Maybe Lena would sense that when she saw me again.

I pulled the sheet off my chest so the fan would cool me, and I went to sleep, smiling.

CHAPTER THIRTEEN

BLOOD IN THE WATER

THE BANDIT SHOVED me toward the doorway leading into the galley. He stepped back to hide while I opened it and called for Frederick as he'd ordered me to do.

I felt horrible dragging Frederick into this, but I didn't have a choice. There were three of the pirates aboard already, and they had rifles strapped across their chests. They knew some English, so they had likely done this many times. I could not hope for amateur mistakes. One man had a red bandana tied over his long, matted hair and wore aviator sunglasses so I could not see his eyes. The other two men had shaved heads, with a zigzag pattern left behind in the stubble. It was one of these two that had crept up on me at the railing. He waved for me to step away from the stairway. He grabbed me again, twisting my arm behind my back. It hurt but I stayed silent, my jaw clenched.

"What is it?" Frederick asked as he walked upstairs. Took a look around. "Shit." He raised his hands over his head.

The other two men grabbed Frederick. They tied us up quickly, each to a mast. The rope dug into my wrists. A machete at my throat now. The man's face near mine, his square bones sharp under his skin, heavy eyebrows, deep-set black eyes—impossible to read emotion there.

"Where is your money?" said the one in the bandana. The ringleader. A painful light glared off his mirror lenses.

I didn't answer, my heart racing as I looked straight ahead. Shouldn't I be doing something brave or clever right now? I should have used my training and fought back when the first one grabbed me. At Camp X, a Shanghai policeman had taught us martial arts. But we'd only practised kung fu for one day. What the hell could I do with that? We'd mostly done close combat drills with weapons, and I didn't have one now. Only the crooks had weapons.

"Somebody answer me!" the leader yelled.

"There's a box in the kitchen downstairs," Frederick said. "Under the seat."

That was Frederick's money. He was trying to save mine—five hundred American dollars in my suitcase, in the front cabin. I also had a few Siamese bills sewn into the dress I was wearing, reserved for emergencies on my landing. It looked like there was going to be an emergency. Sweat dripped into my eyes, and I squinted from the sting of salt that I couldn't wipe away.

"Seat flips right up, so no need to wreck it." Frederick spoke to the back of the man running downstairs. He was admirably calm. Our bank robber days had stayed with him enough to steel his nerves, it seemed. I just felt detached in a way that left me paralyzed. All I could think of was the irony. We, who had robbed so often, were now the victims of robbery. Though of a much baser sort, I thought. The banks were insured, but these thieves would leave us in desperate straits, and they did not care one jot.

Why had I frozen up so badly? I tugged against the ropes.

"Pretty lady," my captor said. "Why you try to get away? Tired of your African? You will like me much more."

He caressed my face with his dirty hand, ran rough fingertips down my neck and onto my breast. I spit in his face. He flinched and wiped his eye. He stepped closer to me, his breath hot.

"You regret that," he said.

I felt something running down my neck, below the machete that pressed against my skin. Was it blood? I wondered distantly, giddy. Would he kill me?

The leader spoke in a language that was abrupt yet musical. It sounded angry, but some languages always sounded angry to the foreign ear. My thoughts were drifting in funny directions but it seemed to take too much effort to rein them in. I thought more about languages, and if there was objective beauty in them? If so, English was partway beautiful, or maybe more like ugly-beautiful. There were people that had these confusing looks, too. They could provoke different feelings depending on the day, or the character of the observer. The Japanese language I had always thought soft and elegant when I was eavesdropping on the pilots earlier in the war. Except when they were shot down. Scattershot and hysterical words, then. It was horrible. But all speech deteriorated in times of panic. I wondered what a scream for mercy in English would sound like to these men's ears. Beautiful or ugly?

The machete was still at my throat, and I waited for what would come next.

Banging noises came from below as the third bandit did his work. He was obviously not content with the stash that Frederick had admitted to. Frederick sagged against the mast, a picture of hopelessness as he heard the damage being done to his ship. By contrast, the head pirate was cheerful now, while my guard stared at me with barely suppressed lust and rage. I felt sure he would choose between the two as the seconds passed. Neither would be good.

The shouting downstairs got louder, and both men fixed their attention on it. They watched keenly while the flunky emerged onto the deck. He smirked and held up the small wooden box with Frederick's money, as well as my drawstring purse with the roll of us bills. My mission was unravelling before it even began. My landing would be much more difficult with no cash.

That was assuming they would let us live.

A shiver ran over my body. I wasn't ready to die yet. I had too much left to do. I tried to remember if I had heard of any murders of foreigners in these parts. No, I had not, but news agencies were not exactly thick on the ground here, either. It was a blank spot in the Western consciousness. Until I learned Link was here, I'd never heard anything about Siam.

I watched their faces for a clue to their thoughts. Yes, they were jolly. I thought if they planned murder they would look serious, with such business left to do. Then I remembered the boys' excitement when we were chased by the police and they fired at our pursuers. That was different, I told myself. That was the thrill of the chase, while Frederick and I were trussed up like farm animals. There was no sport in that. Even criminals differentiated, didn't they?

Oh God, I didn't know what would happen to me now. I felt faint.

The pirates moved their lips, whispering a greedy novena as they counted out the bills. When they were done, the man who had captured me shoved the money into a pouch at the waist of his sarong.

"The police will not help you," the leader said.

My heart lifted: he was imagining our future. We would not die here. I would wake up another morning, in this muggy heat and hot sun, and the thought was glorious.

The three bandits turned their backs as they laid down a board to breach the gap between our ships. Frederick was suddenly moving quickly and quietly across the deck to the lifejacket box, free from his bonds. He had the cold, bloodless look that I remembered from our heists, and I realized I hadn't seen it since then. He pulled out a lever-action rifle and as he cocked it, the pirates froze in place. The leader screamed, jerked back, and fell off the edge of the boat. In the same split second I heard a shot. There was a splash, then silence. The two men remaining looked stunned.

"Put all the money back in the purse and lay it on the deck," Frederick said, the gun trained on them. "No funny business."

Frederick's former captor stared overboard and looked back at him with fear. "You kill him," he said.

Frederick did not answer. He kept his gun aimed, unwavering. Would he kill them too? On the run, Frederick had fired in defence, but I'd never seen him kill coldly. He might well have—he had a history of crime before I knew him. Even after all my target shooting in Alaska, I did not know if I could have pulled the trigger to kill a man the way Frederick had. The real thing was very different.

The bandits did not appear to doubt Frederick's intention. Their hands shaking, the men took the money out of their waist pouches. Hands in the air, my captor shoved the purse toward us with a filthy toe. I couldn't help but think I would never want to use that purse again.

Frederick pulled back the lever action, *clack ka-clack*. The sound of death. My captor squeezed shut his eyes and suddenly looked very young. The other one's hands dangled helplessly at his sides. They were lost now that they had no leader and were faced with superior firepower.

The hard look fled from Frederick's eyes, and I saw doubt flash. "Just get out of here," he said. "Mend your ways, boys."

After a startled pause, they stared at each other and jumped into action. They threw down their plank and ran onto their boat. As they yanked back their escape route, the *Quarlo* rocked gently. How could their evil presence have been so light? They fired up their motor, deafening, and it spewed black smoke as they departed northward.

I tugged against the ropes around my wrists.

"Stay still, Lena. I'll get you."

Frederick laid his gun down on the lifejacket box and pulled a small knife from a sheath around his calf. That must be how he had got loose. When I thought he had given in to despair about his boat, he had reached down for the knife when he sagged against the mast. He had cut his ropes when the bandits were distracted by counting our money. He had been prepared, and I needed to be more like that.

By the time the boat disappeared around the point, Frederick had freed my hands. Swaying a little, I leaned forward and a drop of blood fell onto the deck. Then another.

"Hang on to the mast. Just one more minute." He whipped off his shirt. "Now press this tight on your neck," he said. "It's not as bad as it looks."

I laughed. I sounded a little hysterical, I thought. But I couldn't see my neck—how could I see how bad it looked?

The boat started spinning around me.

CHAPTER FOURTEEN

JANUARY 11, 1946

BILL, WARNER, AND I were ensconced in the back corner table of the Oriental dining room, away from prying eyes and ears. The small talk was going well. I felt good about myself, since I was the one who had made this meeting happen. If a business deal came out of it, I'd have proved my worth to Bill. I wouldn't feel like I was sponging off him at the palazzo any longer.

Warner looked dapper in a white linen suit jacket and he already had a tan, which was set off nicely against the white. I was still pale as a fish's belly since I tried to stay out of the sun. Otherwise I just burned and got a red face that made me look like a drunk. Bill matched Warner linen suit for linen suit, but he was in a dove grey jacket. Like a gangster on holiday, I thought. Pretty much what he was.

"Your Burmese gems sound interesting," Warner said.

A Siamese waiter set down a tray with a crystal decanter, three glasses, and a bucket of ice. Bill waved him off and served us out, tonging a single cube into each glass.

"I have something even better," Bill said. "Guns. It's a good business to get into right now. The world is more unsettled than ever."

"I don't know. Guns create a lot of hassles," Warner said. "This is good bourbon." He raised the glass to admire the golden tones as they glowed under the chandelier.

"The gems could be premature. They're not cut yet. I brought in an appraiser from the States to see if they're worth anything, but I don't have his report yet. This guy Levitsky. I used him before and he knows his beans."

"Levitsky?" Warner asked, still studying his drink, which was already nearly empty. "Is that a Jew?"

"Yeah, go figure, a gem guy who's a Jew. Hazard of the business," Bill said. "But I ain't asking you to buy my gems. My main aim, forgive the pun, is to sell my guns to you." He raised his thumb and finger to Warner, like he was firing at him. It didn't feel like a joke somehow, and I poured another round for everyone, in case it would jolly things up.

Warner said nothing, but just looked around the restaurant, as though hoping that someone would come to his aid.

"I heard there's a German in Burma who's appraising," Bill continued, staring intently at Warner's face. "If that's more to your liking."

"No need," Warner said. He stood up, downed his drink, and slammed the glass on the table. "Good night, gentlemen," he said, and turned for the door.

"That really set him off," I said. "What's his problem?"

"His problems are increasing every day," Bill said with satisfaction. His eyes followed the backs of two men who, just after Warner, left the room.

Bill topped up my glass, which I took as a signal to stay. About ten minutes later, he sidled out of the booth, and I followed him through the hotel gardens and back to the car. Despite the botched deal, Bill was in a grand mood. Other things were going well, apparently. There was a bumper crop of opium, he said, and he'd got it for a good price. As we drove over a pothole, Bill gripped the door handle as the car jolted.

"Watch it," he growled at Dass, who was driving. Bill's mood was changeable as always, and he seemed suddenly dour. Perhaps it was because he had downed much of a bottle of bourbon.

Dass gave him a grim look in the rearview mirror. "It is not I who put these potholes in the road. Could you not ask your government friends to spend some money on the paving?"

The old Bill would have torn a strip off anyone who gave a saucy retort, if anybody even dared to try it. He'd as like throw you out of the car, back in the day. I was a little sorry to see that Dass would not be getting any such comeuppance. Bill was still the boss, after all.

"I can't fucking believe they're here," he muttered. "Just like she said."

"What are you talking about?"

He wiped his hands across his face. "Forget it. Some crazy old fortune teller. Just keep an eye on Warner. What a smug bastard."

"I didn't like him."

Bill whacked me on the back, surprising me. "You're a good man, By God." His face was suddenly illuminated as another car approached and the headlights beamed through our window. His expression was serious. Another effect of the massive quantity of bourbon, I supposed.

"We've never talked about your cut in my new venture," he said. "I won't leave you hanging." He pulled a pad of paper out of his suit pocket and scrawled something in pencil there. As another car passed us, lighting up the interior, I saw "25" writ there under the brief glare and I couldn't help smiling. It was more than fair.

"What about him?" I asked quietly, jerking a thumb at Dass. I was partway sticking up for his interests, and partway just curious. I wasn't sure which feeling was stronger. In any case, I had to perform the accounting of it, so I might as well find out.

"Ten," Bill said, but there was no response from the front. "Hear that, you nosy bastard? You get *ten percent*."

Dass still said nothing.

"What exactly does he do?" I couldn't keep the bitter tone out of my voice. I was tired of competing with Bill's never-ending string of new sidekicks. I reminded myself I had a bigger share. I deserved it, because I'd been with him longer.

"He does what he's told," Bill growled. "Don't think that's so easy. I demand loyalty to the bitter end. I need men who'd take a bullet for me. That applies to you too, By God."

"You know I would."

"You didn't quite, that last time. In Washington. You ran for it." But he was grinning at me, to show there were no hard feelings. Or at least that's what I hoped his expression meant.

"I did get shot, remember?" I rolled up my sleeve to show the scar on my right forearm. There was a red dint in the centre with white raised around it, the size of a quarter. The same scar was mirrored on the front and back of my arm, because the bullet had exited clean. That was lucky, since it was not treated by a doctor but in a Chinese opium den. I wished the scars were more perfectly round so people might actually guess it was a bullet. They probably thought I burned myself cooking or got stabbed by falling onto a stick. Anyhow, I wore long sleeves.

"Well, I'd do that for you. One bullet anyhow. You can depend on it, or my name's not—" He paused. "Shit. William Yardley." He let out a half-crazed laugh. "You heard that, Dass? I'll take a bullet for you, you do the same for me?"

"To the death," Dass said.

"No need to go that far. Just take it to the leg or something."

We were at the pier now and Dass pulled into the parking garage. It was quiet on the sidewalk except for a few late-night vendors crouched over their charcoal fires, waiting to roast slim skewers of meat when they found a purchaser. I knew the meat sat outside raw for hours, but I was suddenly hungry and bought a couple of skewers. I felt proud that I had understood the man say "chicken" in the Siamese tongue when I pointed at the meat I wanted. I had no gift for language but I was making progress. I was pleased also to help the white-bearded old man with some money because he looked poor, in dirty clothes and no shoes. He smiled with beatific happiness when I handed him my small coins. Shouldn't I learn to be satisfied with less?

As we walked the last thirty feet to the dock, I bit into the skewer, but it was hard against my teeth. "What is this, anyways?" I said, staring at it in puzzlement.

"That is the leg, sahib."

Bill burst out laughing again. "Enjoying your peasant's gristle?"

Chickens in Siam were much different than the fat white ones at home. I'd seen them wandering the streets of Bangkok, small brown birds on tall lean legs. They were made to run, and I was eating nothing but the shin bones.

"It was only a nickel," I said.

"Could be worse. Could've been the foot."

Standing on the dock, Bill pulled out a flashlight to shine on the yellow flag as he waved it, so the boatman would see us from the other side. Where we were standing was otherwise dark. There were no streetlights, and only the occasional mansion along the river had lights burning.

I had not relished the two strings of meat I had wrestled off the leg with my teeth, so I threw the other skewer in the water. A moment later there was a surge where the skewer had landed, and a sheen, on eyes. Gigantic lizard eyes. "Oh Christ, it's one of those water monitors."

"*Varanus salvator*," said Dass.

This one was the biggest I'd seen, about five feet long and its tail was as thick as my thigh. "Do they attack people?"

"I would not willingly swim with it," said Dass. "They have a venomous bite and attack other creatures. I have not heard of them eating a man, but they do eat corpses."

"I'll try not to be a corpse," I said.

Our longtail boat cut smoothly through the water and the driver turned it sideways to the dock where it bumped gently, twice. He threw a rope to Dass, who held the boat steady while Bill and I climbed on board and settled on the seats in the centre. Dass jumped on, sitting on the seat across from us near the gunwales, closer to the water, as the driver pulled away.

"If Lena ever comes," I said, "what do you want me to say?"

Bill turned his face away, suddenly interested in the black water. "You can explain how you've seen me and I've changed. You can swear to it I'm clean. I think it's best to set her up elsewhere until she's ready to see me. She might need to adjust."

"Sounds like a good idea," I said, and this was the truth. It might take her a very, very long time to adjust. As long as eternity, perhaps. In any case, I was glad the moment of her arrival was reserved for me alone. For old time's sake. I would hear about her life from her own mouth and for once I would know more than Bill did.

He was always one step ahead of me. I had discovered Warner, but Bill seemed to know things about him that he would not tell. Yet he hadn't ruled out working with the man. What kind of queer fish was he? There must be plenty of other people who would be interested in our products. I would talk to Bill about it when the time seemed right. For now, I would keep a close eye on Warner. I did not trust him.

AT THE TRAIN station, I waited an extra hour past the time Bill said, my eyes darting from the tracks to my wristwatch to the giant clock above the doors. Had Bill got it wrong? No, of course not, I thought, as the train from Sattahip finally arrived with a slow gasp. It was the train that was off schedule. As the dirty crowds streamed off, I felt a pang that Lena would have had to endure such lowness. Why did she have to be on a third-class train? What a shabby introduction to the country. Men and women alike spit foul red betel juice onto the platform, making a mess. I had asked Bill to explain the allure of this habit that left the teeth black. It did not even stop the women, though it spoiled their beauty before age thirty. "It's addictive, of course. Narcotic and stimulant. Ride the roller coaster," he said, and his eyes blazed up for a moment. "But it's unrefined and weak. Too cheap for my interest."

I stood on the platform a long while after the last person came off the Sattahip train, to make sure I had not missed Lena somehow. I could not fail Bill in this. The station was quiet now, and idly I watched a woman sitting cross-legged in front of a low table where she brushed white paste onto a small square of shiny leaf. She added a pinch of chopped betel nut, and folded it up into a tiny packet. She did a brisk business in small coins.

Lena was not coming.

Maybe she felt Bill's presence here, somehow, and it was keeping her away like a magnet's pole reversed. Or had Bill's mysterious sources been stringing him along, telling him what he wanted to hear? If so, I hoped Shively would pay for this infamy. I walked out the main doors and threw my arm across my eyes to shield them from the sudden glare. The one cab driver malingering outside jumped to life at the sight of me, no doubt dreaming of the American dollars in my pocket. He approached me expecting to carry my luggage, but I showed him my empty hands and he opened the door for me.

"Pier thirteen," I said, and thought for the first time of its unluckiness. Strange that I hadn't before. I hung my head out the window, hoping to catch a cool breeze across my face. Like a dog, I thought. I realized how these sensitive creatures must feel as the smell of the city assaulted my nose: rotten fruit, ox dung, and the general tragedy of dead things. My eardrums were also under trial. When the Siamese people were not utterly silent they were capable of astonishing shouting, especially when organizing crowds. I could relate to such differences between the personal and the public performance.

When I finally got back to the palazzo—the boatman did not jump to his duty so promptly when I was not with Bill—I walked into the airy sitting room on the ground floor. It had an echoey feel. Bill's furniture was top quality, but there was not enough of it to fill the large space. The old owners had to clear out in a rush in their disgrace, but they took all their favourite things. It made the place feel sad and incomplete.

"Bill?" I called out. He would not be happy with my report.

"Sahib?"

I was startled to find Dass suddenly at my elbow. "Jesus, man, you're like a cat," I said.

"He's at the warehouse. He wants you to meet him there."

"He could've told the boatman," I grumbled. "Now I've got to cross the river again."

Dass smiled and shrugged. "He has his ways."

I trudged down to the boat again. At least the breeze over the river was fresher than elsewhere, though it was just a few minutes of reprieve. There were no cabs at the pier when I got there, so I took a rickshaw. I always felt guilty relaxing while some poor fellow peddled away under the tropical sun. At least I was not a heavy load, and he seemed glad to get my handful of coins. Such is life, I reflected, as I stood at the warehouse door, waiting for my knock to be answered. I could not fix the driver's misfortune by not riding in his rickshaw—it would require fixing the whole society.

The door swung open and I moved quickly to lock it behind me, pulling the heavy iron bar into place. It was blessedly cool in the dimness. My eyes took a moment to adjust and I made out Bill approaching. Wooden chests were stacked along the walls. I whistled. "That's some haul."

"Yes," he said, distractedly. "Any news?"

I paused a moment, thinking how to soften it, but I could not. "She wasn't there."

"Damn it, what went wrong?"

He ran his hands through his hair and drifted over to the opium boxes. I followed him to where he stared down at his fortune, forlorn. "This is top grade, but what's the point of it all?"

"Riches?" I said.

"True enough, but it made the general and the chief greedy. They took a larger cut."

"How much?"

"Ten percent each, off the top. But they have me over a barrel. They control the mountain passes through Burma and northern Siam. To protect me from bandits—which is mainly themselves."

"How much did you get to keep?"

"About seven hundred pounds." He shifted aside a box to make a chair. "A fortune is always a comfortable place to rest your dogs," he said, patting the space beside him.

I sat down, though I did not find it so comfortable as he suggested. A pile of hay would be softer and have a less bitter smell. Actually, after a moment I felt a bit nauseous. It was hard to imagine the attraction of this stuff now that I was up close to it.

"So she wasn't there," he said. "I don't understand. He said it would be today."

"Who said?"

"A little birdie."

"Did your birdie tell you anything about her life now?"

"She's wrapped up in military things." He waved his hand as though her doings were some kind of magic.

"Still? The war's over."

"You think the War Department is going to roll over and die? They're finding new projects. For one thing, Uncle Sam sent that money to Chief Phao. He's building his army with it."

"But the chief's insane. Remember the story where he drowned a man with his bare hands? He seemed to enjoy the whole thing too much."

"He can keep order, and that's worth something to a lot of people. He helped me out, after all." He patted his opium box fondly. "Want to grab a drink and celebrate my haul?"

His haul—as though he had no partners in it. That was the Bill I remembered.

CHAPTER FIFTEEN

TO FORGIVE A THIEF

I WOKE UP lying across the kitchen bench of the *Quarlo*.

"Sorry it ain't so comfortable," Frederick said. His blurry form resolved, though at first I could only focus on details, like his gold cufflinks in the shape of anchors. I hadn't seen them before, nor the blue-striped dress shirt he wore to replace the white one he'd stripped off for my bandage. He looked dapper. "Bastards sliced up my cushions even though I told them where the money was," he said. "Crooks got no morals these days."

"I'm glad you let them go."

"Hope I judged right. Specially that one that molested you. But he was just a kid acting tough. Their fight left them when I killed the head man. That was enough for me. Not every thief deserves to be shot, does he?"

I started to shake my head, but a thousand shards of pain sparked behind my eyes and stopped me short. I reached toward my neck, but Frederick grabbed my arm.

"Don't touch it. I did a couple stitches, teensy weensy. Used alcohol to sterilize it, and it's bandaged up real nice."

"Will I have a scar?"

"Not with my pretty work. Anyway, it's right below the chin, so you'd never see it."

I told myself to calm down about the scar business. I was lucky to be alive. I sat up and the room wobbled, so I grabbed the table to steady myself.

"I gave you a shot of morphine," he said.

So that explained it. I felt strangely good, and warm, as though wrapped in a silk sheet. Everything in the snug little room looked appealing.

"You got to rest a few days, so I'll need more supplies," Frederick said. "Closest port is Sattahip."

I remembered a symbol marked on our map. "Isn't that a naval base?"

"Before the Japanese came, it was. Don't know how much is going on there now."

It was possible that Miss Maggie would suspect I was headed to Siam. She could have discovered a Russian cable about Link through her other agents. It was best not to linger near a base where there might be intelligence officers posted. The Siamese would be keen to cooperate with America now.

"What about Indo-China?" I asked.

"Kampot isn't too far away. Old French city, a pretty good size."

I was not happy to have more delays when I was so close to Bangkok, but it seemed the safer option. There would be other foreigners and we would not stand out so much—the French even had African soldiers, I'd heard. "Let's go there. But just for one night."

"One night?" he said doubtfully, but didn't argue.

Satisfied, I lay back down on the padded bench. "Let me know how much it costs to repair the boat, and I'll send you the money as soon as I can."

"No need. It wasn't your fault. I'll be glad to get back home to work on her, and Bill will pay for it."

Bill, I thought, and closed my eyes. If he wanted to see me, I would refuse him.

TOO WEAK TO stand, I sat on deck while we sailed for Kampot, the lever-action rifle weighing on my lap as I scanned the waters and plumbed my soul. No wonder Miss Maggie hadn't used me as a field agent. I hadn't done anything right when we were robbed by those pirates, short of not dying. I had to prove myself more resourceful in everything that might come next. Once I left this boat, I had no one else to depend on.

I wished Frederick had told me about the gun he had hidden. I could have grabbed it with lightning speed and dealt with those pirates before Frederick even knew they were aboard. With the muzzle I traced the arc of a large white bird flying by. No, that would be bad luck. It was the first thing I'd seen in the Gulf of Siam—my welcome committee. I put the gun back in my lap. It was heavy anyhow. I needed to save my strength for real dangers.

In Kampot, I stayed sleeping in my tiny bedroom in the ship's bow. I peeked out the porthole a couple of times, but all I could see were the masts of other ships in the marina. Sometimes I heard the hollow drumbeat of footsteps on the wooden dock, and once two Frenchmen drifted by, speaking of the weather. It was hot, just as they said, and my brow was coated in sweat. I went back to sleep. It was right, anyhow, that my first experience on land should be in Siam.

Sailing north again, Frederick kept his distance from the islands, avoiding coves and tricky shorelines. Able to stand now, I continued my watch on deck with the rifle, certain I could at least hit the broad side of a boat. But all was quiet and we made it without mishap to Bang Saray just after sundown. Frederick let the anchor chain loose and it whirred over the roller, splashing into the sea. Once the ship was steady he lowered the dinghy, his muscles straining at the winch. He unfurled the rope ladder down the side of the *Quarlo* and gestured for me to go first. I grabbed the gunwales to steady myself in the dinghy. Frederick followed gracefully, barely rocking it as he climbed aboard.

"Wish I had your sea legs," I said, trying my best to be jaunty. I didn't feel very good.

"All these years living on a boat, I tip over walking on land now," he said, and started to row. The night sky was clear and his face shone with sweat in the moonlight as we drew near the shore. Strange fishing craft, high-bowed, were resting on sand that glowed blue-white under the half moon. Nets hung over bamboo frames. There was no sign of motion. The dinghy jolted as we hit the sand and I let out a quiet *Oof.*

"Best leave your shoes on. Could be stingrays," Frederick said.

I must have looked alarmed.

"Shuffle your feet and if you touch one it'll just swim away. They don't mean to hurt anybody." He held my arm as I got out of the boat and I lowered my feet gingerly into the water until they reached the sandy bottom.

"Good luck, Lena."

"Thanks for bringing me here. I hope I'll see you again."

"Oh, you will."

Though the ocean resisted me, I hurried through the dark, shallow water, shuffling as he advised and wishing I could see my feet. My neck throbbed but I tried to ignore it. I paused over Frederick's parting words, wondering if he thought I'd need his help later. But I wouldn't be able to reach him until he was back in Hawaii, and by then it would be too late. A jolt seared through my leg and I froze. Had I already stepped on a stingray? I shuffled my feet, but I didn't feel any creature down there. Staring into the water, I saw a ghostly blob glowing near the surface, tendrils streaming. Jellyfish. There had been jellyfish in the waters off British Columbia, though I'd never heard of anyone stung by them. I kept moving toward shore, my leg electric but still functioning.

I was relieved when I made it to the soft sand on the beach, and I couldn't resist turning to watch Frederick's dinghy getting smaller as he rowed away. Losing my old friend for a second time reminded me of how alone I was in the world. I took a deep breath. Bill sent him. Bill planned everything. Bill wanted to see me, and Link most likely did not. Could Bill protect him from the Russians until I arrived? I put my palm to my forehead: I had a headache, dull and throbbing, and my thoughts stalled like confused soldiers doubting orders. I needed to get my bearings and leave the exposed beach. A gap in the trees showed a road cutting inland, which I had expected from the map, so I took the hard-packed dirt track. I wasn't sure if I was walking straight. I felt unsteady, like I was still on the boat.

It was strange to think I was in a foreign country for the first time in my life. America did not count. Being from Canada, it was familiar to me the first time I went there. With Bill. I pushed the thought of him aside. I was in the Far East, land of pagodas and opium dreams, or at least that's what people said. So far, Siam seemed humbler than the legend. Passing stilted huts, I heard faint snuffling barnyard sounds—the strangely peaceful sleep of animals doomed to die. The village was timeless, like agrarian life from a history book, though the hot, humid air and palm trees told me I was not in old England. I wondered what the Siamese people would be like. Hopefully those bandits were not representative. Feeling thirsty, I paused at a well with a wooden bucket and dipper beside the road, but decided the water would not be safe to drink. I'd wait until I was on the train and buy some bottled spring water or cola. The train. I would soon be in Bangkok. Would I be the person I needed to be when I saw Link? I probably had only one chance at forgiveness. I wished I knew what I'd say.

I sneezed and stopped in alarm to listen into the dark, but nothing stirred and I carried on, trying to walk more carefully so the dust didn't fly up from the road and give me away. The farming village was behind me now and the air was better, laced with the scent of tropical flowers. Soon the railway tracks shone silver ahead of me, cutting across the dirt road. Stopping at the last stand of trees, I leaned against one to steady myself. The bark was strangely smooth under my hand and I found myself caressing it gently. The pleasant sensation vanished the moment I realized there were people nearby, though there was no station at this remote spot. About twenty feet away stood two peasants, a father and son I guessed, beside the rail line. They were very thin and wore no shirt or shoes. Their clothing was as strange to me as encountering men wrapped only in a bath towel. They cut short their quiet talking, but they did not try to look at me. I suppose the war had trained them to hide their curiosity from strangers. Had they cooperated happily with the Japanese or chafed under their yoke? Probably the latter. Poor people had only their sweat to offer, or their beautiful daughters. They gained nothing under any regime.

I would rather have been alone, but it wasn't like I could hide from the locals much longer. I planned to take a third-class carriage where at least there would not be any foreigners. They were the ones I was worried about. It seemed unlikely Miss Maggie would recruit native Siamese agents, because she'd have to give away too much of her game to unpredictable outsiders.

With the father and son here, at least I didn't have to figure out how to hail the train. Even the effort of lifting my arm above my head seemed like too much. I had a vision of myself standing helplessly like a deer in the path of the train, being mowed down. As though conjured by my grim thoughts, in the distance a train whistled—eerie in every land known to God and sounding like a warning. It was earlier than I expected, but the only schedule Frederick could obtain in Kampot was from before the war. The father and son waved madly and the train slowed on its approach, the front light glaring, a single yellow beam illuminating the smoke of the old steam engine as it came to a halt with a giant's sigh. A man in a conductor's uniform hung by one arm out the door, returning their wave. The boy picked up a large wooden signboard with a white X painted on it, and dragged it away so it was no longer facing the track. So that was how they signalled the train. I moved quickly out of the trees and approached the family while the conductor lowered the stairs and dropped a small footstool onto the ground. The father nudged me ahead and the conductor took my arm to help me up. The attention was alarming, but they seemed like good people. Were they not surprised to see a white woman in this remote spot? I supposed I might be a familiar creature to them, since in Bangkok there must be British people passing through, or would have been before the war. The locals might be used to seeing them on the trains. The conductor gestured to me to stay put while he pulled up the stool and the stairs. I focused on his uniform, because it was the same uniform as anywhere in the world. It helped me feel I wasn't dreaming all this. I was dizzy though the train was not moving—yet somehow, it tipped around me like water sloshing in a bath. I gripped the railing in the gangway. As the train started up the conductor took my arm again, uttering short syllables I could not understand, and tugged me in the opposite direction from where the father and son had disappeared. I tried hard not to lean on him. That would surely seem strange.

In the locomotive, I was surprised but relieved when he settled me beside the engineer. I needed to sit down. The conductor was speaking to me, and I finally realized what he was saying was in English with a thick accent. "VIP," he said again, smiling. I almost wanted to cry at this act of kindness after so many days at sea and the treatment I'd received at the pirates' hands. "Bangkok?" I asked.

The conductor said something I couldn't understand but he was still smiling, so I took it as a yes and handed him some unfamiliar Siamese bills. He pressed several back into my hand, indicating I had paid too much. Perhaps the pirates were not Siamese—I could not reconcile the differences between them otherwise.

"Cap koon ka," I said, *thank you*, as the grammar book had spelled phonetically in English. He stared at me blankly. Apparently, I had to work on my pronunciation. Then he bowed and left.

I sat feeling a little awkward beside the engineer, thinking that conversation must be expected. Realistically though, how could it be, when I was so obviously a foreigner? Soon I decided that the engineer was content to stare out the front window into the night, watching for stray animals, I supposed. He sounded the whistle any time a dirt road intersected the tracks, warning farmers of his passing. In between the blasts I nodded off, but somehow the noise always woke me from a dream in which I was with the gang and we planned to rob a train. We had never done that. It seemed like a bad idea, because once the heist was over you would be trapped on a train. Every time I thought that panicked thought I made an effort to keep my heavy eyelids open, but it was impossible to stay awake.

A cup sat on the dashboard, and the driver pulled a small, square tablet from it. He popped it into his mouth, chewed for a long time, and spit a stream of dark juice out the window. It must be some kind of tobacco, I thought. He held out the cup to me, but I smiled and shook my head to decline it. VIP, I sighed to myself. I had begun to worry that all this attention was making my arrival in Siam memorable, to be recounted to any curious police officer. On the bright side, being in the engine car limited my contact with the rest of the passengers, who would have given me a good stare while I sat with them. I reminded myself that staying invisible was not the same as not being seen. It mattered more who was doing the seeing. Anyone curious about the comings and goings of foreigners would monitor the upscale hotels and restaurants, the first-class trains and ocean liners.

There was no way Miss Maggie could have traced me here. My sailing with Frederick was private and undocumented. He knew not to turn on the radio because I told him the transmission could be located. *But she's always one step ahead.* I brushed the thought away as I fell into another unsettled doze, rocked to sleep by the hypnotic rhythm of the train.

"BANGKOK," THE CONDUCTOR yelled. I yawned and stared out the window into the morning. We had already entered the long outdoor canopy of the railway station. Waving goodbye to the engineer, I walked through the car to the gangway, lurched toward the railing, and grabbed it to steady myself. Though the conductor clearly wanted me to exit first, in the place of honour, I waited until the crowds started down the stairs, my sweaty hand slipping on the metal bar. The air was hot even at this early hour, and I missed the breeze through the train window. I stayed in the middle of a tightly packed group and hoped that the chaos in the station would obscure me from any watching eyes. Looking at my arm where it was nearly pressed against another, I was conscious of how pale I was compared to the Siamese women, and how different my clothes were. They had sarongs and wraps of cloth around their chest that exposed one shoulder, and some had their black hair cut short, in little pompadours. My blond hair shone like a lighthouse among them. I paused and let the local people flow around me. The next platform over had an express train arriving from Butterworth, the sign read in English. I smiled. I didn't know where that was, but it looked so solid, the blocky English letters, among the scribbles of Siamese. I fell in with hale fellows speaking in British accents alongside pretty women twirling parasols. I felt suddenly shabby as I looked at my dirty clothes and shoes. I made myself walk in a straight line to the end of the platform, looking for a washroom to freshen up in. I joined a line of women leading to an anonymous doorway. I hadn't had a proper look at myself since Mercie Gordon's hair salon, back in Honolulu. Frederick only had a small shaving mirror on the *Quarlo*. Waiting to move ahead, I leaned against the wall. The white paint was surprisingly cool and clean, and I felt badly when I raised my head and saw I had left a dirty smear. When I finally got near the front, I saw that inside each wooden cubicle there was only a filthy hole in the ground. Liquid sloshed on the floors and the smell nearly made me retch. I left the lineup with my hand over my mouth. There were first-class trains, so there must be first-class bathrooms somewhere. I drifted with the crowds through the double doors into the station proper, where English signs pointed up a staircase toward a restaurant catering to foreigners. My feet were heavy and it felt very high, but I made it to the second floor where there was a well-lit powder room with an attendant. I handed her a Siamese bill and she looked delighted. How much had I paid her? I'd better get a grip on the exchange rate so I was not remembered as "that generous lady." Keeping my face averted from the Englishwomen standing at the counter, I went into a stall and sat on the modern toilet seat, my head in my hands, resting until I heard them leave. At the counter, I took a white towel from a basket and brushed my dress. The towel turned orange from the dust, but my clothes still weren't what you would call clean. Staring in the mirror I was shocked to see what I looked like. My skin was waxy. I'd avoided a tan by wearing a hat or hiding in the shade on the ship, but now I was beyond pale. I rinsed my face under cold water and raised my chin to examine my wound. Blood had soaked through the dressing. I looked a mess. Gingerly, I peeled up the surgical tape and was startled by the deep red gash with three black x's sewn over it. I pressed the tape down again. I didn't have anything to replace the bloody bandage, so I would have to keep my chin down to avoid drawing attention to myself.

CHAPTER SIXTEEN

JANUARY 14, 1946

BILL HAD TOLD me with perfect confidence that Lena would arrive today on the train originating from Sattahip, most likely on the first local at eight o'clock. I'd pay a deal of money to find out how he knew such a thing. Could the two of them be in touch? I chewed absently on a hangnail. No, that wasn't possible. Bill said she never even answered his telegram when he invited her here. Lured, more like, with that Link Hughes. Who we still had not found. This was a problem, and Bill had left me standing alone in the dung pile. Somehow I'd have to distract Lena from any demands to see Hughes.

I'd never heard of such a place as Sattahip. Wouldn't she come from a major port such as Rangoon or Saigon? Could be Bill was just off his nut, and she wasn't coming at all.

This time I was determined to wait all day if I had to. There'd be hell to pay if she did arrive and I missed her somehow. I would not be surprised if Bill sent old Shively as a backup, to catch me out. Shively would take pleasure in doing it. Of course, I had to admit I was also pretty keen to see her. It was a natural nostalgia for old times. Wasn't it? Having been cured once of unreturned love, surely that would make me immune. Until Bill had thrown her name around, I had hardly thought of her at all for the last few years. So why did my heart have to leap up like it wanted to get out of my chest when I thought of seeing her? It must be like a doctor testing your reflexes. You can't help reacting, but it doesn't mean you feel anything.

Already I had inspected the crowds coming off the eight o'clock train, but I hadn't seen her. It was difficult with so many cars to watch, and so many doors. There was an Eastern Line local from Sattahip every two hours, and a first-class express in the afternoon. My eyeballs would be tired out by then from staring around at everybody. Why did this place have to be so busy?

Now that the train had unloaded, I would stake out the main exit, near the cab stand, until the next local was scheduled to come. Even if I had missed Lena stepping off the train, she might not have left the station yet. She would have to pass through this door. From my post I could see both inside and out. I had run here and was still recovering my breath. I made a bit of a spectacle of myself— nobody runs in the tropics.

A motion at the top of the stairs leading to the British restaurant drew my attention. A woman, blond, flicking her hair from her eyes. She was luminous—like an orchid shining from the depths of the rainforest. Lena. I knew without a doubt it was her, even from this distance. I knew it in the way that Dass could tell an unusual bird from a long way off, simply by the way it carried itself. And so with Lena: stately yet calm. She was a stillness in the chaotic station packed with people, brown and white, silk and rags. As she walked slowly down the stairs, still unconscious of me, I could see that her dress was different, too. Though dusty with the fine orange powder distinctive to the country earth here, I sensed it was expensive from the fabric and tailoring, and you could tell it was American somehow, too. Bolder than the European clothes. There weren't many American women here, and they stood out.

I went to the bottom of the stairs to intercept her. I may have measured my steps—thirty inches seemed like a good length for a casual stride. I cleared my throat. I supposed the station must be dusty.

"Lena," I said, carefully choosing a moderate volume. So she could hear me but I would not attract undue attention.

She stared at me. For a moment her face seemed blank and without understanding, she did not know who I was, Oh God, I was nothing, just like I had always been. Then her eyes lit up. "Byron?" It was the first time in my life that my name had sounded good to me.

She smiled, for me. It was a perfect moment.

Now I saw how her eyes stayed a little sad, and the softness had fallen away from her face. Bill used to pinch her full cheeks, rather too hard and without the sweet joking such a gesture should involve, I always thought. No one, not even Bill, would try to do that now. She was a woman, not a girl.

"Yes, it's me," I said. "Did you have a good trip? Where's your luggage? What's new? Did you know that I own a saloon in Sequim, Washington?" I was running at the mouth, and I stopped myself.

She gave me a hug. I hugged her back, torn between the wish to hold her tight and the fear of seeming to cling. Then I realized I had to hold on to her. She was slipping downward.

She raised her chin and said "Byron?" again, weakly, and I saw a bandage underneath, on her neck, soaked through with blood.

She needed immediate care. What I had thought luminous about her skin I saw now was pallid and sickly. And that sweet look in her eyes was simply staring into a distant land beyond the here and now, having moved beyond pain.

There was no way I was going to take her to the shabby, inconspicuous hotel where Bill had unaccountably arranged for Lena to stay while I was reconciling her to his existence. She needed a soft bed and servants. Bill could stuff his plan and hide himself out of the way if he didn't have the nerve to face her yet. However, I wouldn't mention it was Bill's place in case she refused it. "I have a nice home nearby. Would you like to rest there?"

She opened her mouth as though to speak, gave it up, sighed, and nodded.

"Please, let me help you," I said, and offered her my arm. She leaned heavily, her strength flagging. "The driver is close by," I said into her ear. She nodded again, almost imperceptibly this time. I worried I would not be able to hold her up, but then she straightened her shoulders and continued on her own power.

Dass was where I'd left him, idling the Rolls Royce just behind where the taxis waited. I kept underneath the shady colonnade until we were at the car. I guided her in the door and shut it gently, too gently at first and the latch didn't catch, so that I had to close it again, more manfully. I smiled encouragingly at her through the glass and hurried to the other door, closing myself in with her. She looked a little better now that she was sitting down.

Dass was eyeballing us in the rearview mirror. I was dead tired of never having any privacy, but there was nothing to be done about it.

"Well, here we go," I said loudly. "Back to the palazzo." I prayed that Dass would do this without any backtalk. He knew this wasn't the plan, so I breathed a quiet sigh of relief when, after a lag, Dass pulled the Rolls out and we entered the fray of rickshaws and horse carts on the road.

Lena just closed her eyes. At least she was still conscious, because she did not slide down in the seat. I wished I could find out what happened, but I could not rouse her.

Now that my surprise at seeing her beside me was fading, I was left only with the lead weight of knowing that she had come halfway around the world for this fellow Link Hughes. This was, frankly, a horrible position to be in, but Bill was in it too. If she was here for Hughes, she wasn't here for Bill. We would sink in this swamp together.

I hoped that she had built up this man Hughes during their separation, and his reality would prove a disappointment. I would like to be there to see her face, when we found him. So I could comfort her.

We arrived at the pier, and Dass took her other arm as we left the car. I settled Lena at the prow of the longtail and the driver set off at my nod. It gave me a pang to see her there, leaned against the polished teak, the shimmering water as a backdrop while the wind tousled her hair. It echoed the memory I held of her on our journey to Vancouver Island, before the biggest heist of our career. Those were golden times. I hadn't loved anyone since then. I had a steady girlfriend for a couple of years in Sequim, but when she pressed for marriage I ended the relationship instead. I could not get over the idea that at any time I might have to go on the run if my past was discovered. That was no way to settle down with anyone. Not when your heart felt tepid as a sink of forgotten dishwater. I had resigned myself to not being a passionate man. Passion was only for youth, for the wild roller coaster of being twenty-five. It was hard sometimes to get used to the flatness of life that followed, but maybe such things were inevitable.

I shook myself from my thoughts when I noticed Dass gesturing to me from the far end of the boat, where he stood beside the boatman, and I walked over. Even if Lena was aware of her surroundings, she would not hear anything he said with the wind and the engine noise.

"What are you doing?" Dass muttered. "He does not want to see her yet. Or her to see him."

"I know," I hissed back, "but look at the state she's in. Run ahead and make sure he's not at home, and signal me if it's all right."

Dass just gave me a look, which I knew from experience was his way of disagreeing.

"I'll take the blame if anything goes wrong," I said, as the long-tail bumped against the dock by the palazzo gate.

"I'll hold you to your word." And with that he turned his back to me and stepped off the boat. How could a man who wore pink pants manage to look so superior? He ran ahead silently while I helped Lena off the boat. She was paler by the moment, it seemed— her face was like moonlight.

"You okay?" I asked. She did not answer and just leaned harder against me.

I felt like a cad, delaying her rest, but I had to wait until I knew the coast was clear. I led her to the lawn chair where I had first parleyed with Bill, which was situated to take in the view of the river. Flowering trees framed a sculpted tower on the far shore. It was unfortunate she was in no condition to appreciate it. As I waited impatiently for Dass, the bird I thought of as the panic bird started its wailing. "Oh no oh no oh no oh no," in a crescendo of disasters foreseen. Why did even nature conspire to plague me? No one else ever seemed to hear the panic bird. It never wailed when Dass was with me, for instance, or I would have remembered to ask him its name. Birds just had it in for me. Back in Washington, there was some yellow one always calling, "Gotta getta date, gotta getta date" spring after spring, year after year, needling me. Its wish was never answered, I guess. Mine neither. I hoped the panic bird's nervousness was equally deluded.

Finally, I spotted Dass peering out from behind a shady column, and he waved me inside. The guest bedroom was always made up, and was in a different wing from Bill's room, so that's where I headed, my arm around Lena's waist to support her. If she hadn't seemed so unwell I would have been perfectly happy.

I settled Lena onto the cool white sheets, the fan gently turning overhead. "Just ring this bell if you need anything. Loud. This place is huge."

I didn't think she heard me, and resolved to call the doctor. First, I hurried to the window to make sure the shutters were locked. They had intricate designs carved in them to let in the breeze, but not direct light. In Siam, sun was the devil to be avoided. The key thing was that Lena would not see any doings in the palazzo, should Bill return. Any person passing by would be just a shadow.

Her breathing had shifted to the deeper cadence of someone asleep, and I eased myself from the room. In the hallway near the library sat the main telephone, made of white Bakelite with a crank handle. It was twenty years out of date but the best in its day, like everything else in the mansion. The operator put me through to the doctor and I told him it was an emergency. He was an Englishman, chill and snobby until I repeated Bill's name, and then he said he'd come right away. He was one of the expats who came to Bangkok in some murky time not *quite* before the war was over. His morals were dubious but his training, impeccable.

Hanging up the phone, I continued through the hall, with one more urgent task to see to. I headed for a bedroom around the corner, where boxes of dresses were stacked in a wardrobe. Bill had them ready for me to take to the hotel we'd planned for Lena after she arrived. He said she was travelling light. Indeed, she had no luggage at all. It seemed unlikely Lena would find the dresses, but who knew what exploring she might do when she revived. The first instinct of any robber is to case the joint. Not to say she was still a robber, but these habits die hard. I didn't want her to wonder whose they were, or worse, if they were meant for her, since they were in her size and taste from when she was in the gang.

I had the shock of my life when I entered the room. Bill was kneeling on the floor, his face buried in a dress he was clutching, and the boxes were strewn everywhere. Most of the dresses were new, but the one he held I remembered distinctly from a night we three spent at the Bergonian ballroom in Seattle thirteen years ago. He'd kept it all this time? I cleared my throat.

He leapt up and turned to face me, nimble as a boxer. "I thought I saw Lena, in the garden," he said. "Am I crazy?"

"Dass said you weren't here."

"That's no answer. You fucking with my plans?" He grabbed me round the neck with both hands and I could hardly breathe.

"She's hurt," I sputtered, and he let me go. I gasped. "Knifed. Needs a doctor."

"Holy Christ. I'll call him right now."

"I already did."

"He'll get here quicker if it comes from me." Like a madman he ran into the hall, and I heard the old phone's crank whirring, turning faster than it ever had.

CHAPTER SEVENTEEN

BANGKOK BELONGS TO HIM

I WOKE IN a dark room. How long had I slept? A sheet fluttered on my chest, moved by the breeze of a ceiling fan. I touched the bandage on my neck and winced. I had a vague memory of a mono-cled stranger with a stethoscope leaning over me and putting a cloth over my mouth, sickly sweet. I remembered the glint of a curved needle with a long thread hanging from it, and how I had stared at it with dread.

I remembered landing on a beach and taking a train that hurtled through the night. I saw a brass bell with a dark wood handle on the bedside table. Someone had told me to ring it if I needed anything. I jangled it fiercely.

A man came into the room and I tugged the sheet to my chin. A moment later, I realized it was Byron. He had a beard, which was new.

Byron, from the Clockwork Gang?

"How are you?" he asked, sitting in a rattan chair beside my bed.

"Fine," I said. I didn't want to admit I was muddled, or there was something important that he wouldn't let me do. My voice had come out hoarsely. "Could I have some water, please?"

He jumped up to grab a glass pitcher on an antique side table that had a foreign look, Chinese maybe. As he fussed with the ice cubes, I decided that the beard suited him. Unlike most people, he looked more handsome now that he was older, though of course he hadn't been a lady-killer before. His features had sharpened and the craggy lines about his eyes proved he'd seen more of life. He still looked uncomfortable in his own skin, but I was glad of it, because his vulnerability was the sweetness in him. Wherever I was, I knew that I was safe with him.

The image of a foreign man in a cap, yelling, came to me. "Is this Bangkok?" I asked.

"Yes."

Link Hughes was the reason I was in Bangkok. He was in danger. Where were my shoes? The high-ceilinged room, sparsely decorated, yielded no clues about where they might be. The floor was bare. Getting up to look seemed too challenging.

Byron handed me the glass of water with an expression of concern. I supposed I must look terrible. "Why are you here?" I asked.

"I live here, remember?"

"Yes, of course." I hadn't until he told me, but things were starting to come back.

"What on earth happened to your neck?"

"Some men boarded our ship to steal our money."

"Good lord, men who steal things on ships are called *pirates*. You were attacked by *pirates*?" His face transformed from frantic to angry—he seemed to take the whole thing personally.

Gathering my strength, I sat up, ignoring the stabbing pain in my neck as I pushed my legs off the bed and onto the floor. Time was short. Link could die of his battle injuries or the Russians could take him for some dark purpose. Byron gripped my arm.

"You will *not* get out of bed." He smiled to soften his words. "That's what the doctor said."

"Your doctor doesn't know me. Look, I came here to find someone and that's what I'm going to do. I suppose if you're here, you must know about him?"

"Mostly. Link Hughes, you mean." Byron sounded cautious.

"So you're in with Bill again. How could you, after all he's done?" I tried to stand up, but my head started spinning. I put my hands over my face, hoping the world would settle. It was only my wound that made me feel this way. "After he let us think him dead for three years? Or did you always know?"

"I was as shocked as anyone. Only heard a few months back, when I was in Washington. I don't know. When a dead man summons, don't you go?"

I stared at him silently.

"You came."

I was amazed Byron had the nerve to say such a thing. It wasn't like the old Byron at all, but it was true. "Only because of Link Hughes. Bill tried to ruin my life when he was in jail. He threatened to tell everything he knew about me."

"Jesus. That's low. Did he do it?"

"He seems to have told one person, at least. That was enough." I lay on the pillow with my eyes closed. "Please tell me about Link."

"Bill was working with the British in Siam right after the war, liberating the prisoners who worked on the Death Railway—"

"Oh God. Death Railway?" I felt sick. What had I done?

"I'm sorry. I thought you would know that. At least your friend lived."

Bill probably had some plan to keep Link away from me as long as possible, so I'd have to talk to him instead. I would not do it. There were other ways. I gathered all my strength to smile at Byron sweetly, and took his hand. He flushed. Byron had always been a simple puzzle.

"Can I see him? Right away?" I asked.

He whispered something, a single syllable.

"What was that?" I prodded.

"No."

"Why not?"

"He disappeared from the POW hospital in Nakom Paton, but don't worry. We've got men combing the city for him. You need to rest now."

I couldn't stand it. I'd come all this way and been so close. What if the Russians had him? But I could not move, or even open my eyes. Once again the world seemed to slide away.

I WOKE WHEN the darkness was broken by a pattern tossed on the floor by the pale blue dawn, coming in through the perforated wooden screens. The air was hot and humid, and I remembered right away I was in Bangkok. I felt a momentary sense of panic, wondering if Miss Maggie could be tracing me every step of the way. But how? I had to focus on Link. He was the reason I'd taken these risks. I had to get moving. I rang the bell by my bed.

A few minutes later there was a gentle knock at the door, which swung open with a creak. The light flared on over my bed, a crystal chandelier that I found too bright. Byron had some dresses hooked over one arm, and he was also carrying a tray. He must have been awake already.

"You look better," he said, and put the tray carefully on my lap. "Eat up, you need your strength."

"Does that mean you have news about Link?"

He sighed and sat down, moving the dress he had draped over the crook of one arm onto the rattan chair. "There've been some sightings that sound promising, but we haven't got him yet."

"He's in danger. There are people who are out to get him." I tried to sit up, and Byron propped up my pillows for me.

"There's nothing we can do in the next five minutes. Will you please eat?"

"It does smell good," I admitted as my stomach growled. I hadn't eaten since I was on the *Quarlo* with Frederick, I realized. A day ago, if not longer. I had a clear memory of his wooden sailboat now. Surely I would soon be strong enough to look for Link myself. I supposed there'd be time to grill Byron further when I was done eating. He wasn't going anywhere. I cut up the meat, which seemed to be kidney, and pushed it with my knife onto some warm buttered toast.

"Sorry it's so British. These heavy breakfasts are all you can get," he said. "Only a handful of Americans live here."

"It's delicious," I said, between mouthfuls. Finished in only a few minutes, I laid down my silverware with a clatter and leaned back against my pillow.

Fidgeting in his chair, Byron stood up again, and held up the dress. "Do you like it? The one you're wearing got wrecked."

I looked down and saw the orange dust on it, a rip at the sleeve, and splotches of dried blood down the front. "You're not kidding."

He still looked at me anxiously.

"Yes, I like it," I said. And I did. At least I would look pretty when I finally saw Link again—if I ever did see him.

Byron lifted the tray from my lap and put it on a side table.

"So, from the beginning, Byron," I said. "How did you end up in Bangkok?"

He settled himself back into the rattan chair, steepling his fingers in front of his mouth. He looked nervous, but he'd always been nervous around me. "I owned a little bar in Washington. Then I got a message out of the blue from Bill, inviting me to join his business here. He said he'd gone clean, or I never would have considered it."

"And is he clean?"

Byron looked pained, hesitated, and picked up a red fan from the side table. He flipped it open and shut, open and shut. "The business is opium, but he seems to be." He waved the fan in front of his face. "Believe it or not, the drug's legal here. The government runs opium dens, and any extra is sold to the British for their Indian hospitals. There's strict quotas. It's pretty mundane and bureaucratic, really."

"But lucrative, from the looks of your house."

"Yes," he said, smiling.

"So how did Bill escape from jail?"

"A powerful person was involved and it was covered up. That's all I know."

"How'd Bill know where to find me?"

"Shively, the navy man. He was on the Esquimalt base."

The name was familiar and I tried to place it. Goddamn it, it was the dreadful little man who brought me Bill's threats three years ago. I should have known he'd been tracking me, but it hadn't seemed to matter after I thought Bill died. A dog never does any tricks when the master is gone.

"Did you know about Frederick?" I asked.

"Who's Frederick?"

His puzzlement seemed genuine. I studied his face a moment longer. "Sho-nuff. He changed his name and got that boat he always wanted. He sailed me here from Honolulu. Bill asked him to do it."

"Sho-nuff? That's strange. Bill never mentioned it. It's like he's bringing the gang back together."

I ignored that comment. I wanted no part of it. Bill's schemes were an eternal wheel, crushing everything in its path, and I did not want to get dragged under it.

"Frederick did my stitches," was all I said.

"The doctor added a few more, but he admitted the ones you had were done well enough, for an amateur job." Byron paused and seemed to join me for a moment in wondering at the strangeness of it all. "It's funny to hear him called Frederick," he said. "It sounds so formal."

"I guess we've all changed in some way, and don't want to be seen as we were before."

"I've certainly changed."

I thought of what I'd seen of this mansion when we arrived yesterday. Byron had no need for such show. It wasn't his style, and he didn't seem to have changed so much to me. "This is Bill's place, isn't it," I said. I stared around the room, panic and rage battling in me, past Byron drooping in his chair, almost expecting Bill to be somewhere nearby, grinning. The man I once loved more than anything. The man who sold my freedom to Miss Maggie.

Byron nodded miserably. "I'm sorry."

"I won't stay here another second. I don't ever want to see him." I raised myself in bed, suppressing a groan, and put my feet onto the ground. The bastard probably took pleasure in thinking of me crying over his death. I'd never tell him, or Byron for that matter, that I had. Tears were transient, just water, after all—they would sizzle into nothing under a hot sun. It was only sorrow for the time I wasted on him, that was all.

"You need help," he said. "I'll take you to a hotel."

I didn't answer.

"I know Bangkok, and you don't. I can help you look for Link Hughes. If you'll let me. I'm on your side."

I felt like I was tumbling into a pit in which my old and new life, and all the mistakes from both, were roiling around together, a bunch of bloody crocodiles. I was angry with Byron for going along with it all, but I had to take my allies as I found them. He was easily influenced by Bill, but in the end I meant more to him—or at least I had, in the old days. Maybe Byron would lead me to Link Hughes and I could bypass Bill entirely.

"Fine. Get me out of here," I said.

CHAPTER EIGHTEEN

JANUARY 16, 1946—MORNING

I SETTLED LENA into the Sawasdee Hotel near the obscure Ratchini Pier, where Bill had originally planned because it was an area with no curious foreigners. I apologized about the rundown wood-frame building, but Lena said it was lovely to have her own room after the military dormitories she was used to. I steeled myself to answer questions about Bill, but she said no more about him. Her focus on Hughes was single-minded. This did not bode well for Bill. It would have been better if Hughes were here and she could have got him out of her system. Bill had said he hadn't seemed like much—the man must have still been in the regular ward then, rather than a mental patient, or Bill would have commented on it. I don't know, maybe Bill even arranged his disappearance. Then Lena would never see Hughes, and the way would be clear for him. Or so he would think. I could not see Lena taking him back. She didn't need anyone, least of all him.

"No hope, no hope," came a call through the screened window from the hotel courtyard. That damn bird. I couldn't see it, but I knew what it looked like: plump and brown and white, its kind lazed around in the garden of the palazzo. It would likely be good eating. But its feelings had no bearing on me. I glanced at Lena where she sat in an armchair in the corner of the room. She seemed concentrated on something on the floor, though I couldn't see anything.

"Don't worry, we'll find him," I said. "We'll turn over every rock." Chief Phao would certainly be doing that, but lord knew what would crawl out when he did. I didn't think I'd mention Chief Phao's involvement to Lena yet. I'd leave that up to Bill.

I'd tried to convince her to let me look for Hughes while she rested, but she pointed out that I didn't know what he looked like, while she did, so I was forced to give way. She didn't have a photograph of him. Somehow that fact pepped me up, as though he couldn't really be that special.

Wake up, Byron, I told myself. She had come around the world to find him.

We tried the ports and the train stations—anywhere a traveller would need to pass through if he wanted to leave the country. When the sun set on our hot and fruitless day of searching the city, we returned to her hotel. I could see she felt discouraged and tired, her hand touching delicately, absently, the bandage on her neck. I told her to stay put and I'd get some food, though there would only be noodles. No food for *farangs*, as they called white foreigners, in this district. She said that was fine and settled into the one chair to wait. Through the slats in the wooden window screen there was a view of thatched rooftops and the shiny blade of a canal slicing through the city, the rotting smell of which wafted over on the wind. I borrowed a lidded bowl from the manager and went outside to look for a vendor that was busy and clean. Every time I walked on the streets of Bangkok it shocked me anew, being more chaotic than you could ever conceive of back home. I'd sheltered Lena from it by taking taxis all day. An ox team pulling a cart jangled past, nearly knocking me over. I found a little restaurant decorated with calendars from years past, each featuring a picture of the old king until 1936, when Prince Ananda appeared as a child. He was a scrawny little thing, and I pitied him. I rather hoped that Bill was brewing something up to save him from shadowy enemies. Might as well. Whatever Bill's plan was in the palace—robbery, rescue, or murder—it was going to involve me. Of the three, a rescue sat easiest in my mind.

Out front, I handed my bowl to a Chinese boy stirring a soup pot, and stood with my hands in my pockets while he threw in some some noodles and what I'd call meatballs, which hopefully weren't stuffed with strange things. Restaurants in Siam were designed backwards from what I was used to, with the kitchens outside to let the heat from cooking escape.

I grabbed a *South China Morning Post* someone had left behind and sat down on a dark wooden stool polished smooth from generations of sitting. The ink smell wafted up as I turned the pages. It was not soothing reading. The rice-factory workers were planning a rally near the Parliament, since the king's appointed government had legalized labour activity recently. I wondered where it would all lead. With neighbouring China nearly taken over by the Communists, Western governments were nervous about such displays. Maybe the Americans really were sending money to Chief Phao. One thing he was not was a Communist.

It was not an easy life being a king, I reflected. The old king, Ananda's father, had abdicated after a coup, and lived in exile with his family in Switzerland. They had been allowed to keep their wealth and status as long as they rubber-stamped the new government. However, winners and losers could change places quickly in this country, and it would be a delicate balancing act. This King Ananda, with his European education, supported democracy and made it clear he would endorse a new constitution that allowed free elections. Pridi, the most popular leader right now, was branded a Communist. Could Siam be the first country in the world where the people elected a Communist government?

The Chinese boy called out that my soup was ready, and I folded up the newspaper. He ladled the meatballs and soup into my bowl with a tidy flick of his wrist, and he smiled at me shyly. I put the lid on and kept shifting my fingers along the hot rim, trying not to burn myself as I carried it back to the hotel.

Back at Lena's room, I locked the door behind me. Lena sniffed at the soup, tasted it, and declared it delicious. I felt as proud as if I had made it myself. At least I'd done something that pleased her. Seated at the single small desk, she finished it off, and dabbed her lips with a napkin. The lock in the door turned by itself and Lena and I stared at each other, my heart thumping. Maybe it was just the maid service, but suddenly I wished I had a gun. Could it be the people who followed Lena? She had said she was probably tailed from Alaska to Hawaii. Funny that life as a bank robber seemed an easy lifestyle compared to whatever she was into now. Her face back then had been open, looking forward to the next adventure. Now I would say that dread composed her outlook.

"We need to talk." It was Smile with his tally-ho accent and ill-matched thuggish appearance.

"You could knock," Lena said, and I admired her sangfroid in the face of this alarming stranger. "Whoever you are. And who gave you a key?"

Smile ignored her. "Outside, Byron," he said. There was no need for him to act so bossy, I thought.

"I'll just be a minute," I said to Lena.

Sheepishly I followed Smile into the dingy hall, closing the door carefully behind me, and moved well away from Lena's room.

"The chief found Link Hughes," he said, speaking low. "Bill has him. You'd better move quickly."

"Where?"

"The Oriental Hotel bar."

"We'll leave now."

I watched him depart through the dark hallway and down the stairs with doubt in my mind. Did Bill know what he was doing with this meeting? Of course Bill assumed he was the better specimen now, but physical fitness alone did not win a woman's heart. Plus, he did not know the image she might hold of this man in her mind, and it might override the present-day reality. That might equally hold true for Bill, and her memory of him could not be pretty. Except for whatever happened between them during her prison visit, which Bill said went poorly, the last time she saw him was when he hit her and she ran away.

Yet Bill was right about me. I would do as he wanted. I would take Lena to the Oriental and set her down between two men who she would be torn between, and I would just be a bystander. Wouldn't it at least make her grateful to me? Later, when the dust cleared and she realized both men were part of the past, or just not worthy, I would be standing beside her—her loyal friend. That was something.

The Oriental Hotel. As always, Bill was either crazy or a deep genius. That's where the crooked politicians went, the corrupt businessmen, and the underworld kingpins who earned their riches God knows how. Taking Lena there was like trying to hide yourself in the eye of a hurricane.

I don't know, maybe it's safe in there. No one else wants to go in.

I went back into the room. As soon as I told Lena I knew where Hughes was, she grabbed her purse and said, breathlessly, "Let's go."

We ran downstairs and I had the manager call us a cab, handing him a baht note. "Make it quick."

Sitting in the cab, Lena put on some lipstick, her hand steady despite the occasional jounce on the road. Then she carefully blotted her lips with tissue. Thinking of the expression *Don't shoot the messenger* made me hold my silence. I hoped she understood that Bill would be there. Could she have forgotten how he was? He wouldn't just watch things unfold. He would control everything, somehow. I didn't know what his game was, besides seeing Lena, of course. He had seemed very interested in Link Hughes—beyond what you would expect of a rival for a lady's heart. Admittedly, his story was unusual. I'd had it in dribs and drabs from both Bill and Lena. It could not be typical to be transferred from a desk job to a British guerrilla force behind enemy lines in Burma. But war yanked people out of all corners of the world and placed them in strange situations. I'd heard about that from the soldiers who came into my bar in Sequim. Farm boys who'd never left Washington

State were suddenly perched on the Sphinx in Egypt for a photograph, their legs splayed as though casually riding a mare back home. War seemed to make people good at pretending.

I kind of wished I'd been in the war.

CHAPTER NINETEEN

THE MENTAL PATIENT

THE LONG DRIVEWAY through the hotel grounds was already filled with vehicles, so the cab idled at the gateway. This final delay before seeing Link was maddening. I stared ahead at the native bellboys, in pith helmets and uncomfortable-looking leather boots polished to a high sheen, who waited with excellent posture to open the doors to the hotel. The Victorian eminence was chockablock with archways and half-moon windows, and above its two stories a plaster curlicue loomed, looking ready to tip over from its heavy adornments. I had expected something with less flash and more discretion as a meeting place. I clutched my purse, ready to jump out of the car, impatient with the expats who took their time emerging from their limousines, like lazy butterflies. Oh, lord. The women wore cocktail gowns. I looked down with dismay at my cotton dress. Is this how Link would see me—looking like some afternoon housewife? I sank back into my seat again, suddenly wishing to not go in at all.

"You look pretty," Byron said.

I stared at him, dubious.

"I'm sorry. I didn't know we'd be going out on the town when I brought your clothes," he said, "but none of these women hold a candle to you."

The driver walked around to open my door, and I held up my chin as I got out of the cab. It would not help to slink around ashamed—and I had to admit that Byron's compliment buttressed me.

Inside, the place was packed. There was a sea of tables in the main area and the walls were lined with secretive booths, the usual gloom of a dark-wood British pub made strange by Siamese fretwork. It was noisy with chatter and I couldn't focus. I desperately wanted to see Link before he saw me. I needed time to get over the shock, and to find a way to compose my face. My eyes scoured each table. Fans whirred overhead, the blades whipping round as though aeroplanes were descending, and I felt a sense of dread. It made me think of the battle of Midway, when I listened on the radio as the pilots went down. Link had been listening too, that day.

At the far wall on a small stage, there was a singer at the piano, wearing a tight black dress, cut low, and belting out jazz tunes. She wasn't that talented, but the men kept their eyes glued to her. I guessed she was popular for visual reasons. Then my attention was arrested by the only two men in the room who were not looking at the singer.

"Oh Jesus," I whispered, unable to stop the words. Byron gripped my hand and then quickly let it go.

The man I recognized was Bill, as he stared right at me. My breath caught in my throat. Bill, darkly handsome, looking just as I remembered him from our happiest days, dressed up to go out on the town. Not haggard and ruined like he was in jail. It was as though time had gone backwards. I was too far away to read the expression in his eyes, but they emanated intensity. He had that power, to take up more space than anyone else.

I took a step forward and he smiled.

Smiled! I was outraged. Did he think this would be easy? I wanted to scream at him: *"You let me think you were dead all this time. Jesus Christ, three years!"* And all the harm he did me before his so-called death. I felt my fists clenching. I weaved around the tables, closing in on him with Byron trailing after me.

Sitting beside Bill was a man so gaunt he looked lost in his rumpled clothes. I suddenly realized it was Link Hughes. His eyes were vacant, staring at nothing. He had horrible patchy scars on his arms, and one small round dint on each cheek, like dimples, but he had never had dimples. I realized from the spherical shape they must have come from a bullet shot through his face. Oh, Link.

Why did I have to report him to Miss Maggie? I had not foreseen his exile to the doomed Burma campaign when I wrote about his meeting with the Spanish Consul, but that was because I was not capable of thinking of other people. I believed I was, now, but it only made me sadder because the past could not be changed. All I could do was ask for Link's forgiveness, but I could not expect to receive it. The only thing I could hope to regain from this was self-respect. I supposed that was no small thing.

I didn't know how I was going to get through this. I'd never been so close to unravelling. And there was Bill beside him, smiling like a Cheshire cat. He was in the centre of things, as always. He had spoiled my reunion with Link. I could not say what I needed to say to him—I didn't want anyone else to hear what I was apologizing for. What a goddamn mess.

I took a deep breath and sat down.

"Didn't I say I never wanted to see him?" I asked. I looked only at Byron. I would not look at Bill. I would not.

"That's no way to treat a man who came back from the dead to see you," Bill said, in his jovial manner that I remembered so well. Joy flared for a moment, the old desire fulfilled: that Bill would come back to me, cured. And here he was. He looked too hearty, too *present*, to be using drugs. He was wearing a linen suit, crisp in contrast to Link's old clothes. Then my cynicism crept in—Bill had planned every detail, no doubt. He would revel in the contrast.

"Me and Link have a lot in common," he said. "You should be happy how it all worked out. I can help him."

I'd waited years for an apology, and apparently I would never get one. He had not changed, but I was thrown by his offer. Why would he help Link? I reminded myself that he always had some plan, drugs or no drugs, and he always put himself first. He was using Link to get to me, or perhaps Link had some other value to him. Cautiously I studied Link's blank face, the angular cheekbones and the chin, the shape the same as I remembered, but stripped bare, like a couch waiting to be reupholstered, just the structure underneath left. His mouth hung a little slack, his lips not the full, soft lips I once kissed.

I could deal with Bill later. Link was the one I had come to see. I touched his arm gently. "Do you know me?"

He did not look at me, and I might as well have touched a block of wood. He did not pay any attention to his arm and I withdrew my hand. "I'm sorry. I didn't mean to do it. You have every right to hate me." My words just tumbled out in a heap, like garbage. He did not react at all.

"His mind's scattered," Bill said. I felt gratitude, and squelched it. That was just the sort of opening Bill would look for.

Link did not react to this observation. He sat impassively, not even smoking the cigarette smoldering in an ashtray beside his hand. Bill, meanwhile, was almost merry, ordering drinks, holding up four fingers to the waiter. He was the only one in a social mood. Byron looked uncomfortable, Link was drifting in the stratosphere, and I just wanted to get out of the bar. Nothing important that I had to say could be said in public.

I was so angry at Bill. He had used Link as bait to get me here, when Link deserved to be left in peace. He must have shell shock from what he'd been through.

Seeing Link again, I had to ask myself honestly what there was to our relationship. The grounds were flimsy. I had obsessed over him for a few months from afar, since he had a wife. We had danced, once. We had kissed, once, by the creek on Craigflower Road. At the time these things had loomed large, I admit. I was so surprised when he pulled me close, to lead me in the true

Argentinean tango. He whispered that we should move together like lovers and I melted. Maybe that moment had been real for him, too. I'd never know.

It was easy enough to be attracted to someone. Trust is something else again, and I made the mistake of giving it to him. The time I thought we were closest—a team—was when he was actually betraying me. I had shared with him a coded message I discovered on a banded pigeon. He encouraged me to keep it from the others and decrypt it myself. He told me I deserved the credit, and that's what I wanted to believe. What he actually did was take advantage of my pride to keep secret what he knew: it really was from the Japanese. He lied to me, saying it was a meaningless message between fishermen in the local militias. Then he destroyed it. So Miss Maggie hadn't been wrong about him, not in broad strokes. He was the spy she was looking for. But it did not matter to me anymore what kind of a spy Link had been or why. He was not evil, I knew that much. He did not deserve three years of slavery under the Japanese, which Miss Maggie consigned him to when she sent him to Burma. *Or does he only blame me?* I wondered.

The four of us were silent until the waiter returned. "Seagram's, sir," he said, setting our drinks on coasters with a muffled thunk. Bill had always liked Canadian liquor during Prohibition—the American stuff had been brain-burning moonshine. Seagram's had been my favourite too, and for a moment I wondered if Bill remembered. But I doubted that factored into anything. Bill only ever thought of himself.

"I was telling Link this is a good place for us to meet—once," Bill said. "It's busy and loud enough that no one can hear your business. It's like Switzerland, this place. Neutral territory. The devil could drink with you and no one would raise an eyebrow. Santé." He raised his glass. I couldn't help but think Bill was that devil, and maybe that was his intention. Byron clinked his glass half-heartedly, while I kept mine on the table. Link didn't seem to know he had a drink at all. Bill drained his whisky and grinned at each of us in turn. He was the only one enjoying himself at this table, that was for sure. I wished he'd shut up, but at the same time I was glued to his every word. He was leading me somewhere—I'd just have to wait and find out how I fit into his plans. That's all this was. He didn't really care for me still. I was just useful to him. If I waited and found out how, maybe I could thwart him.

"But we should never come here together again," Bill continued. "Link, it was a little rash of you to choose this place, though I admit it is the nicest bar in town. But we have been marked. Only you know who might have cause to mark you, like I know who marks me. That fellow Warner at the bar, for instance. He might buy my gems or my opium. Which is legal here." Bill glanced at me, as though he wished me to register that last point. Well, he wasn't about to win some Boy Scout prize. Drugs were drugs, and some underworld business had to come into it somewhere. He was still a crook. I refused to meet his eyes, and stared stubbornly into my tumbler of whisky. Perhaps I would have one sip.

This man Warner's back was turned, so I could only see he had broad shoulders and wavy blond hair. After a moment he talked to the man beside him, and I had the chance to study his profile. Warner was handsome with refined features. He was about Bill's age, I thought, though they couldn't be more opposite. Bill was dark and rugged. While you would not immediately call Bill handsome, he had a presence that drew your attention until he was somehow the most attractive man in the room. Back in the day, of course. I had to admit Bill looked better than I could have imagined, and not much older than when we first met, before the drugs had ravaged his mind and reflected that fact on his face. Now his cheeks were tan from time out of doors, in apparently healthy pursuits. It seemed very wrong that he would sell drugs to other people after what they'd done to him. I supposed I should not be surprised at any contradiction in him. He was constructed from opposing forces, always at war.

Bill continued with his monologue. "So it helps for Warner to see me talk to you. If he thinks there's other interested parties, that'll make him more eager. He might think Link here is in the opium business—he has that look. While Lena has a regal bearing that suggests the gem trade. First lady gem dealer in the country, why not? She can do such things easily. And Warner will see that in her immediately. Warner is perceptive."

Was he proposing I should go into business with him? Oh, he was maddening. But I needed to keep calm and think about what he really meant by all this. He must be drawing my attention to Warner for a reason.

Here I was, falling for Bill's ploy and getting wrapped up in his world. He was deflecting me from doing what I came to do, which was reconcile with Link, or at least to tend to him. He clearly needed help. I would only speak to Link, not Bill.

"Link, you don't seem well yet. Why'd you leave the hospital?"

If Bill was behind it, I wanted to know. Link pressed a finger to a small clear tube protruding from his throat that I had not noticed until he did so. I tried not to stare at it, but it was a horrible invasion of his person. It should not be there. "No choice," he said, his voice raw. He had to plug the tube to speak, and the words cost him an effort. I wanted to cry.

"Your neck. What happened?"

"Japs got me." He spoke slowly and had to pause often, wheezing between words. It sounded so painful. "But I killed some first. I was a patriot."

It was a statement meant for me, but we were in no position to speak frankly. I interpreted it as a message that he had not meant to betray his country. A weight came off my chest—it was as I thought. He'd been duped by the Spanish Consul. I knew he would never want to harm the Captain.

"Is it permanent, the tube?" I asked hesitantly.

He shook his head. "Take it out. Soon. They said."

"Can you go back there?"

He shook his head, more violently this time, and had to take a moment to place his finger back on the tube. "Russians."

I had a thousand questions I wanted to ask. Had he actually spoken to a Soviet agent? What did they want with him? Had they learned he was branded a traitor to the West? How did they know about him in the first place?

"Listen to this knucklehead," Bill said. "Russians? He needs to rest."

Link really should not speak of such things. Could he be on morphine still from the hospital? My doubts about Link were creeping back in. After being tortured, he might be controllable by any side. I needed to question Link privately. If I could tell Miss Maggie what the Soviets were doing in Siam, it would be an important contribution in the new war.

God, how could I think of my work right now? What about the debt I owed Link? Whatever he'd done, it was partly my fault he'd been sent behind the front lines. He'd been tortured. No one should have to endure that. I downed my drink.

"Lena, you okay?" Byron asked.

"My neck still aches, but I can't complain when other people have injuries much worse than mine." I couldn't bring myself to say Link's name aloud. "I'm fine. Really." My neck actually was fine. I hadn't felt it much today. I just needed an excuse for my agitation.

My world was crumbling. I had held onto the idea of Link these three years: my obsession with him was tied to my guilt. But guilt and love do not co-exist well. Maybe one murdered the other. My guilt could not be stronger, short of him having died from his capture. But love? I realized I felt no passion when I looked at him now, and it wasn't just because he had changed. In his gaunt face, I could still see the man he had been. But those eyes did not burn any more when they looked at me. Passion required that spark to survive. Three years ago, I would see him desiring me, and I would imagine our skin touching as he undressed me. The idea of him animated my days. But now, nothing. Passion was a fire, but fire ended as ash. Love was the thing left standing in the wreckage after the fire burned out. Like a safe to which only one person knows the combination.

"This fellow needs a comfortable bed," Bill said, "and I aim to provide it. He'll stay at my palazzo."

Damn that man. The gears of his plan were turning, relentless. I did not want to be like Saint Catherine, lying pliant on the wheel. He knew I wouldn't want to let Link out of my sight, now that I'd found him, and that least of all would I want him in the exclusive company of Bill. If he did not yet know them, Bill would pry out all the details of our relationship. Also, I did not want to see Link fall further under his influence. I turned to Byron.

"Link would recover better under my care. Is there a spare room at my hotel?"

"Most likely," Byron said, looking every which way except at Bill.

"That's not so comfortable," Bill said. "Lena, you can stay at my place also. It's big enough that even I get lost in it, so you don't got to worry about bumping into me."

"Byron, please take me back to my hotel."

"I have to agree with Bill on this one," Byron said, swallowing hard. "There's good security at his place. After those pirates, I worry about you."

"Pirates are only at sea, Byron. We're on land." I glanced at Bill. "Though I admit there are bandits there as well."

Bill just smiled. "I got nothing to do with banditry now. Don't you see I've changed?" I did not answer, and he frowned into the silence. "What the hell are you talking about, pirates?"

"You—" I took a deep breath, and turned to speak to Byron as I had resolved. "I think he knows what I'm talking about. Since he's apparently spying on me all the time."

Byron opened his mouth, but Bill cut him off. "I heard her, damn it, she's right here beside me. Acting like a child, I must say. Anyhoo, I been keeping an eye on her, and helped her. She should be grateful."

"I wouldn't have needed help if it wasn't for you."

Unperturbed, Bill waved his hand for the waiter to bring him another whisky.

I stood up, straightening my dress and grabbing my purse from the back of the chair. The strap snagged on the teak fretwork.

Frustrated, I yanked it upward to free it. "I'm disappointed in you, Byron. Helping this maniac with his little games."

"Don't go, Lena."

He started to stand up, the chair legs shrieking across the tile floor, but I gestured him to be still. He sat down again quickly as a dog admonished.

Bill waited calmly as the waiter took away his empty drink and put down another, the outside of the glass already slick with moisture from the heat in the air. "I'll send my associate Smile to watch over you," Bill said. "He can let me know when you're ready to speak to me. You'll have to, if you want to talk to him." He hooked a thumb at Link, who was absently stirring the ice in his untouched whisky.

"Link?" I said weakly, but he did not look up. Any chance for me to make amends seemed further away than ever. Feeling defeated and more alone than ever in my life, I threaded slowly through the crowds to the gaping door, hoping Link would call me back, but he never did.

CHAPTER TWENTY

JANUARY 16, 1946—EVENING

AS THE LONGTAIL boat cut through the Chao Phraya, I stared glumly into the dark water, and the moon reflected like a thousand shards in the wake. I stood alone in the stern. Lena was mad at me, and maybe she'd never forgive me. I was too tightly bound to Bill. That was what I had run from those years ago in Washington, when I knew the cops had him and it was my chance to be free. And here I was, like a chump, his sidekick again of my own free will. Or was it? Shively would have allowed no refusal.

The shadowy form of a temple pierced the moonlit sky as we motored against the current, while wind rustled the palm trees and shook the banyans. No, I had to admit I wanted to come here. To Siam for adventure—me, who had never left Washington until I met Bill. I'd been an accountant and then a barkeep. That had been the extent of my exploits on my own. I sighed, but it was like the sound never existed, drowned as it was in the murmur of wind, river, and boat.

Bill and Link sat together in the front of the longtail in silence. It was no great joy that Link was staying with us. I was baffled and angered by this new alliance. If I had to give up Lena for Bill's friendship, at least he could show appreciation for my loyalty. And on Bill's end, he could be making a terrible mistake. I didn't know how he could stand to be in such close quarters with his rival for Lena's affection, although looking at Link, I had to agree with Bill's assessment that he was a shattered wreck. It was hard to imagine what Lena had seen in him, and harder to imagine her seeing it still. But shades of horror and sadness had passed through her eyes when she looked at him, especially when she first noticed the tube in his neck, and her hangdog ways signified guilt. Guilt was like a glue between people. I knew that.

The palazzo grounds were silent but for a no-hope bird sighing in its sleep in the trees. I passed through the front doors where two servants stood sentry in the place where Dass usually had his post, and walked past the library. A hand shot out and grabbed my lapels. It was Bill, and he pulled me inside.

"Some queer things are going to happen tonight, but don't mind them nor interfere," Bill said.

"Okay," I said, not wanting to give him the satisfaction of asking what he meant. I drifted over to Bill's favourite armchair, where a reading lamp shone a bright circle onto a book with a cheap paper cover: *Handbook of Irregular Warfare*. I picked it up and looked over the page it was open to, where a passage was underlined. "Never give the enemy a chance. Every soldier must be a potential gangster." It was crossed out and altered to say, "Every gangster must be a potential soldier."

"A little light reading?" I asked.

"I like to stay informed. Call me a renaissance man." Bill took the book from my hands, marked the page with a bookmark, and put it in a drawer.

"What queer things might I expect tonight?" I was curious despite myself.

"Shouting, crying, banging, caterwauling, and general commotion. From the servant's room on the third floor."

I felt a sudden alarm that he meant to kill Link with his

bare hands. No matter my feelings for him, I could not stand by for that.

"I'm doing him a favour. He's a junkie. I'm getting him clean. I judge it'll take four days. He's not so far gone." Bill sat down in his green velvet armchair. "But he's going to suffer."

"This is a new one. Get a man *off* drugs? You'll lose a customer through this." I stared at the books on the shelves, left behind by the previous owner, in all languages under the sun. The bindings were tooled leather embossed with gold. Bill only clung to this collection, remnants of a finer intellect, to put on a pose for his guests.

"By God, you misunderstand me. I have no pity for people who get into drugs for a lark. That's what I did, and it was my own damn foolery. But a nurse shot up this man with morphine, day after day in that hospital, and he became an addict against his will. That's not right."

"True enough. Good luck, then." I left the library. I don't know why Bill's words bothered me. I should want him to be a decent man.

I HARDLY SLEPT a wink that night. There wasn't exactly cater-wauling as Bill predicted, but it sounded like someone was tap-dancing across the ceiling and Link yammered on and on. After I heard him yell "Lena" once, I muffled my head with pillows. At least I knew Dass was standing guard outside Link's door, so there was no likelihood that he would rampage through the house.

Bill and I took breakfast in the conservatory surrounded by orchids. The peace was welcome after the disruptions of the night. I cracked open my egg with a small silver knife, and Bill did the same. I sipped coffee from a porcelain cup painted with hale peasants performing mysterious tasks in fields full of windmills. Bill hated these porcelains but he kept them for display after having the mansion's contents appraised. He had shaken his head, saying, "God knows why but they're worth a goddamn mint."

"I know you're going to see Lena today," he said out of the blue, and my face felt hot. It was not possible to have a single thought in your head without Bill knowing it. "I advise against it," he said, cutting up his toast. "She'll be mad as a hornet. Smile isn't letting her leave the room. I know she wants to see Link again on the sly. I could see her squirming at that table in the bar, wishing to say things to him but not able to with us around. I would give a deal to know what those things are," he mused.

"So you're holding her prisoner."

"That's a little harsh, my friend. She's actually in danger. Some unsavoury elements noted her arrival at the Oriental, and I'm protecting her." He cut the crusts off his toast one by one.

I banged my fist on the table. "But you're the one that took her to the Oriental!"

There was a pause, and I was relieved when Bill decided to overlook my outburst.

"No, By God, she took herself. She knows best what risks she's willing to take to see the lieutenant."

I wondered what unsavoury elements he meant. His supposed pal, the psychotic chief of police? Those Russians Link mentioned? There were a lot of choices. I undid the top button of my shirt. The sun had risen above the treetops across the river and was glaring through the thousand panes of the conservatory. "We should breakfast earlier if we're going to do it in a glass box."

"I like it in here. It's my favourite thing, to contemplate the flowers," Bill said. "Ever since I got out of jail."

I just nodded my head, uncertain what to make of Bill's strange new poetic leanings, which despite his reformed ways were still at odds with his lifestyle. I tugged on my collar, which was sticking to my neck from sweat.

"Look, go visit her if you want," he said. "Tell her she can see Link as soon as he settles down. She'll forgive you."

"Aren't you worried about her pity for the lieutenant? Pity is like a drug to some women."

"Not Lena." He pushed his cut-up toast pieces through the soft yolk on his plate and took a bite. "She hardly knew him. Shively told me that much. What's more important is she should spend more time around me. It's your job to make it happen." He pointed his fork at me. "You'll convince her to go to the hospital ball with me at the royal palace. I'm one of the biggest donors. The king will be there, and you can tell her that. Bring her one of the dresses I bought to soften her up."

I stared at him. He had lost his reason. Lena would not want to go to a party with him, dress or no dress. She hated to be manipulated. My job was doomed from the start.

"Wipe that look off your face, By God. If she wants to see the lieutenant, that's the condition. She'll come."

BILL WAS RIGHT about one thing. Lena opened the door to me when I said it was about Link. But as soon as I proposed the ball, she refused completely.

"What could it hurt?" I asked, grasping at straws, I knew. But this was the only job Bill had given me and I didn't want to bungle it.

She told me to sit down, giving me the only chair while she sat on the bed. The room was dim with the shutters pulled to keep out the heat. She looked at me with sudden seriousness, then stepped past me to lock the door. She was tired of that goon Smile barging in all the time, she explained.

"Why do you do Bill's work? He betrays everyone eventually. Including you," she said as she sat down again. "A copy of your journal turned up on my doorstep three years ago. It was his warning. If he showed it to anyone else, I was done for. My military career meant everything to me."

I felt like throwing up. "He sent you my private journal?"

"Yes."

"You were only supposed to get it if I was *dead*. That was the condition in my will, which the lawyer had, along with the only key. Bill must have corrupted him somehow."

"Of course he did." She smiled ironically.

I put my head in my hands, humiliated and not knowing where to look. "I suppose you could always tell how I felt about you, anyhow. That was no secret."

"I'm sorry how I acted back then." She took my hand, and hers felt cool, the skin smooth and soft. There was a quiet strength in it also. I was embarrassed that my own hand was sweaty, but what could one do in the tropics? "In the years since, I've thought back on how good you were to me," she said, "and believe me, if I didn't have the sense to value it then, I do now."

"I didn't approve of this scheme."

"He never listens. I know."

She was still holding my hand. It was a moment I could have enjoyed forever, except that my humiliation over the idea of Lena reading my journal was so deep. Thinking of it, my anger grew.

"Did you know Bill has a wife in Burma?" I kept out the part that there was no Western ceremony, but he had technically paid the bride price. The Burmese locals considered them married, at least.

"When did he marry?" Her voice was crisp, businesslike.

"About six months ago."

The warmth in Lena's eyes had vanished, and her mouth was set in a thin, hard line. I had worried at the Oriental bar when, despite her attempts to ignore Bill, she had accidentally addressed him. And even when she spoke to me, she couldn't help looking at him briefly each time, before tearing her gaze away. Once Bill saw an open door, he was quick to walk all the way in. I was pretty sure the door was slammed tight again.

"Some rich Englishwoman, I suppose?"

"No. Some tribal girl who rides a horse. That's all I know. I never saw her."

"A horse. I see."

She nodded grimly. I wasn't sure why equestrian ability was more disturbing than money, but it seemed to be.

"Tell him I'll come to his damn party," she said.

I didn't understand how she agreed after that revelation. She must have some revenge in mind. I did not allow myself a smile until I was outside, on the way back to the palazzo.

Bill was pleased as punch at my news, completely unaware of his doomed position with Lena. Yet he was hardly around for me to gloat over secretly, because in the days of Link's cure Bill spent hours at a time with him in his room. If Dass was not still on guard at the door, I would have pressed my ear to it to listen. Was Bill spooning him broth and wiping his brow in sympathetic silence, a fellow junkie, or was Link becoming central to Bill's plans? Surely it was my right to know if someone else was going to be cut into the business. I had to do the accounting of it.

In one of the rare moments when he emerged from Link's room, I finally approached Bill about it. He was sitting in the library, continuing to ignore his exquisite book collection in favour of the shabby cardboard-bound text on irregular warfare that was placed open, face down, on the side table. He guffawed at my concern.

"He'll get no money out of me. I'm pleased to turn his brain inside out, is all. Know thine enemy, isn't that what the Bible says?"

"I don't think so. That's more a 'turn the other cheek' kind of book."

"Not the Old Testament. There's lots of smiting and bloodshed in it."

I let it go.

"Did Lena like the dress I sent?" he asked.

For half a second I almost felt sorry for him. But only half. "She loved it."

She had flung it carelessly on the bed. I thought it would be more of a blow if her disgust at everything to do with him hit as a full-force surprise when she arrived.

CHAPTER TWENTY-ONE

FIRST TIME TWICE

THE DAY APPOINTED for my meeting with Link was finally here, but I was irritated that I had to follow Bill's conditions. I couldn't believe that, after effectively coming back from the dead to barge into my life, Bill was blackmailing me again, and trading this visit for my involvement in one of his schemes. What was the purpose, except to prove that he could control me? Byron had suggested some business agenda Bill wanted me to advance. Perhaps it really was as simple as that. The royal family would clearly be important customers for his gems. But couldn't his *wife* do it?

Wife. Who would marry him? Some illiterate girl, I supposed, out for his money and a ticket to America someday. Not knowing that he could never go back there. Why hadn't he brought her to Bangkok with him? It was not like *newlyweds* to be separated. Maybe she hated him as much as I did right now. No, that wasn't possible.

I laid out my five dresses on the bed. Byron had warned me that Link did not remember speaking to me at the Oriental because of his condition. How unbearable, when I thought that the difficulties of seeing him for the first time were not actually over with—that this was the first time all over again. Blue dress, yellow dress, red dress? White or black? It was just as well he did not remember, I thought, because it was not like it had gone well. I was glad to know it was because he was in an altered state. Why were the men in my life plagued with drugs? First Bill, now Link. But at least Link had an excuse, because the hospital had given it to him.

Yellow dress, I thought, holding it up against my face while I peered in the tall mirror on the antique wardrobe. My image wavered in the glass, eaten away by dark voids where the silver had blackened with time. Yellow was an innocent colour, of friendship, roses, and truces. White would have been going too far into surrender and virginity. Though wasn't yellow also for cowards? I tossed it back on the bed and picked up the blue. I would wear this one. Though I wished it was not so conservative—down past the knees and up to the neck, but all the dresses were like that now. I missed the risqué styles from when I was a teen, but those freewheeling times were long gone.

As I did up the buttons on the back, straining to reach the ones near my shoulder blades, I wished that Byron would be at the palazzo. The knowledge would have calmed me while I waited to see Link, and I'd feel safer if Bill barged in. Byron claimed he had some business to attend to today. I could not blame him, I supposed. He had once cared for me and did not want to deliver me into the hands of someone I had loved, and for all he knew, perhaps still loved. I did not think Byron loved me anymore, what with so much time having gone by, but obviously he still had a soft spot for me. I had wanted to stay angry at him, but I needed him as an ally.

I had to knock on the door to let myself out. As always, Smile stood in the hallway blocking it, my jailor more than my protector.

Smile did not speak the whole way to the palazzo, either in the cab or on the boat. He followed me up to the entrance, where an equally silent Indian man took his place at my side. Bill had always surrounded himself with gregarious types in the past, to add to his merriment. Times had changed. It was apparently all about security and secrets now.

"I'm here to see Link Hughes," I said, in case he imagined that I was visiting his boss instead. He gave me an almost imperceptible nod. I followed him up the curved stairway, with the brief thought that I was entering the thousand and one Arabian nights, what with his pink turban and white pantaloons. That was an unfortunate parallel, I realized, since the woman in that story could only save her life if the story she told was good enough for the king. Today, Link would be my judge.

The Indian deposited me in a large sitting room with pukka fans deranging the air. I stared with confusion at the many chairs scattered about, wondering where to put myself until Link arrived. As my eyes adjusted to the dim, I became aware that a figure was already sitting in the corner.

"Link?"

He didn't answer.

I sat in the chair beside him, a beautiful antique that turned out to be lumpy and uncomfortable. I was relieved to see that his tube had been removed.

"Your neck is better?" I touched his hand, but he didn't react. He seemed dissociated from everything, including his own flesh. His eyes were like dry pebbles.

"After I got pneumonia in the camp, there was an infection in my throat. It's clear now." His voice still sounded ragged, but he could speak more easily than the other night.

"I heard you don't remember seeing me at the Oriental. I said sorry then. I'll say it again. I'll say it a thousand times if that could make things right."

"You just did what anyone would do."

He spoke mechanically. Touching him was worse than not touching him given that there was no response, and I withdrew my hand. I stood and paced nervously, staring through the slits in the shutter, but a tree in front of the window blocked any hope of a view.

"Miss Maggie was blackmailing me. She made me write a report on you and two other men." I waited for him to ask what she had over me, and wasn't sure what I'd answer, but he sat in stony silence. "I didn't think it was you she was after, Link. I didn't know about the Spanish Consul, or I never would have said anything about him."

"You probably knew about the Spanish Consul, deep down," he said in the same monotone.

Did I? Was I the person he must be imagining, who would sell him out for some abstract concept of patriotic duty—which really meant saving myself from Miss Maggie?

"I did," he continued, "but I let myself be fooled. I was desperate for money. My family lost everything in the Depression. Spain was a neutral country so I told myself there wasn't any harm in it. After the bombing, I realized the Consul was giving my intel to the Japs. That was the last thing I wanted."

"I knew it had to be something like that. I knew you didn't want to hurt the Captain." I took a deep breath. "I cared about you."

From far across the river came the sound of a piano, wispy and melancholy. The further away the piano was, the longer it had been since the player struck the keys. The player's thoughts and emotions could have changed completely since then. I thought of Einstein's theories—was the space of this room the same as time? I supposed it would be, if I crossed it; so I stayed standing where I was. I was afraid for time to move forward.

"I was glad when Miss Maggie sent me behind the lines," he said. "I wish I'd died. But my damn body wouldn't stop living."

I tried to think of what to say, but I was at a complete loss. I needed to know exactly what he'd been through, so that I could calculate how large my sin was. Frankly, I didn't think I could take it. In any case, it wouldn't be fair to ask him to relive it. Still standing at the window, I felt claustrophobic with the wooden screens shut, and I pushed them open a crack. There was a scuffle in the shrubberies below. Broad shiny leaves twitched and petals fell from pale pink flowers. My shoulders tensed.

"What?" Link said, reaching my side with surprising speed.

"Someone's down there."

Nothing for long seconds, and then the shrubs heaved. Something large and grey-green, carbuncled, weathered, and ancient, darted out and away, toward the river.

"Monitor lizard," Link said.

I buried my face in his chest, and he did not resist. But I wasn't going to cry over a lizard. What was wrong with me? "I went AWOL to find you, when I heard the Russians were after you. This is the next war." I stared up at him. "You need to be careful."

"There's nothing left anyone can do to me."

"What happened?" I whispered. I traced my finger on his gaunt cheek, felt the dint of the bullet scar.

He took my hand and gently removed it from his face, a more stinging rebuke than any anger he might show. "One of those miracles of war. I got shot through the head, clean, and it only took out my back molars. Didn't need them anyways. The Japs only fed us a cup of rice a day. Once we finished building the railroad, fall of forty-three, they moved my camp into Siam, and we repaired the line after Allied bombings. I got pretty sick. Beriberi, dysentery, typhus, and malaria, but at least it took me off the work crew sometimes. The British found my camp about a month after the Japanese surrender and put me in their hospital."

It was like he was talking about someone else, someone he didn't much interest himself in. I could hardly imagine the horror of what he'd been through. If what had been between us was love, I would have sat at Link's side, holding his hand, waiting for the healing to come, forever if need be. However, he clearly did not want me to do that. I could hardly bear his indifference, but I would have to learn to accept it. I still owed him a debt.

"Is there any way I can help you now?" I asked.

"Talk to Bill. He'll tell you."

CHAPTER TWENTY-TWO

JANUARY 25, 1946—NOON

BILL HAD INSISTED that I stay with him in the library, which I found strange because he wasn't speaking to me at all. He sat in his green velvet armchair, for once reading one of the leather-tooled books from the library's original collection: Sun Tzu's *The Art of War*. I remembered it from our bookshelves when I was a boy. My father had liked to read it, as instruction for cutthroat business practices, I supposed. Later I made my way through those shelves when I was a lonely teenager, trying to understand the man who had abandoned us. I never did.

"Remember you said to me the other day, 'Know thine enemy'?" I finally said to Bill. "It's from that book you're reading. Not the Bible."

"What do you know. You're right," he said, looking at the cover and returning to his reading. Had he just brought me here for the pleasure of ignoring me?

I stood up and examined the aspidistra by the window, which looked droopy. I liked looking after plants. I remembered I was dusting my favourite agave when Bill came to my office in Seattle back in the day and first offered me work with his gang, fixing his taxes. I pressed my finger in the soil and it was bone dry. "I'm going to water the plant."

"Not now, By God. It'll keep."

I stared at the clock and wondered at how time crawled. After a while I decided the hands weren't actually moving. It must need winding. No matter how impatient you are, at least *one* minute goes by, even when it feels like ten.

Then Lena burst through the doors in a rage. She stood there like Joan of Arc with her hands on her hips. No wonder Bill needed to prepare himself with that book.

"What have you got Link into?" she asked.

"The question is, what have you got him into? Or really, let's lay this on the proper doorstep." He calmly put a bookmark in at his place, closed the book, and laid *The Art of War* on the table near his hand. "What's Miss Maggie got him into?"

That seemed to take the air right out of her. "Miss Maggie?"

"Yeah."

Her lips formed into silent words that I took to be, *Oh God*. Lena looked hesitantly to where I was sitting in the corner. "Does he know about her?"

"Nope. But he might as well. He's my associate in all my undertakings. This is my current undertaking."

Lena seemed upset and nervous, and I got up to leave. "You two can hash this out."

"Sit you down, By God." His voice bore no argument and I sat. I hated witnessing their fights in the old days. If he tried to hit her again, goddamn it, nothing would hold me back from defending her.

She had gathered her strength up, her posture ramrod straight as she advanced toward him with her hands clenched into fists. "You're lying."

"Don't you remember, I never lie?" He laid a hand on his heart. And it was true, when I thought of it, he never had, although he'd been known to keep me in the dark a good long while. He was like a river at night, its course unseen. Deep and dangerous. You had to be a damn good swimmer.

They stared each other down, but it was Lena who looked away.

"By God, will you please help Lena to a chair? I think she would be more comfortable sitting while we wait."

"Wait for what?" I asked, but he didn't answer.

Lena did seem unsteady on her feet so I did as Bill asked. Like a maître d' at a fine restaurant, I pushed the chair in for Lena while she sat. Meanwhile Bill went to the library door and whispered something to a person outside. I saw the flash of a pink turban, and was irritated to think that Dass must know things that I didn't.

Minutes passed, the silence not even relieved by the ticking of the clock, long since run down. The aspidistra yearned for water. Then the old phone in the hall jangled. The three of us turned our heads as one toward the harsh ringing outside the door.

"It's for you, Lena," Bill said.

Like a sleepwalker she headed toward the sound, and disappeared into the dark of the corridor. The ringing stopped.

"Can I water the plant now?" I asked.

"Not if you got to leave the room," Bill said.

I sighed. He was not a nurturing personality. I fidgeted with a paperweight on the table, until I realized it was a scorpion encased in the glass and nearly dropped it. "This is a dreadful artifact."

"I don't pretend to understand the mind of the man who last owned this place, but I kind of like that thing. Better than the porcelains."

This banter was just a way to pass the time until Lena returned. I could sense that Bill wasn't really listening, and all his energy was focused on the door that Lena would walk through. Unless this strange telephone call made her run for the hills. I hoped one of them would explain what was going on.

Finally, she returned, sat on the velvet chair, and crossed her slender hands in her lap. She looked like someone at a funeral.

"So?" Bill asked. "What did Miss Maggie say?"

"That I should follow the orders of William Yardley."

"By God, could you confirm that *I'm* William Yardley?" Bill said.

"Yes."

"That's a stupid alias," she said. I was glad this backtalk seemed to shake her a little from her daze.

He smiled. "Made Miss Maggie madder than a hornet. That's why I picked it."

"Could someone please tell me who Miss Maggie is?" I said. "Everybody else seems to know."

"I'll go first," Bill said. "Lena is used to keeping everything clammed up in her line of work. Remember how I told you that I had a benefactor that got me out of jail?"

"Yes."

"That was Miss Maggie."

"So you told her everything," Lena said. "That's how she got her hooks into me."

"Frankly, I don't know what I said in my ravings when she dried me out. But blame yourself. You're the one that led her straight to me when you visited the jail."

She groaned with rage. "You were threatening to blackmail me!"

"You didn't have to visit me in person."

"Bloody hell, I wish I'd never met you," she said, and jerked her head away to look at the point in the room furthest from him.

"You got to take responsibility for your past," he said, walking toward Lena. She cringed and he halted, but he kept up his jocular tone. "Like I have. If you think rational-like, you'll see it worked out for the best. You got a fancy secret service job. Isn't that something?"

When she spoke, it was to the far corner. "Yes, my work is important to me. I made it to second-in-command of my decryption unit. But because of you blabbing about my past, Miss Maggie can throw me in jail whenever she wants."

"Lena, don't you get it? She never will. She recruited you *because* you were a crook. That's Miss Maggie's game. The other spymasters are building their units out of their Harvard pals. Nancy boys. That's fine if you want gossip from an ambassador, but you want an operation done? They don't know their ass from an assassin! You want to steal something, blow something up? The skills you need belong to a crook. I got to credit Miss Maggie with being a visionary."

Lena stood up and walked over to the shelves, where she kept her back turned as she made a show of studying the titles. "These are not your books," she said.

"I own them."

She pulled one down. "Not the same thing. I bet you've never read Shakespeare."

Bill closed his eyes and took a deep breath. "Lena, sit you down. We have work to do."

She remained standing, the ceiling fan ruffling her hair. She wouldn't look at Bill. It was high noon in Bangkok, and even the birds outside had gone quiet. I was glad of the reprieve. The birds of this land were unusually sinister and cold-hearted. Back home, all the innocent barred owl asked was, "Who cooks for you?" I missed the simple days at my saloon in Sequim. When Link was in the mountains of Assam, he told me, he heard the constant cry of "brainfever!" from birds in the trees. It had haunted him. When he got malaria, that was all he heard running through his burning mind. He later found out from Dass it was a common hawk-cuckoo, making up for its dull brown appearance with its startling message. Dass had also told him that the Bengalese thought the same bird said, "My eyes are gone," while in the Hindi tongue they argued it was, "Where's my love?" Maybe all those messages were the same thing.

"I'm not really AWOL, am I?" Lena said.

"Miss Maggie sees all and knows all," Bill said. "You're here with her blessing. She knows what a great team we used to be."

"Why didn't she just transfer me to Bangkok?"

"This is a very deep operation. I don't believe she's authorized for it."

"Oh God. What do I have to do?"

I didn't want Lena to be unhappy, but I couldn't help feeling excited about the idea of us all working together again. Surely Bill had a place for me in all this. He always did.

"The Harvard men have the President's ear," Bill said, evading her question. "Miss Maggie's networks could get axed. But it's not for Miss Maggie that I'm concerned. You understand the fallout if she's cut, honeylamb?"

"Don't call me that."

I gave her a sympathetic smile, to no effect. She was staring at the pattern in the Persian carpet.

"We'd no longer be protected by her, and we could be called to account for our crimes. That would mean jail for you, death row for me. So the Harvard men got to fail. To be particular, Knowlton Gaige's unit. He has something planned here in Bangkok that's part of a bigger strategy against the Commies. It boggles the mind."

At this Lena finally looked at Bill. "He's using Nazis. Here?"

Bill nodded. "Gaige will do anything to stop Siam from electing a Communist government. Siam has always been a leader in the Far East. If they vote red, other countries would follow."

"This man would really kill a king?" I asked.

"Some piss-pot crown is just a chess piece to him. After the war, killing is easy. When it's the leader, you win faster." Bill strolled over to the window and absently picked some leaves from the aspidistra. I wanted to say, *Hold on, what did that plant ever do to you?* but Bill was on a roll. He explained that Prime Minister Pridi, a war hero hand-chosen by the king, had rallied an influential group of Communists around him. The peasants and factory workers were on board. They were only waiting for King Ananda to approve the new constitution and the Communists would seek an official majority in Parliament. The Russians were delighted and the Americans, apparently, alarmed. Gaige's mission—his obsession, really—was to keep the Communists from gaining power.

King Ananda's brother, next in line for the throne, did not have these same ideals. He would not ratify the new constitution and the Communists would be outlawed again. If an assassination was required, so be it.

"So when we break into the palace, we really aren't stealing that Emerald Buddha," I said, and Bill laughed.

"I wish. That would have been more fun," he said. "This is all politics. What a pain."

The US government openly supported the anti-Communist Chinese Nationalist Army, he continued. Meanwhile, Gaige had private dealings with the Chinese Nationalist warlord who escorted Bill's drug shipments through Burma. Under the table, Bill said, Gaige supported various key players in the Far East opium business because they were prepared to fight Communists. Communists were bad for business. This was a cheaper way to fund a war, and technically opium was legal here, so the Americans had a defence if their involvement in the trade ever came to light.

"Now you know why I'm an opium dealer," Bill said, snapping another frond off the poor plant. "Miss Maggie wanted me in the centre of it all, and with my past it adds up. Gaige is the one funding Chief Phao's drug empire here in Bangkok. And Phao is my buddy now."

"Oh Jesus," I said.

"Wouldn't trust him as far as I could throw him. The chief would be a dictator, but he'd keep the peace and he's far right. So Gaige will overlook the rest."

"Chief Phao is bad enough, but no one in America knows who he is. I still don't get how we could work with Nazis," I said. "After all the American soldiers they killed in Europe? And the death camps? It's like dealing with the devil."

"There's always got to be a new devil. To Gaige and his buddies, the Commies are it. The Nazi intel on them is the best there is. So Gaige is recruiting fascists from the SS. Interrogation, murder, whatever you want. They're efficient, you got to admit. Only a few people know about it. Like a bunch of gazooneys, the US army is out hunting for Nazis to bring to trial, not knowing some of the worst are hid by their own government."

I must have had a dubious expression on my face, because Lena said, "It's true. I decoded a cable about the American secret service recruiting Nazis in Berlin."

"That's where you come in, Lena," Bill said. "Find Gaige's transmissions and figure out his plan. We need the date. Byron, can you get a couple of radios in here?"

"An American model," she said. "The SSTR-1 portable has the best range. But that was OSS issue. Could be tricky."

"I can find anything," I said, perhaps a little too proudly. "The Japs captured a lot of Allied gear in Burma, and it's all for sale now." I took a few steps toward the door. Then a thought struck me. "Wait a minute. Does Miss Maggie know I was in the Clockwork Gang too?"

Bill rolled his eyes, and Lena gave me a pitying look. Well, dang it. Every time I learned something new, it turned out there was somebody else out there bossing me around, which made the bottom of the totem pole ever further from the top.

"You still haven't told me what Link's got to do with this," Lena said. "After all he's been through—"

Bill held up his hand to cut her off. "It's not me. He's a bit obsessed with this Nazi business. For starters, he'll take shifts listening to the radio." He lowered his hand and his face softened until he looked almost shy, a state I hadn't seen in him since he first courted Lena. "Like when you're at the party with me tonight. You are coming, aren't you?"

"Yes," she sighed.

The party. Of course, I was not invited.

CHAPTER TWENTY-THREE

EVENING AT THE PALACE

THE DRESS BILL gave me was not what I would choose, but I had to admit it was beautiful: hand-woven silk in shimmering pink and green, with a demure princess neckline, short sleeves and a long, fitted skirt. Bill said all the women would wear traditional gowns because it was a royal event. So he was controlling everything, right down to the wardrobe. Typical, I thought as I combed my hair, wincing as a tangle yanked at my scalp. My feelings about this operation were mixed, to say the least. While I was used to keeping secrets, I had never been undercover before. I was relieved that Miss Maggie thought I could do this after my lacklustre showing at Camp X. I never thought she'd give me the chance to go into the field. Of course, that made me worry I might fail, and the opportunity would never be repeated.

On the other hand, I suspected that she couldn't get anyone else to do this. Only people who had more to lose if they refused. Like me. This mission to destroy a Nazi agent was at odds with other spymasters' schemes. Was I just mixed up in the naturally vicious jockeying for promotions or a bigger budget in the secret service—or could this job be treason? No, I thought, pulling apart a tangle with my fingers. Surely the President could not approve of using Nazis. Not with public sentiment against them so hard in the war. And I felt that Miss Maggie would not make a move if the penalty to herself was too steep.

If we got caught, might she just cut us loose?

I thought back to her Shemya visit, and the way she had so quickly approved my leave. At the time I had wondered what her purpose on the island was, and felt wounded that she didn't need me there at all. Now, I understood. I had been her mission. Whether I was valuable or expendable remained to be discovered.

I smoothed my skirt in the looking glass and patted my hair, jamming in another bobby pin. I could hardly recognize myself in this foreign dress. How did my life end up like this, with me going to a royal party in Siam as a spy? Well, I could keep my face blank. I'd been hiding things for a long time.

Was I on the right side? I didn't know if Miss Maggie actually opposed using Nazi agents. All I could tell was that she was against some ssu leaders who were using Nazi agents. That would have to be enough, for now, because Miss Maggie had me boxed in. Just thinking of the Nazis filled me with rage. What had the war been for? I would be glad to derail these men's plans. I wondered how far the rot spread—but one or two key men would be enough. The old oss structure, with individual units walled off for security, meant they could keep their doings concealed. In the war, our budgets did not need to be detailed or explained. A sense of untouchability had developed, and the ssu leaders had apparently become warped by their growing power, until they lost grip of what the common person found morally acceptable. It was always possible to justify your actions to yourself. I was guilty of that too. I had robbed banks after I decided the rich were corrupt. In the Depression they looked on coldly while others suffered, while postmen like my father lost their jobs and died of poverty and broken hearts. But I had to admit I had also done it for the thrill. It was a point of pride that we never harmed an innocent bystander in our jobs, but it was a horrible truth that some policemen had died in hunting us. Kill or be killed, I could imagine Miss Maggie whispering.

As the gang's driver, I had never shot a gun, but soon it would be my turn.

My hand shook a little as I jammed in the final bobby pin. I took a deep breath and waited until my face looked calm in the mirror.

All I had to do right now was go to a party.

"Looks good on you," Bill commented when I came down the stairs. "Shows off them pipes." I flushed. I hoped I didn't look too mannish. My arms *were* bigger than when he first knew me. What else could I expect after countless days in Alaska holding up guns—a Springfield rifle was nearly nine pounds—when I was aiming at targets in the Aleutian fog.

"I'm only going to this party because it's part of the assignment," I said. The last thing I wanted was for Bill to think I actually wanted to be with him. I absolutely did not.

The business was compelling enough. Bill said we were looking for intel about the Nazi agent: how would he carry out his assassination of the king? Assassination. The word still gave me shivers. Someone in the new Strategic Services Unit was willing to go that far to prevent Communism from taking hold in Siam.

Byron watched our repartee from the corner of the marble foyer where he stood in the shadows. A silly place to hide, I thought: anyone like me looks in the shadows first.

"It'll be fun," Bill said. "It's in a castle, for God's sake."

Bill held out his arm, but I did not take it. He was not winning any points just because he had an invitation to a palace.

"I see my role as the wife who can't stand her husband," I said. "That happens a lot, I've heard."

Bill stormed off ahead of me in his tuxedo, and I followed, grimly satisfied that I punctured his smug attitude.

"Have a good time," Byron called out feebly. He was always trying to smooth things over.

Bill seethed silently on the boat and in the car as we drove toward the palace. As we turned onto a large boulevard, it was blocked with people chanting, pumping their fists, and waving empty burlap rice sacks in the air like flags. At the end of the street, a man stood on a pillar, inciting the crowd with a bullhorn.

"Commie rally," Bill muttered. "Could get ugly." He leaned forward to address the driver. "Better go back. Try Maharat Road."

The driver reversed the car. The next street he turned onto was empty except for a huge fire burning in the middle of it. This seemed more ominous than the crowds. Around the next corner there was a little more life and the cab picked up speed, weaving between bicycles and ox carts. We passed a little girl sitting on the ground in front of a thatch hut, intently cutting wood into kindling with a large machete. It seemed a task well above her years. She had to be only four years old. I hoped the machete was dull, so she wouldn't get injured if she slipped. Where were her parents?

"You know that Hughes doesn't love you, right?" Bill said. His face was in darkness save an orange flash when we passed an oil-drum fire flaring. He looked like a warrior dreaming of vengeance in the savage light.

The words hit me like a sucker punch, coming out of the blue like that, and I struggled to keep a calm tone. "What would you know about it?"

"Plenty. I've loved you more in one hour than he could in his whole life."

I brooded over that statement, absently snapping the metal clasp on my purse open and shut, open and shut. Past tense, yes? Yet ambiguous. I didn't want to go there at all. What about the wife Byron told me about? I should be recording this little exchange to send her and see how she felt about it. What kind of field operative was I, anyhow?

I wasn't, that's what. I was an analyst. I wished I was back at the palazzo, listening to radio signals. God, I was sick of men who had wives. Link and Bill were like warped funhouse reflections of each other—and I had chosen them both. Ten years between them and I'd apparently learned nothing.

"He's not himself," I said. "He has no feelings about anything right now. He needs to recover from his ordeal." I wasn't really sure why I was defending the possibility of his love. I had given up on it myself.

"He won't ever be the same. He's been through too much, and he don't have the character for it. Forget about him." Bill cleared his throat. "Can't you see I've changed?"

I glanced at him, and my heart ached. I told myself I was only seeing the past, before things got bad. If anything, he looked too much the same, and I didn't want to get suckered in again. "I see a drug kingpin. I see a man who uses other people to his own ends. How's that change? What you did is too much to forgive. You hit me. You betrayed me to Miss Maggie. Why would I ever trust you again?"

"Byron does."

"Byron is a soft-hearted fool."

"He's a good man. He ran from the old me also. He came back."

"It would take about a thousand years to make up for what you did to me."

"My time on death row was hell. Don't that count for at least nine hundred and ninety-nine?"

"No," I said, and closed my purse with a decisive snap. Why did he even care, with that wife he had in Burma? I was tempted to bring her up, but I didn't want him to think that I cared. He would think that was progress. And I really wasn't jealous. Looking out the window, I saw that we had reached a tall white wall, stretching block after block. I was relieved at the chance to change the subject. "Is this the palace?"

Bill wiped his hand over his face and turned to me with a grin that frightened me a little. His eyes had a malicious glint. "Yes. We're going to play Spot the Nazi tonight. You'll tell me who you think it is."

"You already know?"

"Sure. I just want to see how you judge character. To assess your operational usefulness."

"Listen to you. Miss Maggie *has* got her claws into you," I said. But my insult felt hollow. I was scared I would fail at this, as he hinted. He had the power to report my shortcomings to the only person who really mattered.

He was silent a moment as he adjusted his bowtie in the rear-view mirror and then, catching me observing him, his eyes locked on mine. I looked away. "Just act your part, wife. But don't go too far. This is a state occasion."

The car slowed at the iron gate where two guards nodded us in, and Bill gave a friendly salute through the window. I stared down the long carriageway, visualizing it within Bill's sketch that we'd studied before leaving tonight. There was a bewildering array of temples and mansions belonging to the extended royal family, and I feared I had not memorized them all. The secret tunnel in the temple, however, I knew. If it was real, a voice whispered in my head. This supposed tunnel would be the key to our next visit to the palace, once we found out when the Nazi agent planned to kill the king. There was no indication it would be tonight. It would be rash, with so many foreigners present to witness or wonder. Most likely Gaige would wait to make it look like some local madman or internal politicking. The engine purred as we continued along the rolled gravel drive at a crawl. We stopped behind some other luxury cars—Bill's Rolls Royce as slick as any of them, I had to admit—and the driver came around to open the door for me. I struggled with the long skirt tight around my legs. Bill scooted out his side and came around, at the ready with his arm proffered. I stayed sitting in the car.

"Please," he said. He looked like a little boy with his hopeful eyes.

I took his arm—only because of the damn dress.

I was impressed by the scene despite myself. The Italianate palace glittered with lanterns along the outer colonnade, while the windows blazed with lights. Behind us, the golden roofs of exotic temples gleamed. "It's beautiful," I said.

I felt a stab of insecurity when I saw the other women stepping out of their cars, bedecked with pearls and diamonds. I touched my throat to remind myself of the ruby necklace I wore, made from gems Bill had procured in Burma. "Advertisement. For our cover," he'd said as he clasped it round my neck back at the palazzo, his fingers brushing my collarbone, making me shiver and draw away. Now, reflexively, my hand continued up my neck to where I'd been cut, but the bandage was gone. The wound was healing well, though the stitches weren't out yet. Byron had assured me a person would have to be short indeed to notice them.

Some of the Siamese women were very short. I hoped they would not inquire, but Bill had concocted a story about a horse-riding accident and a wire fence. I was angry about the horses when I thought of his tribal wife in Burma, but I had not come up with anything better.

Entering the reception hall, we stood in the receiving line. I was nervous to meet foreign royalty in case I forgot the protocol—Bill said that a curtsey would do, but to look at the floor. Eye contact was not polite here. He said not to worry too much about it, though, because the king was raised in Switzerland and was used to European ways. "In the old days, you had to crawl across the floor," Bill whispered in my ear. "The king is next to a god here. Not a bad gig."

You'd like that, wouldn't you, I thought, but held my tongue.

The line progressed quickly. Three aides flanked the king, one briefing him discreetly before each guest approached. He gave a shy smile and greeting to each.

"I never put you down as my wife," Bill whispered. "Business partner, okay? Maybe you'll be a little more civil?"

There was not time to answer because we were approaching the king, who wore a white military uniform with epaulettes, his chest draped with gold braid and medals. "Mr. Yardley. Your generosity to the hospital is much appreciated."

The king shook Bill's hand in Western style, and Bill answered him in Siamese, looking humbly at the floor. I was impressed without wanting to be.

The king's dark eyes were languid and trusting. I felt a pang of sorrow for him. He looked scarcely more than a boy, but Miss

Maggie claimed he was marked for death—for the simple reason that he would introduce full democracy to Siam. I wouldn't have believed it if I didn't know about the Nazis firsthand. If that was possible, anything was on the table.

I curtsied to the king and we moved into the ballroom, my heels clicking on a stone floor inlaid with candy colours. An orchestra played big-band tunes on a stage while Siamese women with flowers in their hair carried trays of champagne around the room. I took a glass and sipped. "The women are so beautiful here. How are the Burmese women?"

"They're pretty enough," Bill said.

I seethed inwardly. I had only myself to blame for my dig back-firing, but he certainly was not out to charm me. He could have complimented me instead. Hoping to find someone else to talk to, I looked around the room, but of course everyone was a stranger. The majority of the guests were European or American. Even on first glance, I noticed at least four with bristle mustaches that evoked Hitler. Were they all fans, and this foreign country their refuge after the war? Finding the Nazi would not be so simple after all.

Finally, I saw one familiar face: the man that Bill pointed out to me in the Oriental bar as a potential customer. "What's his name again?" I asked.

"Warner. Dance with him so he can see your necklace up close," he said. "I'll introduce you."

As I followed Bill, patting my head to make sure no strands had come loose from the bobby pins, I regretted my intricate hairdo. Being in the military so long had left me unpracticed at the role of civilian female. I didn't appreciate being bait, but if that was my purpose I couldn't bear the humiliation of failing at it. I hoped he'd think I was pretty.

"Warner Knox, this is Vera Pasterfield," Bill said. "Old friend of mine."

"Nice to meet you," I said.

Warner put down his champagne to clasp my hand for a moment longer than was strictly necessary. After chatting briefly, he asked me to dance. As Warner escorted me to the floor, I saw Bill watching and tossed my head. Bill turned his back to talk with the men in Warner's crowd, and he seemed to know most of them already. Bill had certainly insinuated himself into this place, like a worm burrows in the dirt.

"So you've known Mr. Yardley some time?" Warner asked as he took my left hand and placed his other arm gently around my back. He smelled of French cologne and Cuban tobacco. It was pleasant.

"Since before the war," I said, looking up at him and smiling. He was over six feet tall and muscular, like a boxer.

"Were you in gems with him all that time?"

"That's new. But I have every confidence in it," I said, touching my necklace.

"It's beautiful," he said. "Though of course the woman wearing it is influencing my impressions."

"Thank you."

The waltz carried us across the room, our own small circles within the wheel of the other dancers, like planets circling the sky. I had to take small steps so my fitted dress didn't trip me up, but Warner accommodated me easily. "What did Mr. Yardley do during the war?" he asked.

"Lord knows," I smiled. "Except for those who like to brag—who usually lie—most men don't seem to want to talk about what happened."

"True. It's all best forgotten."

We chatted off and on for the rest of the waltz, and I learned he had majored in classics at Cornell, and was fond of Dutch art, particularly Vermeer.

"Not Roman art?" I asked.

"They're best admired for the art of empire. No one knew light like Vermeer. Only he could do justice to a painting of something like this necklace against your pale skin."

I felt warmth in my cheeks, and I tried to turn the topic to business. "Does that mean you're interested in buying some rubies?"

"More and more. Why don't you come by the Oriental tomorrow? You can ask for me at reception." The waltz over, he kissed my hand and bowed as he returned me to Bill.

"See you fellows around," Bill said, abruptly leaving the group. He twitched his head for me to follow, and I glanced over my shoulder to see Warner tracking us with his eyes. Bill grabbed two glasses of champagne from a passing tray. He moved like an eel through the crowds, nodding his hellos while I struggled to keep up in my tight dress, until we stood on an empty balcony overlooking the garden. The heady scent of tropical flowers filled the air and Bill put a glass into my hand.

"Thought you'd taken them both for yourself," I said. Bill closed the French doors behind him and the noise of the party dimmed, leaving us in privacy. We could see into the ballroom, but the reflections from the bright lights inside would obscure us to their eyes.

"I should have, but I didn't. Anyways, what'd you think of him?" I shrugged. "I don't know. He wants to do business."

"With you, I'll bet he does," Bill smirked. "I saw how you gave him the sparkle eyes. You might as well know he's von Roth. The Nazi."

I almost spit out my mouthful of champagne. "I found out where he lives," I said, recovering myself. "At the Oriental. He said we could come by any time."

"That's just tickety boo." Bill stared at the dark garden below, finishing his champagne, and ducked back inside. In a minute he came back onto the balcony, with two more full glasses. "The king left the reception already," he said. "When Warner, or I should say, the Nazi, wasn't staring down your dress, he was eyeballing the king. Von Roth might try to scope out the place. If he leaves the room, follow him. If he makes you, you have your excuse. You found him *so charming*, you wanted to be alone with him."

I ignored Bill's sarcastic tone. "Think he'll try something tonight?"

"No, security's too tight. He's a smart motherfucker. But I'm smarter." He took both my hands in his and I stared at the ground. "I'm going to get him, Lena."

Murder. He was talking murder. "You're going to risk your neck for some foreign king?"

"Did you see Ananda? An innocent. He can't help what he was born into, any more than I could."

Bill had once told me his father was a drunk who beat him, until he ran away at the age of twelve to raise himself up on the streets. He had to steal to survive, and that was how his life of crime began. I felt a stirring of pity for Bill and tamped it down.

"Can't we turn von Roth over to the Nuremberg court?"

"Miss Maggie says that won't work and I agree. He's protected by the authority of the US government, even if it is through Gaige. His identity's been changed. Lena, don't get cold feet. Let me tell you something. Von Roth was one of them who uncovered hidden Jews and sent them to the death camps. And he was a field commander over the massacres in the Ukraine. Even some of his SS troops found it too vicious. If they wouldn't do it, he shot his own men. To make an example."

I had danced with that man. His hands, murderous hands, had touched my neck—with gallantry. His lips, lips that had shouted orders to kill, had pressed against my fingertips, and I had sensed nothing of this. I had no intuition for evil. I was a failure. Weren't agents supposed to know what goes on underneath? "How did he seem so normal? So American?"

"He really did go to Cornell. A slick bastard. Evil takes many forms, I seen that much in my life," Bill said. "He deserves whatever he gets."

Through the glass doors I saw a blond man, taller than most, weaving patiently through the crowds and away from us, toward the main exit of the reception hall. "He's on the move. I'm going to follow him." I put down my champagne glass on the stone balcony ledge behind me, and Bill grabbed my arm as though to stop me. "You said to," I hissed, and brushed past him.

If anything happened to me, it was Bill's fault. He gave the order. It was too bad he never felt sorry, or guilty, or anything. That was always his problem. I snaked my way through the crowds, smiling and apologetic in turn, turning my shoulders sideways to slide through. Warner disappeared out the main door, and I cursed under my breath. Which way would he go? The empty foyer was large and had doors off both sides to other rooms, not opened for the evening. Bill said they were the kings' and queens' galleries, which he had seen on his earlier tourist visit. One of the two doors was open a crack but the room was dark inside. I poked my head in, but all I could see was the glint of moonlight off the polished black sculptures lining the room. The kings, these were. There were two other doors shut tight at the far end of the long gallery. I had to choose quickly. Either try those doors, or go outside. There was no time for mistakes if I wanted to catch up to Warner.

Damn it, I had to think of him as von Roth now. The Nazi.

I rounded the corner and smiled brightly at the stern-faced guards manning the main exit. I hoped they spoke English. "My husband lost his cigarette case. He's so absent-minded." I rolled my eyes, recalling Bill's words from earlier, *Act your part, wife*. I could be anyone's wife. "Did you see where he went?"

"Yes, ma'am. To the automobiles."

"Thank you." I walked down the steps, exultant. The feeling was short-lived when von Roth was nowhere in sight. The visiting automobiles lined the wide drive, the first of them under bright lights from the palace. The more distant vehicles were shadowed in darkness stretching back to the main gate, which had a solitary spotlight beaming down upon it.

I hurried along the row of cars, staring left and right. When I reached the dim middle ground, beyond the easy surveillance of the guards, I spotted a tall man darting around a corner, between some more modern buildings, heading eastward. It had to be von Roth. Who else would dare skulk about the palace grounds? I tried to picture the map Bill showed me and decided these were the administration buildings. The place was a maze. I'd just have to follow as close as I dared. I took off my high heels to move more quickly, and held the straps in one hand. Women's attire was made for baiting, not hunting. The smooth paving stones were still warm on my feet from the heat of the day. A second later I felt cool grass under my toes and shivered at the sudden contrast. I dashed beside a modern white building and poked my head around the corner. Von Roth was making his way south along the temple compound's wall. That was easy enough to identify, with the gold towers glinting on the other side. Von Roth turned east again, then veered suddenly across the wide boulevard. He followed a curved path by a French-styled chateau. One of the king's old sleeping quarters, I recalled from Bill's guidebook, but seldom used today. Did von Roth plan to murder the king in his sleep there one night? I moved from tree to tree along the boulevard. Passing a sort of pagoda that was open to the air, I stepped onto a small pathway, and there was a crunch under my feet. Gravel. Von Roth paused also. I froze in horror. Quickly, I backed against a wooden pillar of the pagoda, pressing myself into it tightly, praying that I could become part of the very wood. I held my breath. Von Roth paused also, but after a few seconds, he continued on. Apparently the darkness was kind. There were so many strange shapes, statues, carved buildings and topiaries. I could conceal myself among them if I was still enough.

Scared now, I stayed where I was. Once von Roth reached the main carriageway, he no longer bothered with stealth. Walking south along the main palace walls, he moved carelessly toward the guards at the southeast gate, which was spotlit like the other gates had been. They did not challenge him. When he reached them he paused. Their muted voices carried across the grounds, but I could not make out any words. He lit a cigarette. The last I saw of him was his white tuxedo gleaming under the spotlight before the guards locked the gate behind him.

The southeast gate. This was most likely where he'd breach the palace. Now, we had to figure out when he meant to strike.

CHAPTER TWENTY-FOUR

JANUARY 25, 1946—NIGHT

THEY GOT BACK to the palazzo around eleven thirty. I hadn't been able to sleep, despite a glass of warm milk, and lay in bed staring at the ceiling. They didn't speak, at least not once they entered the front door, and I heard two sets of footsteps echoing down the halls, each in their separate wing. I was glad of that. Somehow I had imagined Bill making a move tonight, him dressed all dapper and showing off his connections at the palace. If he had played his pawn, or knight, or wherever he was in his game, he had not yet won anything. Lena's footsteps passed by my door, not pausing. I wished there were more wings in this place, so she wasn't so close to me. I'd grown used to my privacy. But between her refusal to be near Bill, and his wish to keep her distant from Hughes, even the palazzo was challenged to accommodate all these social quandaries.

I was disturbed that Bill had taken such an interest in Hughes. Drying him out and involving him in our plans. Even Lena seemed ill at ease about him. I wasn't sure he could be trusted. What had he done that Bill and Lena would not tell me? And was he really cured of his addiction? If not, he would have no moral compass and could sell out any one of us. Not everyone was like Bill, able to give up their drugs once and for all, like discarding a toy after childhood ended.

Bill was usually good at reading people. It was his gift, like a lion senses weakness in a herd of prey. He knew who would do what and why. But was his judgment clouded? Succeeding at this job for the mysterious Miss Maggie was clearly important to him, and he was involving Link for practical reasons. Lena could not be on the radio twenty-four hours a day. Bill might be so focused on this scheme that he failed to see it was not a good idea to throw Lena and Link together in a shared project. God knows Bill could be overconfident about his own charms. I guessed I had to trust him. He'd never been wrong about anyone before—except me. I had betrayed him for Lena. Link might do the same. Maybe Bill was the one in danger.

Given the choice of who to protect, I'd certainly choose Bill over Link. Except when I had hated Bill, when he was in the depths of his addiction, he had been the best friend I'd ever had.

I flopped over onto my side, plumped the pillow, and shoved the sheet down to my waist. It was hot and uncomfortable in my room tonight. Sometimes I wished I had just stayed in Sequim. It was nice and cool there, and while it had been boring I had no worries. Running my saloon, I'd been a big fish in a small pond where there were never any sharks. In the tropics there were dangers everywhere, it seemed.

AT BREAKFAST THERE were three place settings in the conservatory, with three eggs, three toasts, and three guavas. Bill was already sitting down, looking chipper, when I joined him. Lena came down a few minutes later, rubbing her eyes. She grabbed her chair and set it away from us, behind some potted orchids. She came back for her plate and cutlery, and returned to her chair to eat alone in silence.

"Last night was excellent, By God," Bill said, loud enough for Lena to hear. "We eyeballed the Nazi and saw the layout of the

215

palace. We're going to stop this bastard from killing the king. That's what they call Wet Affairs in this business. I don't know why. Maybe because everything ends in blood? These Harvard boys puzzle me. Just call a spade a spade."

I spilled some coffee on my lap. Everything ends in blood? Lena should not be involved in this. Even in our bank robber days, killing someone had been incidental and unfortunate, and certainly not planned out in advance.

"All we need now is to find out the date." He raised his voice. "Lena, get on your radio voodoo. Me, I'll tap my networks. You know, By God, my idea of a criminal has expanded since the old days. They're in all walks of life. The most crooked fuckers are in police, in government, what have you." He took a sip from his glass and smacked his lips. "Do you like this juice?"

I looked at the green liquid dubiously. I hadn't tried mine yet. "What is it?"

"Avocado."

"How do you squeeze an avocado? They're not juicy."

"Squeeze anything hard enough, you can crush it," Bill said.

"Is that one of his mottos?" Lena said from across the room.

"No, Lena. I say a thing, I mean it for what it is. I'm speaking of this here avocado. Wouldn't life be easier if we were all like that?"

"Byron, please pass the coffee," she said, and I carried the silver pot to her. I hesitated, then poured it into her cup, thinking Bill would not like me to leave the coffee on her table. He usually had at least two cups.

Lena gave a little cry as something hit the glass wall of the conservatory and dropped to the ground. "Is it dead?" she asked. I rushed over and found a little bird lying still behind a potted palm. Bill stepped in front of me and wrapped it in his white linen napkin.

"I feel its heart beating," he said. "It just needs to rest a minute in the dark." He cradled it to his chest and Lena returned to her eating, staring intently at her plate. Her knife scraped the porcelain as she cut her toast.

"Check if there's a message on its leg," she said.

I thought she must be joking, but Bill took her request seriously. He opened the napkin and shook his head, no. A minute later he released the bird, tossing it like a magician from the white cloth. It flew off in a dash of blue and yellow, out the open door it had come in. "Sunbird," he said. "They like the nectar from my flowers. I'll have Dass keep that door closed."

Bill returned to his seat, grumbling that his egg was cold now.

"Speaking of closed doors," Lena said. "Byron, I've noticed that Link never comes out of his room. Is he a prisoner?"

"Prisoner?" I looked sideways at Bill. "No." Bill did have some strange hold on him, but I didn't know how.

"He's just keen on his radio work," Bill said. "I'm curious. Was he as good at it as you? That is, before he became a traitor."

I was dying to ask what he'd done, but the atmosphere was more than strained. Maybe I could get Bill to tell me sometime when Lena wasn't around.

"I want to see him today," she said.

"Take her up there, By God. But only for ten minutes. He needs to keep on that radio."

I STOOD AT the door awkwardly, peering inside as Lena went into Hughes' room. I was always some goddamn third wheel. Hughes was sitting and staring into space. The radio was turned on, but only loud static hissed out of the speakers.

"Should you try another frequency?" Lena said, in a voice so gentle I hardly recognized it as hers.

"Right," he said, shaking himself from his daze and reaching for the dial.

Seeing the distress on Lena's face, I withdrew to my room to give them some privacy. I sat at my desk, making origami cranes from old ledger papers with the numbers crossed out. I made a lot of mistakes when I first started the valuation of Bill's goods.

The next thing I knew, Lena was knocking hesitantly on my door, but from my clock I saw that twenty minutes had passed. I hoped Bill wouldn't be sore at me for letting her overstay the time. I told her to come on in, shoving the cranes into a drawer.

"May I?" she asked, gesturing at the leather club chair beside my desk. I nodded and she sat down.

"I need your help."

"With what?"

"Link intends to kill the Nazi."

I quirked an eyebrow, thinking uncharitably, *and why would I care about that*? But Lena attributed some Christian concern to me and grabbed my hand. "We can't let him do it. It's a death wish. Bill will take advantage of it because Miss Maggie's orders are to kill the Nazi. How nice for him, not to get his hands dirty. But if Link dies it would be my fault."

"How would it be *your* fault?"

"Oh Byron, I can't stand to tell you what I did." She buried her head in her arms on the desk. The breeze of her collapse ruffled the wings of a paper crane I'd failed to corral, and I swept it into the drawer with the others. "But the short story is, it was because of me he was sent to Burma."

"He must have done something himself, surely? Bill hinted at something."

"He made a mistake. He's paid for it and then some. But he said he's got nothing to live for." Her voice had been muffled in her arms, but then she stared up at me and spoke clearly. "I'm going with him. I'll try to protect him. I got some special training in the war."

"But von Roth was ss. It's too dangerous."

"Well, I'm going."

The expression in her granite green eyes left no room for doubt. Why was she willing to risk death for that man? I didn't know what had been between them before, but Bill was right—Hughes didn't love her now. I doubted he would love anyone again. He was already dead, you just had to look at his eyes to know it. She should let him do what he had to do. It might at least bring him peace.

Had anyone ever been ready to die for me? I doubted it. Rachel, the girl in Sequim who had wanted to marry me, was already married to someone else, so clearly I was not the be all and end all to her. Life was nothing more than a series of letdowns.

"Can I be your driver?"

She jumped up and hugged me. "Thank you," she said, and she was so close to me that the words caressed my cheek. I had to fight the urge to put my hand there.

CHAPTER TWENTY-FIVE

THE MISSION

BYRON SCROUNGED A crystal oscillator to improve my receiver's range, and a week later I found the channel von Roth used to transmit coded messages to his American handler, who was based in Hong Kong. There was a Morse communication once daily, at five o'clock, and I kept at it until I found the one I needed: "Deliver package February 11, 21:00 hours." We had two days to prepare our own plan to prevent the assassination. I told the others with confidence that von Roth would use the southeast gate, where I'd seen him speak to the guards. In my heart I had some doubts, but the only use for doubts was making better plans.

At the centre of it all was Link. I was so angry at Bill. I had believed him to be brave, when we spoke on the palace balcony, and I thought he intended to kill the Nazi himself. Bill must have known, even then, that Link was determined to do it. When that became clear, I insisted that I would go with Link as a lookout and backup shooter.

Gaige's team was surprisingly sloppy, and they didn't change the code's keys the whole time that I monitored the channel. Maybe they believed no one would be watching, so far from the world's headlines. Or maybe the American intelligence service was actually inferior to the Soviets'. The Russian transmissions that I intercepted in Alaska used a new key every day, which had been the practice on all sides during the war. I wondered if the Soviets knew everything we were doing, which would be catastrophic. By "we," I meant the secret service in general. I was sheltered—I hoped—by Miss Maggie's unsinkable deviousness. She had insisted that I change keys daily for my own reports from Alaska, though she said that her superiors grumbled about the extra expense in the postwar cutbacks. Because she was a woman, she was probably thought "fussy" and it would be a black mark against her. Miss Maggie wouldn't care, because she knew the bad results of too much pride. The Japanese had believed their Purple Machine unbreakable, and so had ignored obvious signs that we had advance knowledge of their missions. Then we crushed them at Midway, which was the turning point of the Pacific war. Miss Maggie herself was a technical genius, capable of wiring her own Purple Machine. Bill rightly scorned the dilettante spymasters, former lawyers who jumped out of a plane into France once during the war, blew up a bridge and thought it was fun. Given the choices, I preferred to be on her team, even if it wasn't exactly voluntary.

I stood on a chair to unhook the wire from the light fixture, where I'd set up my makeshift antennae in a room on the third floor to get better reception. I very much hoped it would turn out Miss Maggie had principles, and that she was against using the Nazi agents on moral grounds. Not just that she was driven to get the remaining agency funding for her own unit. Well, I supposed, what of it? It wasn't fair these men had the President's ear just because they were men. Miss Maggie had been a decryption master for twenty years, and her work was more worthy of being continued. Although, I wondered, what *was* the purpose of America's intelligence service before the war? Was it mostly tracking down Communist agitators in the labour movement? Had Miss Maggie fixated on the Soviets simply because she had a deep and irrational hatred of their ideas?

In any case, I didn't have the luxury of doubting my mission. My only choice was to take the cards I'd been dealt.

I wound the fifty-foot wire round my arm so that it would fit in the suitcase with the three canisters holding the radio. Certainly, eliminating a Nazi agent could only be considered a good thing. Then my conscience kicked in. I had to stop using the foggy language of the Morale Operations branch. Not eliminated, killed. We were going to kill a man. A man who had looked into my eyes and danced with me.

I grabbed the chairback as I stepped down to the floor. Von Roth was a war criminal. It was not right for our government to shelter people like him from prosecution at Nuremberg. When the proper channels were subverted, the law must go into the people's hands.

From the teak table beneath the lamp, I gathered all my pieces of paper, coded and decoded. I heaped them in a porcelain basin on the dresser and lit a match, dropping it in. Watching the flames die out, I prayed that Link would still be alive in two days' time. That I would be. What was I doing, going up against a seasoned ss officer?

Paying for my sins, that's what.

BYRON AND I were going to cross the river to the warehouse to inspect the guns Bill arranged for this job. They were Nazi weapons of the kind the Soviets captured on the Eastern Front, so it would appear that Germans or Russians killed von Roth. Either was a logical conclusion. The Nazis still at large were killing any turn-coats, knowing the Americans used the collaborators to rat out other war criminals for the Nuremberg trials. Meanwhile, the Russians would do anything to stop von Roth from using his knowl-edge of the Soviet regime to aid the Americans. During the Nazi occupation of the Ukraine for three years, von Roth had access to the Communist government records, and would have learned their tricks and secrets.

I walked downstairs to Link's room, where he sat by the radio, the static hissing as always. I found it disturbing. Bill insisted he was not an addict any longer, but he acted as strange as one. I turned the dial gently to shut it off.

"We got what we need," I said. "You don't have to listen anymore."

"I like the emptiness."

"You sure you won't come? If you're really going to do this, shouldn't you look at the guns?"

"I know all I need to know. I've shot a lot of men."

I stood awkwardly beside him, wondering what else I could say, but when he put on the headphones and turned the radio on again, his back to me, I walked out the door. A good solid door, the kind you could slam behind you if you wanted. He didn't care that I was helping him, and even risking my life for him. What would it take to heal him? Maybe shooting the Nazi would give him the redemption he needed, but I had a bad feeling about this mission. Link looked healthier now, his cheeks had filled out, but his mind was still funny. I could only hope that Bill's clockwork planning, and the element of surprise, would win the day.

THE GATE TO the river closed behind us with a shriek that made us both jump. "Needs oiling," Byron muttered. I stared at two boys in sarongs who stared right back at me, wide-eyed, one with his finger in his mouth. Bill wouldn't tell them to stay off the path, because it was an ancient right of way, but he told us never to speak when they were there. Just in case. He knew how the unimportant folk could be used for intelligence, since it was what he himself had always done, even before he was a spy. Bill, a spy. It was so strange. But Miss Maggie was right—the skills were mostly the same. He had always had networks of informants.

My clothes stuck to me with the heat as I stepped silently into the longtail boat and made for the shady spot in the middle, under the awning. Even without the children lurking, I would have stayed silent. I did not care to speak to Byron right now. When I was alone in my third-floor radio room this morning, Byron had come in and sat down, watching me work the frequencies a while. Then, out of the blue, he asked what led me to love men like Bill and Link. What kind of man was that, I demanded. He had coughed and turned red and stared at the ceiling, and finally said, "Bad men." And I'd wanted to cry. "I thought Link was one of the good ones," I'd said. "I thought I'd learned a lesson after Bill. I was wrong." I didn't like getting older. You were supposed to get wiser. Instead I just felt more aware of my flaws and mistakes, but still helpless to fix them.

"I brought some limeade," Byron said, pulling a green thermos out of his satchel. "Want some?"

It was hot, even on the river. I nodded and took the bottle without looking at him. I drank some and couldn't decide if it was more sweet or more sour. It was mostly bitter, I thought.

"I'm sorry about what I said. Bill's not so bad now," Byron said.

As we moved upriver I looked at the warehouses on the waterfront a while, white plaster edifices of surprising beauty given their mundane purpose. Men on the docks loaded rusty barges with sacks of rice. The men were scrawny as hyenas and I wondered how they had the strength to work.

"He's not so good either," I said finally. "Why did you go back to work for him?"

"My life in Sequim was a little too quiet. You're always at the centre of things with Bill."

"True, but sometimes you might wish otherwise."

The longtail bumped against the landing, and the tillerman jumped out to hook the rope on a metal post. Bill's warehouse did not have a privileged position, not being by one of the larger docks, but its inconspicuous placement in a nearby alley suited Bill perfectly. He was not shipping teak or rice by the ton, but opium and guns. The building was still close enough to the river to allow small shipments by that route, or he could use the newer roads. We stepped out of the boat and Byron hailed a rickshaw. I felt lazy using one for such a short distance, but I had learned that a few blocks in the tropics could feel like an eternity when walking under the open sun. I was glad when the rickshaw that pulled up had back-to-back seating, because then I did not have to discuss Bill any more.

We entered the warehouse and Byron locked the door behind us. It took my eyes a moment to adjust to the dim. "They're supposed to be over here," Byron said, waving me ahead as he moved toward the spiral staircase on our right. He stopped in front of a metal army trunk and turned the padlock's dial, left, right, left. He yanked in annoyance at the rusty old lock, tried it again, and it opened with a rattle. He raised the lid and read off a piece of paper: "Three Walther PP pistols, two Mauser Karabiners, and an StG 44. That look right to you?"

"I've never seen German guns. I've shot pistols and rifles kind of like those Karabiners, but not the other. That's a sniper rifle. I assume Link knows how to use it."

"Bill wouldn't have ordered it otherwise."

Byron's continuing faith in Bill was touching, and made me feel a little better somehow. I picked up the German pistol and it felt heavy, smooth and cool. A nice ivory grip, crosshatched. Must have belonged to an officer. I supposed he was dead now, and this was suddenly all too real. "What exactly did you do in that place, Sequim?" I asked, trying to distract myself from grim thoughts. I put the gun back in the trunk.

"Tended bar. Hunted ducks," Byron said. "A goose for Christmas sometimes."

I became genuinely curious about his life since the gang. "Who did you spend the holidays with?"

"Myself, mostly. I always had too many leftovers." He dropped the trunk's lid heavily and coughed at the dust it kicked up.

"Was it true what Bill said, that Link was a traitor?" he asked, fiddling with the old padlock to close it. "I'm a bit concerned, since we've got to work with him and all."

"He gave information to the Spanish, who were neutral in the war. It was supposed to stop there, but it ended up with the Japanese. So." I decided not to tell him about the part where our base was bombed as a result. It wouldn't exactly increase Byron's confidence in Link.

"Kind of like how I thought I was working for Bill, but turns out it's Miss Maggie."

Surprised at the comparison, I laughed, but the sound was small and hollow in the warehouse. "Miss Maggie is not the enemy."

"You all seem afraid of her."

"She knows too much about us. Nobody likes that."

We made to leave and our footfalls echoed, one-two, left-right, reminding me of the drills at Camp X. At which I had failed. Or had I? Had Miss Maggie been saving me for this? No, I was flattering myself. I was only one of the few who was cornered enough to take on a mission against others in my own agency. Dust motes swirled in the air, like miniature tornadoes.

The warehouse door, which looked like something from a medieval castle, slammed shut behind us, and the sudden daylight was shattering as a migraine. A motion caught my eye and I stared into the searing sky.

"Vultures," I said, trying to shield my eyes from the sun with my hand without losing sight of them. The bright light made my eyes watery. "Chasing death."

"Can't avoid death or taxes, they say." Byron smiled at me. "Though I've always found ways for Bill not to pay taxes."

I wanted to hug Byron for that. He always could make me feel better.

AFTER DINNER, SITTING at the table underneath the leers of the baby angels that I had not been able to ignore since Byron pointed them out one day, Bill was silent until the servants had cleared the last of the cutlery. The knives scraped jarringly against the platters with their peasant windmills. Were they the sort Don Quixote would have tilted against, I wondered idly. A sweet-natured Byron sort of project. I hated to admit I was nervous about the operation tomorrow. I had spoken little during the meal.

"So. I have some news. About tomorrow night," Bill said, his eyes anywhere but on mine.

"This doesn't sound good," I said. I started reaching for the wine bottle to steel myself, but stopped my arm mid-air. I needed to be clear-headed.

"Lena, you'll be leading the operation."

I felt both fear and excitement—Miss Maggie must think I was ready. For once Bill would have to follow my orders, too.

"I'm going to be strictly backup," Bill said. He held a silver fork in his hand that he quivered in the air, over and over, in some kind of nervous tic. "I won't be out there with you."

I stared at him. He'd been on every bank job I'd ever done. He was the leader. He gave us confidence in his plans by coming and risking his own neck equally with ours. And his joy in the moment had been my courage. I didn't know what to say, but I didn't want him to think that I needed him, that I wanted him with me.

"What if Link won't listen to me?" Because he was insane, I did not add. Because he had not forgiven me. Only trust or fear created followers who actually followed. He clearly had neither when it came to me.

"He'll listen." Bill set his fork down and lined it up exactly against his knife. "I told him if he wants the Nazi dead, he's got to."

Did Bill think this job would fail? "You're using him. You've always looked out for yourself first," I said, and shoved my chair away from the table.

He fingered his linen napkin. "She said it had to be like that. Anyways, now you can win this one, for you. Don't you *want* to prove yourself to Miss Maggie?"

"You're a coward," I said, and ran from the room. My footsteps echoed hollow in the empty hall, my breathing ragged as I slammed shut my bedroom door. He was using me most of all.

CHAPTER TWENTY-SIX

FEBRUARY 11, 1946— LATE AFTERNOON

AS THE SUN prepared to set, the library was suffused with a soft pink light, unsettling in its beauty and innocence that suggested naïve hopes. The three of us stood over a large table, going over the plan one last time. Bill traced his finger along the tunnel at the Talad canal. Link was nowhere to be seen. Lena asked where he was, but Bill just shrugged, saying a man had to prepare in his own way and to let him be. If we could not kill von Roth outside the palace gate, our plan hinged on the story of the ancient tunnel that Bill had wormed from Silanon the palace guard. He'd pointed out the location of a barred-up entrance concealed with hanging vines, but how did we know it really led into the royal temple? And if it did, might we emerge from the tunnel into a trap? In exchange for the information, the guard had been warned of the date of von Roth's attack so he could absent himself from any danger or blame. Of course, this would also give him the perfect ability to betray our plan.

"How can you trust him?" Lena dared to ask, echoing my secret worries.

Bill stared at her with a flash of hurt that quickly turned to anger. "I been cultivating him a long time. I paid for his son's surgery, rushed him to my own doctor and damn well saved his life. I think he's mine." He slammed his fist on the table. "In fact, I know it. Don't I always know who's mine? I got an instinct to see in people's souls."

She looked unsettled when he said that but did not answer, and returned to studying the hand-drawn map unrolled on the table under his fist. I joined her, trying to commit the detailed drawing to memory. Our ability to do so and the accuracy of our source were the things on which our lives depended. I thought back to our shakedown of the guard. I decided he *thought* he was telling the truth, but we'd have to see about the reality of this tunnel. Some people liked to believe in the most unlikely stories.

Last thing before we left, I watched Lena put on the leather holster for the Walther PP semiautomatic, which gave me a sense of dread. Guns always meant the possibility of death. Next she tried to strap a dagger under her sleeve, for emergency close combat. I didn't bother with such-like, since I didn't have her training. Really, you needed two hands to manage the buckles, and she was struggling, so Bill went over and did it up for her. It was a weirdly tender act as he brushed the skin of her wrist and she averted her eyes. *Lena, don't let him get to you again*, I thought angrily.

Link drifted into the library and we took it as our signal to leave. We trooped silently down to the dock. As the three of us sat in the longtail boat heading toward the palace, the setting sun impaling itself on the temple spires, Lena looked as glum as I felt. It was hard not to think Bill was abandoning us. Tonight Link was going after von Roth, with Lena and me as the only backup. Link stood alone in the prow, staring into the sunset as if to blind himself in the last searing light. Lena leaned her head against a post of the awning, her eyes closed. What Link was about to do was dangerous, and it was foolish for me to be involved. We were all drawn together by allegiances that were against our own happiness, or maybe even survival. I wanted to protect Lena and Lena wanted to protect Hughes. Bill needed to get the job done for Miss Maggie—her way, apparently. That must stick in Bill's craw. In this mess, Bill and I were eye to eye on one thing, at least: Hughes would have to look out for his own skin. He was the only one who seemed hell-bent on this operation.

At least Bill had planned everything, and that made me feel better. When he ran the gang, before the drugs, no one could beat him for plans, and that's why the newspapermen called us the Clockwork Gang. Bill knew our skills and how best to use them. It seemed that Lena had been in this spy business during the war, and Link had been some kind of guerrilla fighter in Burma. Me, I'd been a bartender and an accountant. Heaven help me. I could call on some things we'd done in the bank robber days: sneaking around and outsmarting policemen. But the rewards compared to the risks on this job were not as clear. There were no bags of loot, no Emerald Buddha—just the hope of making it out alive. I wasn't sure I could get attached to the idea of saving this king. I mean, nobody should be shot in his own bed, but there were guards paid to look out for his safety. For some reason Bill seemed to actually support King Ananda, beyond Miss Maggie's orders. I suppose he liked the democracy this king envisioned, which would allow the people to elect any chosen rebel. Bill was a sort of natural-born communist. As long, of course, as it did not interfere too much with his personal riches. He was a puzzle.

As we passed by the mouth of a smaller *klong*, I stared at the one-room houses lining its banks. On stilted porches, women washed laundry in tin buckets and hung it out to dry. Nearby were little patches of greenery, which Bill had told me were floating gardens. Men tossed scraps into the river for the carp to eat, and later they would eat the carp. The circle of life and death. It seemed more vicious than symbiotic.

A train whistle blew somewhere, but it seemed only I felt its urgency. Lena did not rouse herself to look. And why should she?

Sound carried a long way over the river. I studied Lena's face, which was familiar and new at the same time. Sadder and leaner. Was it possible to do anything but think of the past when you heard a train whistle?

The longtail bumped against the dock and we debarked, the sun below the horizon now and the light nearly faded. I felt none of my usual interest in the bustle of carts at the pier, selling their foreign wares, glittering bronze statuettes and clever woven baskets, and the oddments of peasant food. Kerosene lanterns threw guttering shadows which I told myself were not sinister. In the increasing dim away from the market, I looked only for the car that was meant to be parked nearby. Tick one off the list: it was there. We climbed in and I drove silently, not wanting to intrude on Lena's own silence. Link could keep his mouth shut forever as far as I cared. We knew the plan inside out, anyhow. After minutes that passed too quickly, our last in safety for a good while, I pulled over to let Lena out in the back streets behind Saranrom Park. Link and I would meet up with her there shortly on foot, to stake out the southeast gate that Lena had identified as von Roth's chosen entry point. Lena melted quickly into the night, and I couldn't shake the desire to imprint a final image of her in my mind. I told myself I didn't need one, not yet, anyhow. The rendezvous in the park was straightforward enough.

The next street over, I dropped off Hughes. As he got out of the car, he had a strange look in his eye—I didn't know how to describe it, full of purpose I guess, and happy for the first time since I had met him. Was that what a death wish looked like? In any case, it was good that Lena wasn't here to see it. Five blocks from the park, I pulled the car into a garage on a *soi*, a sort of alley, branching off Asdang Road, where the city's chaos reasserted itself beyond the angular walls and rational buildings of the palace district. Unfortunately, there was nowhere closer to keep a car. We could not do as we had done in the old days, when I waited outside the bank with the engine running. There were few private cars on the roads, so lingering would attract attention.

On foot I crossed the street backing on Saranrom Park and entered the trees, which offered cover for our vigil over the southeast palace gate. Thankfully, the street itself was empty. Most of the people of Bangkok were poor, with no electricity to light their activities at home, so why not sleep? Also, they had not yet readjusted since the wartime curfews. Freedom is not just a law, but a feeling in the heart. I buttoned up my shirt against the mosquitoes that rose when I stepped through the grass. I wished I was still in that cozy library where we four gathered last night, the yellow lamplight pooling over the map. Planning was better than doing, in my opinion, just as Christmas Eve was always better than Christmas. The only present I might get tonight is a goddamn shot to the head, I thought, wincing as the Mauser Karabiner jolted against my shoulder blade, metal against bone.

Byron, you are a fool.

Man's finer points of loyalty and bravery were also his undoing. I was just an accountant underneath it all. I'd never shot at anyone, unlike the others in the Clockwork Gang. Damn it, why had I not at least gone on that grizzly hunt last year with the Sequim locals when they invited me? I had shingled my roof instead. I had no place in all this.

I wished Bill was here. We had always followed his lead when we stormed into a bank, but I should not linger over the past. All I needed to think of was tonight, and how I would protect Lena.

I ran over the backup plan in my mind. Earlier this afternoon, Dass had tied up a boat on the Chao Phraya River. If Hughes did not kill von Roth outside the palace, I would head for the boat. Hughes and Lena would run for the Talad canal, which paralleled Ratchini Road, a thousand feet from the palace walls. They would swim across the canal and break into the ancient tunnel, then hunt von Roth from within the grounds. After the shooting, they would flee in one of the palace boats that were supposed to be inside the tunnel, always ready for the king's use in a time of emergency. For this we had to depend on faith, since the guard had never actually been inside. The last barrier they would face on the way out would be the lock between the Talad canal and the Chao Phraya River. Bill had arranged through his contacts to drug the lock-keeper and replace him with one of his own. The dead time trapped in the lock would be agonizing, waiting for it to fill and the gate to open, but once Lena and Hughes made it onto the river, I would be waiting to race them back to the palazzo in an unmarked boat. I wished I could do more, but everyone agreed on my limitations. It was kind of humiliating.

In the darkness, I focused on every shape around me as I moved through the park. There were two deformed trees ahead, which I took to be Hughes' and Lena's bodies pressed against the trunks, to use them as concealment and shields against stray bullets. I dashed from tree to tree until I was close enough that I could see Lena's nod. I pulled the Mauser Karabiner, a light infantry rifle, across my chest and readied my finger near the trigger. Sweat pooled on my forehead and threatened to run into my eyes. At least the darkness was perfect, and I was surely invisible. The moon was only a sliver in the sky, and I could make out the pits and craters on its dark side. I told myself to quit gandering at it, and to keep my eyes on the road and the gatehouse for von Roth.

Last night, when Bill revealed he would not be joining us on the operation at all, it had thrown me. Could Hughes handle this without Bill? Hughes had a queer dependence on him, and he was definitely not right in the head. I suppose some things could be done by willpower alone—he was fixed on killing this Nazi to clear his conscience in some way that only he could understand. Hughes looked brave, and Bill a coward now. I agreed with Lena on that. If Bill really wanted Lena back he should have come on this job, no matter what Miss Maggie said. At this thought I smiled a little, inwardly. He still did not deserve her, and she knew it for certain now.

The strangling branches of the banyan dug into my back. I ignored the discomfort as I scanned the palace wall, back and forth. I could hear myself breathing. I wondered if it was loud, or was everything else just quiet?

In the distance there was a faint growling that soon resolved into the sound of car engines. Headlights illuminated Sanam Chai Road as they approached, and I pressed myself tighter against the banyan. The cars pulled over, idling at the gatehouse, and a group of foreigners poured out, talking loudly and laughing. Americans and Englishmen, from the sounds of it. Servants hefted cases from the trunks. Among the group was a taller blond man, evidently von Roth. What the hell? We had expected him to sneak over the wall alone like a commando, not waltz in through the door with a party. I raised the Karabiner. Tracked, tracked. For a second I had a clear line on him. I made myself forget I'd shared drinks with the man at Bill's club. I could pull the trigger. I could kill him. Couldn't I? This was not duck hunting; I did not have scattershot and I needed my aim to be true. There was only one chance at this. If I botched it, von Roth would shoot back. He might kill Lena. My hand faltered, and a mustachioed old man took his place in my sights. I lowered the gun.

Lena said a silenced weapon was no louder than a door slamming. I heard no door, so the other two must also have their aim blocked by an innocent bystander. Well, I wasn't sure Hughes would care who else might die if he had the shot. I squinted at the tree where he was standing with his sniper rifle ready, but he did not move, and I turned my gaze back to the party. The foreigners piled through the gatehouse with their gear, von Roth still protected in the middle of the group while they chatted with the guards. In a moment they were through, the gate shutting behind them as the cars pulled away.

Von Roth had given us the slip.

So it would be Plan B. Hughes needed to travel fast and light inside the palace walls, so he would only take a pistol. I approached Hughes to relieve him of the beastly Sturmgewehr 44. Only he had the training to use the assault rifle, which had the obliterating power of a machine gun combined with greater portability and control. It was the latest in German engineering, yet ancient as death, with its weird curved magazine that reminded me of an Arab scimitar. The scumbag Bill bought these weapons from said it was a shame the Germans lost the war when their inventions showed such genius. I'd handed him the envelope of American dollars grudgingly, wishing I didn't have to support his living.

I slung the heavy gun crosswise to mine, on the other shoulder, as Link ran off toward the canal. I adjusted the uncomfortable weight as I readied myself to head back to the car. Without waiting for me to take her gun, Lena threw down the Karabiner and ran after Hughes. I had an impulse to call out, but that would be foolish. I could only watch her disappear into the trees, toward the Talad canal where Link was headed. More than anything, I wanted to follow, but I'd be a hindrance not a help. It would be my bumbling presence that would rouse the guards inside the palace and get them shot. Hughes had served behind enemy lines and Lena had her espionage training. Me, I could only claim a basic knowledge of building cocktails. I'd spent my war years rather differently from those two.

I tried to tell myself that Lena could take care of herself, and the only thing I could do now was my assigned part: drive the getaway boat. As I headed back toward the park to retrieve Lena's gun, I felt my face wet with tears. It was unmanly, but I didn't care. There was no one to see me.

CHAPTER TWENTY-SEVEN

THE TUNNEL

VON ROTH WAS inside the palace walls and everything was a shambles. He had been surrounded by an entourage, and Link never got a clear shot. Now we had to go with Plan B. When Byron relieved Link of the German assault rifle, Link started running through the park toward the canal. I followed, and it seemed to be just the two of us. I had feared that Byron would trail me, trying to help after all, though he was not supposed to. I had to trust he would stick with the plan. Meanwhile, Link didn't look back. He seemed completely indifferent to my existence.

Suddenly I felt unreal. *Were these feet my feet? Was this body my body?* I ran faster, panting, the humid air smothering my lungs. It felt like drowning by degrees. This wasn't panic, was it? I'd never felt like this before.

Calm down, Lena. This is it.

I focused on the pounding of my feet on the packed earth, like a drumbeat, like a call to war.

Link looked strong as he ran. He'd regained his strength once the drugs were out of his system, but I was worried about his mental state. Byron let slip that Link had been in a straightjacket in the hospital. He shouldn't be doing this, but he had fixated on this mission as the only thing worth doing with his life. And Bill had gone along, a selfish bastard as always, because it fulfilled his orders from Miss Maggie. Link had already been punished enough by Miss Maggie, so he shouldn't have to die for her now. I would do everything I could to keep him safe.

Reaching the edge of the Talad canal, I could not see anything under the inky black surface, which was about ten feet below street level. The tunnel entrance Bill had seen was about fifty feet west. Thick trees and vines blocked the shore from further foot travel, so we would have to swim now. Just ahead of me, Link set down his pack to pull out his goggles and fins, which he needed to set the limpet bomb underwater. This task was assigned to him by Miss Maggie, Bill said. Of course, since it was the most dangerous. As I finished putting on my own fins, Link dived in, cutting smoothly through the surface. He did not wait for me. I hurried to secure my gun in the rubberized invasion bag, and, fumbling, tightened the shoulder straps. Link was swimming a precise crawl, the distance between us increasing. At least he had not been lying about his abilities. He had claimed to be a strong swimmer, having crossed the lake at his family's cottage in Ontario every summer since he was twelve. I wished we could have met then. We could have pushed each other playfully into the lake, sunned on the dock, and had our first sweet kiss. Those things don't last, but they don't need to. It would be enough to have something pure to remember.

I jumped into the canal, sputtering as I came up. At least the water was warm, and I followed the shining wake that Link left behind him in the water.

Swimming alongside the wall, Link felt underneath the hanging shrubs and vines foot by foot until he found what he was looking for. A metal grille barred the tunnel entrance. Inside, we had been told, there was enough space between the water level and the curved ceiling for a small boat to pass. As we had expected, Link couldn't squeeze through the bars, so he dove underwater to place the bomb. I started swimming away from the blast area, which was supposed to extend less than thirty feet. He was using a short three-minute timer, so I waited anxiously until Link reappeared at the surface and started to move away.

There was a dull whump and the surface boiled. Ripples splashed my face and the water lifted me up, but it soon subsided. Link was about fifteen feet to my right. We each swam back toward the tunnel, though I slowed as my arms grew tired. We had no cottage when I was a girl. I grabbed the gate to rest a second. A gap had opened between it and the wall, and Link had already slipped through. I moved through after him. In the darkness, my hand found a ledge inside the tunnel, and I hauled myself out of the water to sit on it.

Link busied himself taking his gun and flashlight from his frogman's pack, still paying me no attention. I wanted to hiss, *Link*, but that would be foolish. I took my own gun from the waterproof invasion bag, shoved my fins away, and wedged my feet into shoes. Link's beam revealed a low ceiling, and the ledge continued parallel to the waterway as far as I could make out. We crouched down to hurry along the ledge as best we could. The low ceiling prevented running, but it still was faster than swimming. The curved roof was discoloured with green and rust streaks, and stale water dripped onto my head, tepid and unpleasant.

It took about fifteen minutes to reach the end of the tunnel, where three boats were at the ready. So what the guard said was true. Circling them I saw that, while they were old, they had been motorized, which would speed our escape. Link walked over to a metal ladder bolted to the wall, which led to a trapdoor in the ceiling. He checked his naval issue watch. Bill's informant had said the guards passed the temple above us every half hour. Each time they paused a moment, reverently, at the door of the temple that housed the Emerald Buddha. Link climbed the ladder and pushed on the trapdoor, but it didn't budge. It was locked.

Link took out a pouch of small tools. Though we had rehearsed this many times, he stared vacantly at the metal pick as though he'd never seen it before. This was not the time for him to lose it. Climbing up to his level, I grabbed the tools from him. He did not protest as I motioned him down and started on the task of picking the lock. I had always found it peaceful. It required a total focus that blocked all other thoughts and feelings, including fear. I turned the tension wrench left, right, until I found the spot where there was less give. I kept it in place while I inserted the pick to fiddle with each pin in turn, at the same time finessing the pressure on the wrench. Okay, one, two. Two more to go.

"So you were a bank robber?" Link asked from below. His words echoed in the underground room.

My hands froze. I was terrified that he had spoken, but also, in the next instant, I was outraged that he knew. There were only two people who could have told him, and not for a second did I think Byron would do it. Only Bill had holed up for hours on end with Link when he was coming off the drugs, Byron told me that much. Calming myself, I returned to picking the lock. I didn't have time to rage or defend my past to Link. I had to get this done now.

Three, four, then the satisfying release of turning the tension wrench further, just like a key.

Link drew his weapon and gestured at me to come down. It seemed threatening somehow, and I wondered uneasily if Link could still hate me so much that he'd kill me tonight as well as von Roth. Well, there was nothing to do but carry on at this point. I'd just have to watch out for myself. I climbed down, and Link hurried up the ladder to push the trapdoor open. The warmer air struck my face as it spilled down the hole while Link vanished upward into the temple. Though he had not bothered with caution up to that point, he shut the trapdoor softly behind him. I was left behind in total darkness. Feeling my way up the ladder, I peeked through the crack of the door and sensed only the deep silence of emptiness—or so I would have to hope. I flipped the door open fully and climbed up into the temple, scanning a full circle around me with the Walther before I spotted Link heading toward an altar screen. I followed him. Candles flickered everywhere, casting long shadows.

Beside us was a tiered gold throne, and on its highest platform sat the Emerald Buddha, covered in a gold mail robe. The way it shone, it had to be real gold, as were the four statues flanking the icon's base. The richness was incredible, but I was no robber here.

As I reached Link's shoulder, we peered around the altar screen into the vast bare rectangle of the temple proper. Staying close to the wall, ducking to avoid windows, we ran past continuous murals of armies and strange beasts until we reached the exit. I pressed my ear against the door. Link rushed past me, leaving me standing in surprise while he ran into the courtyard, completely exposed. I was scared and angry at his recklessness. I waited for the gunshots, but there was nothing.

As I followed Link with silent footfalls, I was alarmed to notice dark prints behind me on the temple stairs. My clothes were already drying in the warm air, so I prayed these markers of our damp passage would soon evaporate.

In the courtyard, I froze at the sight of men holding spears—but it only took a second to realize they were moving even less than I was. There were statues everywhere. A gang of false men laboured to hold up the base of a stupa. Everything had a sense of pressure. Nearby a dark tower rose from a pagoda like a missile, as though threatening to bust the sacred building to pieces. The silhouette of the temple roof was littered with curved ornaments like scythes, poised to cut down the stars. Would I be able to detect a real person among all these garbled forms? At least this visual confusion would camouflage us, as well. We made our way around corners and through zigzag passages toward the palace. It was strange to think I had arrived once as an invited guest through the main portal, and now we were here to commit murder through the back door.

Did I have to think the word *murder*? Could I not think *justice*, when von Roth was a war criminal? But I had never killed a person. Even at second hand, I had felt sick when I read the part in Byron's journal where Bill murdered an old man in the cabin they wanted to use as a hideout. I reminded myself that was a vicious death by bludgeoning. I hoped that a bullet would feel clean.

We pressed ourselves against the wall that separated the temple precinct from the palace grounds. We were close to the heart of things now. At any time, we might see von Roth—if he didn't see us first. Link looked calm and purposeful. I didn't like that. Fear would offer him more protection, more caution. *Don't die tonight. Please. We're not done yet, you and me.*

Link removed some rope from his rucksack and untied the alpine coil, which had a weighted pouch on one end for momentum. Staring at a finial on the wall's pitched roof, he made the throw. The rope didn't catch and the weight thumped to the ground. Nervously, I scanned the area, but there was no sign of any guards. He gathered up the rope and bent his knees to make the throw again, and this time the rope snagged the finial. Link wrapped the rope around his hip in a mountaineer's belay and flicked his chin at me, to go up. Not friendly, but at least he wasn't abandoning me. He leaned back to brace himself while I climbed the twenty-foot wall, my palms burning as I gripped the rope. I wanted to stop but couldn't, as Link kept taking in the rope, almost hauling me up against my will. I started to feel dizzy, and could hardly make myself take my hands off the stones in the wall to pull myself higher. My hands were sweating. Two-thirds of the way up, I made the mistake of looking down. I clung to the rope. I was paralyzed, but the rope yanked relentlessly against my waist. I had to keep going. I made myself grab another stone in the wall. Upward. Finally reaching the top, I pressed myself against the peaked roof, as far from the edge as I could be, panting with fear. I anchored my feet in the tile gutter as I wound some rope around the finial and held it tight, so Link could follow. Once he was safely crouched beside me, he hauled up the rope and stuffed it into his pack.

Cautiously, we raised our heads above the peaked roofline of the temple wall. A wave of laughter and shouts met our ears. What was going on? Below us was only darkness and silence. From the map I knew the French-style chateau just south of us was the Borom Phiman mansion, where the king sometimes slept for a change from his newer Dusit Palace. To the southwest I could see the larger Chakri hall where the charity reception had been held. From that night, I remembered its three extravagant towers, Asian wedding cakes grafted atop a severe European box. A large, formal garden to the southeast featured rows of trees, each pruned into balls at the end of every branch, like lollipops gathered in a child's hand. These strange topiaries loomed over a shrubbery maze. I thought of Alice in Wonderland and felt that I was through the looking-glass now.

We had to find out where the ruckus was coming from. We ducked below the roofline and ran along the inside gutters, around the corner and onto the western temple wall. In the middle of it, above a doorway, there was another set of multi-level roofs for cover, and we peered into the grassy courtyard below. A burst of machine-gun fire made me duck, my heart racing, until I realized they hadn't shot at *us*. I hazarded another look. Giant floodlights illuminated bull's eyes set up near the outer wall of the palace complex. Some of the targets had been blown to smithereens, with only the stands left behind. Link pulled out binoculars and scanned the crowd. Silently, he handed them to me, but I didn't need them. I could see von Roth's blond head clearly, where he stood right beside the king.

Von Roth. His gall was incredible, and, I had to admit, his genius formidable. King Ananda was known to be a gun connoisseur and keen marksman. So apparently von Roth had organized a shooting party, allowing him to haul in weapons under the very noses of the guards, many of whom had gathered, laughing and cheering, in the courtyard.

For the admiration of the king and his entourage, von Roth held out a rifle, which I recognized immediately as a Sturmgewehr 44. I wished Link still had his. It had a lot more firepower than our pistols. Well, we had one advantage: von Roth did not know we were here. We had to keep it that way.

The men grabbed pistols from a portable table covered with bottles, which were apparently filled with liquor, judging by the men's behaviour. They shot wildly at the remaining targets, making an incredible racket. Perfect cover for silenced weapons, I thought as I stared through my sights. Link steadied his pistol on the ledge. Under the floodlight, von Roth's blond head made a clear target, but he needed to step away from the king. If the shot was more than six inches off, Ananda would be killed instead.

Link took the shot.

Even a silenced weapon is painful to the ear when only a few feet away, and I was stunned. Von Roth jumped backwards, but no one else seemed to have noticed anything. He did not fall. He was not hit, but he must have felt the air disturbed by the bullet. He spoke into the king's ear and made a low bow. The king hardly looked at him, distracted by the shooting and laughter of the other men, while von Roth calmly made his way toward the temple wall. He was still carrying the StG 44 close to his chest. He seemed to know what direction our shot came from and was staying out of the roof's sightline. Frantically, I waved Link forward. We scooched along the inner wall, back to the south side, which had a view toward the main gatehouse through which von Roth had arrived. Link must have guessed the Nazi was planning to leave the same way. Maybe we would have one more shot at him before he reached it. The guards were occupied watching the king's antics in the courtyard, and the shooting party's noise would easily conceal us.

Von Roth should have been on the walkway below us by now, but there was no sign of anyone, either there or around the silent mansion that housed the king's bedroom.

I heard footsteps inside the temple walls. I pushed myself up against the gatehouse roof, putting my arm instinctively across Link's chest to draw him back. Panicked, I had a childlike impulse to close my eyes.

Link took a shot onto a path lining a small pagoda.

Von Roth dived onto the ground, recovered, and disappeared around one of the many dogleg corners in the temple precinct. He was running too fast to be injured.

I wanted to scream at Link. Where was his sense? Blood pounded in my ears. Before I had time to think, Link slid down the roof and grabbed the tiled gutters, hanging on his arms. Then he jumped to the ground, landing in a roll that must be painful on the stone ground. It looked very far down, but I knew I had to follow. I hung, the ground wavering below my dangling feet. Dear God, don't make me do this, I thought. I was scared, but the rough tile edges were digging into my hands. I let go. Pain shot up from my ankles and through my legs. I stumbled, then righted myself.

I drew the Walther and kept my finger on the trigger guard as I ran after Link. My feet pounded on the stonework, and the sound refracted off the walls of the temple maze. I halted at Link's shoulder where he stood at a corner, and he poked his head around it. Then he ran into the square. I followed, keeping close to the wall. I saw no one in the small courtyard, just silhouettes of strange grey statues, men with wings and beaks, standing guard over a pagoda. Dark passageways led off each side.

There was a shout in Siamese. On the wall near Link's head, a spark ricocheted. Link ducked and popped up again, letting off a shot from his silenced Walther. A man fell to the ground in front of him, by the pagoda door, his gold buttons shining in the moonlight. A dark amoeba formed on the white of his uniform. Blood. Link ran and took cover behind the slumped man.

An arm grabbed me in a chokehold and I gagged. I couldn't see who it was. I could only smell something like pine sap, but more cloying. I strangely wondered if it was frankincense, from the Bible, from the death of Christ. Was this von Roth? No, the man seemed to be my size, while von Roth was much taller. It must be a guard. I struggled, but the man's grip was strong. The click of a trigger cocking echoed throughout the courtyard, but Link didn't take the shot. The guard had me as a shield. He raised his revolver to aim at Link. The guard's disembodied arm stretched in front of me, as though it was my own. Now that he only had one arm around me, I tried to grab the gun, but I couldn't breathe and it made me weak. The report of his weapon, unsilenced, exploded in my ears.

Was Link hit?

My blood surging in my panic, I felt the straps tight around my forearm. It was the knife Bill gave me, and it called me to my senses. I yanked it from my sleeve and stabbed behind me, where the man's soft stomach would be. He screamed and let go of me.

The air was displaced beside me, very close. With a surprised yelp, the guard fell to the ground. His white uniform seemed to glow like phosphorescence in the sea. Link had taken the shot. It was risky, but it had missed me and hit its mark. I ran to the pagoda staircase where I'd last seen Link sheltered behind the dead guard. I found him standing behind a pillar.

I tugged at his sleeve, but he would not move. He looked everywhere except at me, scanning the courtyard, his eyes glassy and strange.

"We've got to get out of here," I whispered.

"Not till we get von Roth."

"I know where he is. Come on." I don't know why I said that, but it did the trick and Link followed me. I had the uneasy feeling that we hadn't seen the last of von Roth, and I didn't need to know where he was to find him. He would find us.

We slipped through the claustrophobic passageways, checking around each corner, until we were back at the main temple where the tunnel was. I eased open the giant door. I froze at the sound of chanting, which seemed to be coming from everywhere and nowhere at once. Then my eyes made out the source: at the far end of the temple, in front of the Emerald Buddha, two monks in orange robes were kneeling, their backs to us. They were near the altar gate that accessed the tunnel. How could we get by them?

There was a muted bang, once, twice. The monks slumped forward, silent, blood blooming on their robes. I stared at Link in horror. His arm was still outstretched, holding the pistol. Smoke wisped from the barrel. When he ran, I followed him, desperate now only for escape. *They were monks*, I thought, again and again, like my own dark mantra. How could Link kill them?

We descended through the trapdoor, closing it behind us with a click as I set the lock. I was shocked by the pure blackness. Link found his flashlight and turned it on to illuminate the chamber. The royal boats still sat waiting in the flat, dark pool, and we ran to the largest one. To cut the rope, I reached into my sleeve to pull out my knife, but it wasn't there. I must have dropped it after I stabbed the guard. At least it was unmarked. That in itself could suggest secret service, though hopefully no one would know which country's. Well, nothing could be done now. Link cut the rope with his own knife and we jumped aboard. We each grabbed a long wooden paddle from out of the keel and shoved against the wall to start the boat on its way. We would wait to start the engines until we reached the canal, far enough away that the sound could not be heard from the palace.

As we paddled through the tunnel, the ceiling got gradually lower until we had to fold ourselves forward. I realized I was breathing loudly and quieted myself. The light was getting blue, so we must have been nearing the exit to the canal. I used the paddle to nudge the boat off the far wall toward the small raised ledge by the gate—our escape hatch. I fired up the engine, but Link stayed seated in a dreamy state. Why didn't he open the gate? I nudged his ribs with the paddle and he jumped onto the ledge. He tugged at the gate. Mangled from the blast, it barely moved. He jumped into the water and, bracing his legs against the wall, wrenched it open enough for the slender boat to get through. He climbed back aboard and the boat nosed through the vines, their tendrils dragging across my face as we passed underneath them.

From the canal I looked back at the entrance, which was concealed by the screen of hanging plants. It was as though we'd never been there, and I could not help thinking we were going to make it. Soon we would meet Byron on the river and shove this boat away, to drift with the current to the ocean, while we would race in a speedboat back to the palazzo.

We were escaping, but Link had not killed von Roth. And I was supposed to be in charge of this mess. What would Miss Maggie say—or do—when she learned that von Roth was still free to murder the king? Surely von Roth would abort his mission after the chaos of dead guards and monks we left behind, I told myself. Security around the king would increase tenfold after this. Was that not a form of success?

Maybe not in Miss Maggie's books, but at least I had seen Link out safely. I exhaled.

He'd saved me, too. He'd killed the guard who had grabbed hold of me. Or had he not cared if he killed me also? The bullet had been close, too close. I stole a glance at Link as we travelled down the canal. He was staring back into the distance, a smile on his face. It disturbed me. Was he completely unhinged? I supposed I should be glad he had gone into this strange passive mode, rather than insisting on staying behind to finish off von Roth.

We reached the lock at the end of the canal, the last barrier between us and the river. We were nearly free.

I navigated alongside a hanging cord and pulled it to signal the lock-keeper in the tower to let us out. The engine idled as I kept us in place, and the metal gate slowly, excruciatingly, yawed open. I had time to picture Bill's hired man looking down at us, bemused by the goings-on of these strange visitors to his land, the usual lock-keeper unconscious at his feet. As soon as there was room to pass through, I revved the boat into the lock. The metal gate shut again and the water began to pour in, floating us up to the river's level, slowly, slowly.

"Get down, Lena," Link said, so calmly it took a moment to register it was a warning.

Then I saw the silhouette of a man holding a pistol. He was standing above us on the edge of the lock, which was now our cage. A bullet zinged nearby and cracked the boat's wooden hull. Water surged in. Link stood up, tall and unwavering as a Viking figurehead on a ship's prow.

He took aim and fired.

Von Roth ducked and rolled. He did not cry out or fall off the ledge. Link had missed.

The boat kept rising in the lock, bringing us ever closer to the ledge where the Nazi waited. Von Roth took aim from his prone position and fired. Link stared in stunned amazement at his chest. Then he let off one more shot, wildly, and collapsed.

"Link!" I yelled.

On the floor of the boat, I stayed huddled under my wooden seat. I expected von Roth to kill me at any moment. The water was now six inches deep in the bottom of the boat and my legs were soaked. I would soon be nearly level with von Roth. I stared up at the starry sky, a sight of infinity and beauty. This did not have to be the end. I wanted to live.

I pulled the Walther from my holster.

Von Roth was standing in full view at the edge of the canal, as though waiting to give me his hand to step ashore. His pale hair gleamed ghostly under the moonlight. I knew this man. *Warner*. I raised the pistol and, as it so often did these days, my hand shook.

"The lovely Vera," von Roth said gently.

My hand steadied as I thought, *I'm someone else now*.

After the shock of the gun's report, I heard a moan, and Warner toppled sideways to fall on the cement ledge. The water lifted me until I stared straight into his eyes. They were lost somewhere, whether the past or future, I couldn't say. He was already more dead than alive.

I looked away. Why hadn't he shot at me? He was a Nazi. He'd killed hundreds of people, but he had danced with me. Did he have some strange selective morality that stilled his hand? Or had he believed that I was too weak and would not kill him, that I would now stand beside him, go to bed with him, the conqueror?

Had I been more cold-blooded than a Nazi?

I turned to Link. Blood streamed into the water around him, where he lay face up on the bottom of the boat. My steps sloshing in the deepening water, I rushed to feel the pulse at his wrist. It was faint and erratic. The hole in his chest was small, but I knew the exit wound, at his back, would be large and gaping. There was no time to staunch the blood. Oh God. The boat was over a foot deep in water now, and would sink before I could get it to the dock where Byron waited upriver. I'd have to swim.

I yanked at the lid of a padlocked wooden trunk built into the side of the boat, but it only budged an inch. Through the gap, I could see red lifejackets inside. The trunk's lock was small, the wood old. I leaned down and, averting my eyes from Link's wound, slid the dagger from the sheath on his arm. I used it to pry open the lid. The wood splintered and squealed, the blade bent, but the clasps flew off. The knife was ruined and would not fit back in its scabbard, so I threw it overboard. I pulled out the lifejackets, putting one on myself first. Then I gently raised Link's head to slide it through the neck opening. He was floating a little in the deeper water in the boat now, which made it easier to put the straps behind him and clip them to the front of the lifejacket, though he groaned at the jostling. I made out faint words.

"Is he dead?"

I blinked back tears. "Yes. You got him." A smile played on his lips, or so I thought, and I traced my fingers there.

"I'm sorry," I said, my voice quavering. "I'm so sorry."

The gates of the lock were opening. Somewhere above us, the false lock-keeper looked down on our drama, unwilling to get involved, or uninterested in the outcome. A man doing his job. I jumped into the river and grabbed the gunwale of the sinking boat, to bring it nearly level to the water so I could pull Link out as gently as possible. Once he was floating beside me in the river, I clutched the collar of his lifejacket and started to swim awkwardly toward the dock where Byron was supposed to be waiting. *It's not far*, I told myself. *Swim harder. Byron will be there—he's always there.* I took one last look over my shoulder, but already I couldn't make out von Roth's form on the ledge. All I could see was the tall silver silhouette of the lock tower, like a monument.

I swam away in the dark river, warm as blood, the green mats of lotus parting before me.

CHAPTER TWENTY-EIGHT

FEBRUARY 11, 1946—MIDNIGHT

I HAD BEEN waiting and waiting at the little dock just south of Arthit Pier. The palazzo was just across the way, but hidden by the trees along the banks of the Chao Phraya. I hoped my speedboat was equally concealed among the branches in this obscure spot. Leaves quivered against my face when the ocean breathed up the river from the Gulf of Siam. Bats swooped low over the water, hunting insects, though there were fewer of them now. It was getting late. I'd expected Lena and Hughes at eleven o'clock, and it was now long past the hour, but I would never leave my post, no matter what. Either Lena returned or I would die here waiting, whether living to the end of my natural days as a lunatic boatman who begged alms from passing waterfolk, or shot as an accomplice by palace guards. My devoted skeleton would bleach under the tropical sun. I had not welcomed such visions, but did not shirk them either. They were a distraction, at least, from looking at my watch every few seconds. Now it was closer to midnight.

A faint splashing sound made me stand up and stare into the water once more. I made out three forms in the river, approaching slowly, two of them together and the third trailing behind. Soon I knew for certain that Lena was the first of them. She was identifiable to me always, her head sleek as an otter like in those happier days, when the world was at our feet before the Nanaimo payroll robbery, and she had jumped overboard from our gang's speedboat as a lark. Tonight, everything was different. We were on the other side of the world, and she was grim-faced and struggling. As she approached, I reached out to her with an oar, which she grabbed desperately, and I saw she was dragging Hughes. With a shiver I realized that the third form was one of those monitor lizards, perhaps fifteen feet behind them, cutting patiently and silently through the water like a crocodile.

"Take him," she gasped. I hesitated, thinking to haul her up first, but she pushed Hughes toward me. They don't eat people, I remembered Dass saying. Only corpses.

I grabbed him by the strap on the collar of his lifejacket, and she dragged herself up and over the side of the boat. I struggled with Hughes' weight, at one point nearly dropping him. He gave me no aid.

Lena had drawn herself away from the body, and lay panting on the floor of the boat.

"You're okay now," I said to Lena. I felt for Hughes' pulse, but I already knew what I would find. At least his body looked whole. I shivered at the thought of Lena in the dark water, dragging him, that dismal lizard trailing behind.

"He didn't make it," Lena said. She put her hands over her eyes and shuddered, which I took to be weeping, but was all the more dreadful for its soundlessness.

I didn't know what else to do, so I started up the engine, and the night was obliterated by the roar as the boat cut through the wide, black river.

Bill was waiting in the darkened grounds of the palazzo. He must have been there all evening. It was cool now, but he still wore a short-sleeved shirt and British jungle shorts as he hurried past the hurricane lanterns that lined the pool to meet us. As I walked Lena up from the dock, she leaned against me—when we debarked her knees had buckled and she staggered once, until I caught her. Bill stopped short at the sight of us.

"You okay?" he asked, but Lena did not answer, so he looked to me.

"She needs rest."

"Von Roth?"

Again she did not answer. I myself hadn't had the nerve yet to ask about this, or anything else about the mission.

"Did you get von Roth?" Bill asked again.

"He's dead," Lena said.

She was shivering in her wet clothes, so I walked her past Bill on the sidewalk to get her inside and away from the night air. "There's something in the boat that must be brought in," I said. He nodded and went to see to it. This was the first time he'd ever done a thing I said.

TEN O'CLOCK THE next morning, Lena sat in the library, looking subdued in a grey silk robe wrapped up to her neck. Her eyes were puffy. The shutters were closed to keep out the light, though it was already dim, threatening rain. The heat was unbearable. I felt oppressed by these heavy tropical storms, which held back and held back until they finally exploded. Back in Washington State, it was calm, because it was always raining. I missed the feeling of knowing what was going to happen because it was always the same.

Today was a complete mystery. Would Lena leave now that Hughes was dead?

"You knew he wouldn't make it, didn't you," she said flatly. Her eyes would not meet Bill's, but drifted across the dim gold book spines where they were trapped on crowded shelves in the order the previous owner had chosen.

Bill crossed his arms. "You damn well know there was no talking him out of it. And he got what he wanted. He fixed up his name. He'll get buried with military honours. I'll see to that."

"Is that supposed to make me feel better? He's dead."

"How about this? You chased an assassin out of the palace. Miss Maggie will reward you for ruining Gaige's operation. It proves that Nazis don't work, so why take the extra risk? Gaige's program will be cut, and the funding will go to Miss Maggie."

I looked at Lena. She was tired and worried. I wished there was something I could do for her, but could not think of anything. There wasn't even a pot of tea to pour.

Bill cleared his throat. "I heard from my lock-keeper. So I know you were the one that killed the Nazi. Not Link Hughes like you said."

Lena remained silent.

Bill walked over to his bookshelf and paused in front of the antique black marble clock. If you believed that time was heavy, or unyielding, or cruel, this was the object to embody it. He pushed forward the hands to reset it, though now that I thought of it, I'd never heard it tick. His back still turned, he wound the clock for the first time since he owned it. "Miss Maggie will be pleased," he said.

I stood there, wishing I could be anywhere else, while also hanging on every word. Bill walked over to sit in the chair across from hers, and leaned his elbows on his knees. "Lena, there's no use regretting. That Nazi was evil. You got to be a wolf to survive."

True enough, I thought. Bill was a wolf, and so was Lena, which explained why they could never quite get on. There was only one head of every pack. And I was just a lamb. Where was my flock? These wolves were it, I thought uneasily. I would have to be careful not to go the way of Link Hughes. But I had no plans to sacrifice myself. The name Byron Godfrey was nothing special, but it needed no redeeming either.

Bill walked over to where I stood at the window. "Why so glum, chum? You want a cigar, By God? You did good." He clapped me on the back.

"Thanks."

Bill took a cigar from a dark wood humidor and trimmed it with his silver scissors, just for me.

LENA STUCK AROUND after the von Roth job, drifting through the palazzo and avoiding Bill when he happened to be around, which wasn't often. She couldn't leave because Miss Maggie had ordered her to stay and "await developments." Lena was in a rage about it, but she was under Miss Maggie's thumb as much as Bill. I was curious what my place was in all this, so I'd asked Bill about it. Was I a crab in a trap, who walked in of his own innocence and then, when he turns around, can't figure the way out?

"I brung you here without Miss Maggie knowing," he had assured me. "One of my rebellions against her. I wanted you in my business. I trust you."

I felt happy when he said that. I had to admit, being a spy who only pretended to be a crook was more soothing to my conscience—what I had left of it anyhow, after all I'd done with Bill. Of course our "pretending" was pretty convincing, since Bill actually ran an opium ring.

Practising my new profession, I snuck around the palazzo and tried to overhear when Lena spoke to Bill, which seemed to be almost never. But one time I paused by the library door when I felt a silence heavier than silence, and knew somehow that both of them were there. I put my eye to the crack, and saw Bill kneeling on the floor and gripping her hand.

"I won't ever give up," he said finally. "I'll love you till I'm dead."

"You ruined everything a long time ago."

"You only have a love like this once in a life. That goes for you too, Lena. I'm it and you know it."

She tore her hand from his, and I ran ignobly into a hall closet because I could see she was going to flee. She did so, and her steps echoed on the tile floor, receding from me.

Bill went to Burma shortly after that, and stayed away for a month to tend to his opium business. And his wounds, I supposed. It would not help his case that Lena knew about the wife he had there. Well, he'd made his own bed. Maybe he'd figure out how divorce worked in that tribe.

I asked Lena if she wanted to go for a drink at the Oriental Hotel, and she said yes. I put on a tie.

I will always remember that day, June 10, because on that day we sat in the bar together, drinking a Scotch cocktail called Blood and Sand. There are not many things that mix well with Scotch, since it's usually best sipped alone. But I was not alone, and I did not want my liquor to face that fate either. So it is shaken with orange juice, cherry brandy, and sweet vermouth, and it was very nice, I thought. Lena seemed to enjoy it also.

But our repose was disturbed. Word rippled through the bar that King Ananda had died yesterday in the Royal Palace. The Siamese police proclaimed it an accidental death, but the foreign news reported that the bullet went through the centre of his forehead. By whose hand was such an "accident"? Lena and I looked at each other with wide eyes. The only certainty was that the constitution was in danger, and democracy in Siam was probably over. The Communists would be outlawed in the new regime. Many people in the bar were predicting that, and were happy about that part. Amidst the hubbub, Lena traced her finger slowly around the rim of her glass. I wondered what she was thinking but did not ask.

It wasn't long before I noticed a man lurking at the entrance to the bar. It was Smile, and I knew instantly that Bill was home from Burma. Goddamn it, it was hard to keep one's affairs private around here. I guessed he knew where we were from the boat driver, who had dropped us off at the Oriental Pier. I downed the last of my drink and helped Lena with her chair. I didn't remember about my umbrella until we stepped outside and a heavy rain was falling, so I went back to retrieve it from the holder, which was shaped like an elephant's leg. A scruffy man at the bar was watching me with interest, and I left feeling his eyes on my back. How many people are in this spy business, I wondered.

Outside, I gave the umbrella a shake before raising it to cover myself and Lena. Smile, who had so rudely interrupted our cocktail hour, could figure out his own shelter. In any case he seemed oblivious to the rain. It poured down his shaved head in streams and he did not try to wipe it back. It was kind of eerie, like he was more machine than man.

I was tempted to cut across the manicured lawn, but deep puddles were forming already, and I did not want Lena to ruin her shoes. We stayed to the sidewalk, hanging back a few feet from Smile as he led us to the pier. Lena sat down on the wooden bench underneath the roof of the longtail, quickly shifting to the box in the middle to retreat further from the driving rain. She squeezed water from the ends of her blond hair, and I watched her with a sense of nostalgia. The death of King Ananda signalled the end of something, I thought. Both the old Siam and the future he had promised. History did not always mean progress. Chief Phao had been building his army of police, and now was his chance to come forward. He had no love of democracy. Despite his perfumed pomade, he was just a thug. Meanwhile, we had risked our necks trying to save the king, who had not in the end been saved.

I shook my head—what times we lived in, when crooks were more moral than cops.

CHAPTER TWENTY-NINE

WHEN KINGS DIE

I STARED RESENTFULLY at the back of Smile's head while Byron and I followed him down the hallway of the palazzo, the rubber soles of Byron's shoes squeaking from the soaking they'd got in the rain. My soles were leather, which meant they were quiet but probably ruined. Why couldn't that goon have let us be, happily drinking in the Oriental Hotel, instead of dragging us through a monsoon? I still regarded Smile more as a captor than an associate, since he had kept watch over me at the Sawasdee Hotel. He escorted us to the library, where we found Bill settled in his velvet chair like a king on his throne.

"I heard from Miss Maggie," he said.

Just the sound of her name brought my senses to a pitch of alarm. I sat down in the chair opposite Bill, clutching my pale blue purse. I did not want to speak to him, but this was something I couldn't let pass.

"Is she angry?" I asked.

"Do you think so?"

"King Ananda is dead. We were supposed to protect him."

"We were supposed to kill von Roth. We did that and we derailed Gaige's mission. Miss Maggie was happy. How she felt about saving the king is something else. She is a sphinx." He shook his head, stood up and started pacing. "But do you think she liked a king who was going to allow free elections that included Communists? Maybe they'd form the government. Prime Minister Pridi was getting too popular, and now the rumour mill says he planned the murder."

"Pridi?" Byron asked the window screen, his back still turned. "Don't you support him?"

Byron's behaviour was strange. He was like a statue. Did he hear someone outside? Of course, I was equally paralyzed sitting here in this chair. Bill always wanted to be the one in control, the puppet master. I wouldn't react to his revelations, because I knew it pleased him too well.

"I spread my dollars around," Bill said. "I ain't tarred by him. Anyhow, it will be a while before the local cops go after Pridi. They're waiting to be sure the Americans back them. The police say the king was playing with a gun in his bed. As if!" He stopped his pacing. "You two look wet. Need a towel or something?"

"No thanks," Byron said. I did not deign to answer. All I really wanted to know was what Miss Maggie was thinking or going to do.

"I insist. You're dripping on my floor. Smile!" he yelled. "Can we get some towels in here?"

He stood silently until Smile appeared, two perfectly folded white towels perched in the crook of his arm, this brute somehow playing the butler. Bill plucked a towel off and threw it at Byron, who moved too slowly to catch it, and had to pick it up from the floor. Meanwhile Bill was carrying the other towel to me and held it out, but I refused to take it. After an awkward moment he dropped it in my lap and sat down again.

"I find it interesting that a new director was appointed to the secret service today," Bill said. "Today of all days. General Vandenberg. And they're changing the name again. Now it's the Central Intelligence Group."

Goddamn it, I thought, how did Bill know all this? Did Miss Maggie confide in him to such a degree?

"You think it's connected to the king's murder?" Byron asked.

"Who knows? But we got to be careful until we know what it means for Miss Maggie. Is she on the way up, or down?"

Bill was astute if nothing else. I could not decide if she had hated the idea of using Nazis, or only hated Gaige. Which horse had she backed at the top? But knowing Miss Maggie, she had picked this General Vandenberg. She would frame her own manoeuvres to curry favour with him, even if they ran completely at odds to his agenda. She was capable of that.

"Is it possible Miss Maggie was behind this murder, now that she discredited Gaige?" Byron asked, patting his arms with the towel. "Does she have other agents?"

"By God, I admire your suspicions," Bill said. "But the answer, I do not know."

The idea Byron proposed was disturbing. I knew damn well she had other agents, but outside of a few key cryptologists, I had no idea what they did. However, her ambitions clearly extended beyond gathering intelligence and into covert action. And in that realm, I now believed anything was possible.

Bill picked up an envelope lying on the table. "Read this," he said, holding it out to me.

The envelope, I noted, had been opened—Bill, no doubt. Inside was a letter, encrypted. The last two code groups looked familiar, somehow.

"Pencil?" I asked.

I could tell, from the impatience in his face, that Bill had not been able to read the message. Despite this, he made a production of opening a drawer, pulling out a pencil, and examining it with maddening care. Then he pulled out a knife to sharpen it, the shavings falling to the floor, as I seethed. Finally, he handed it to me, the point sharp as a dagger, and for a moment I wished I could stab it right into his neck.

I fell to work on the transliteration.

It took me a moment to realize, but then I almost laughed. Miss Maggie had used the same key as the last message from her that I had decrypted on Shemya. I couldn't remember it perfectly, but it was enough. She evidently knew Bill would try to break the code and would fail, that he would watch me do it and be impressed by my swiftness. I had to be grateful for small pleasures, I supposed.

I laid down the pencil, nudging it a couple times to make sure it was parallel to the envelope. Link's family had been sent a Burma Star and a Burma Gallantry Medal in his name, I said to Byron. He would have a full military burial, with a flag draped over the casket and a bugler playing "Taps." I supposed Miss Maggie was doing that for me, since the dead have no further use for honour. Or at least, she wanted me to believe our mission had redeemed Link. To lessen my guilt. To ensure my cooperation going forward.

My breath caught in my throat, ragged. There was nothing more I could have done, was there? No one could have stopped him from going after von Roth. Link had died brave. He'd deserved those medals. By rights von Roth was dead because of him. Link led the hunt. I found the strength to kill because I was trying to save Link. I wiped at my eye. He died without forgiving me. How could I expect it, when he couldn't forgive himself, either? There was nothing worse than unfinished business, and sins that could not be undone, but there was no going back. I would just have to be stronger now. Harder. I composed myself.

I returned to the message, and read aloud that Miss Maggie's budget for Far East operations had been approved.

I paused over the last lines.

"What is it?" Byron asked.

"I'm not with the Shemya radio unit anymore. I'm a field agent. Assigned to Detachment 302."

"In case it ain't clear," Bill said, "that's headquartered in this room. We're a team, Lena. Just like old times."

Old times, Bill said. What were old times? Cruelty, blackmail, and lies? I'd told Bill there was nothing left of my love. He was just clutching at the past and wanted to forget all the parts in between.

To carry on with his old life as though he hadn't ruined it by his own actions. He'd never once apologized. We were over. I didn't want to be a team with him again, yet Miss Maggie was making it so.

I had to admit that part of me felt proud: I was a field agent. I had redeemed myself after Camp X, or maybe I had not failed there at all—maybe Miss Maggie had been waiting for the right time to use me. Maybe Bill hadn't abandoned us on the von Roth job as I'd thought. Siam had been my proving ground.

I was also a murderer now. That was something that could never be erased. Miss Maggie had me over a barrel, not only because of my past as a criminal, but because I'd killed an American agent, even if he was a Nazi. These were dark days. I almost longed for the simplicity of war. Everyone had agreed who the enemy was.

There was only silence. I realized that even the antique clock was not ticking. It was dead. Time had stopped.

"What about me?" Byron asked.

"You're in it too, of course," Bill said.

"That's good. I was worried for a minute." His eyes darted toward the window. "Did you know that the brainfever bird says different things, depending on the language of the listener? It makes sense, since everything's a matter of perspective."

I didn't know what the hell Byron was going on about—I hadn't heard any bird at all—but I couldn't be bothered to ask.

Bill went over to the ornate French sideboard and poured amber liquid from a crystal decanter into three glasses, which he put on a tray. "A toast," he said, proffering the tray to each of us. Reluctantly I took a glass, and Bill stared into my eyes so that I couldn't look away. "Now that we're spies," he said, "we'll get rich while we rip the secrets out of everyone." He turned to Byron and clinked his glass. "And you, By God, will count them up."

"What about saving democracy?" I asked. Partly sarcastic, and partly hoping that's what we were really about.

"I leave that to the politicians," Bill said. "The spymasters don't buy it. They just talk the talk when it suits them. What's an ideal except a weak spot? The arrow always goes into the neck, so you keep your neck covered."

Bill was right. Link had died because he wanted to restore his honour. I didn't want an end like that. I would have to predict everything that might come, and fight to make my own way within Miss Maggie's constraints. Bill seemed to have managed it. "I don't want to be bait for men," I said, putting my empty glass down on the sideboard. "That's what they always have women do. It's too boring. I want to be a full part of the front business."

"That's exactly the plan," Bill said. "Gems and opium provide cover to travel to some odd places. The Chinese Commies have spilled into Burma to regroup. Miss Maggie believes they'll win their war. China is next door to the Soviet Union. Commies everywhere now. There's work to do."

The Soviet Union. I felt a surge of excitement. Maybe I'd get there yet, as I'd wanted for so long, to finish my language research from before the war. Alone, if possible. Of course, I could still meet somebody out in the field. Love was a hazard and I apparently lacked judgment in this area. Link and Bill, two strikes. And to be honest with myself, had I not thought von Roth attractive before I knew he was a Nazi? I felt sick to think of it. I had a fifty-fifty chance of picking wrong again, and I did not play the roulette tables for this reason. I'd been independent for thirteen years—since I fled Bill—and wanted to stay that way. Maybe Byron still loved me a little, but not like when we were younger. I supposed that wouldn't interfere with our work. In fact, I could make use of it. He'd be my ally and he would protect me, even from Bill. It would be best if I could get away from Bill, though.

"Will she send me there? I speak Russian. Far as I know, I'm the only one," I said pointedly.

"If it comes to that, we'll all go."

Bill's eyes as he looked at me were so blue, deep and cold as ice off a glacier when it breaks away in spring. In innocent seas, a freed iceberg crushes ships and destroys people.

I would not be destroyed.

ACKNOWLEDGEMENTS

THIS BOOK WAS many years in the making. My most profound thanks to those who had faith in me when faith was hardest to come by: Richard Bausch, my mentor at the Humber School for Writers, and John Pearce, my tireless agent who holds the torch for literature. I am grateful to my great-aunt Sheelagh, who served in the Canadian Air Force in World War II on the West Coast. Hearing that she was involved in radio intelligence against the Japanese inspired Lena's profession. My deepest thanks also to Marcia Markland of Thomas Dunne, whose enthusiasm for *Speakeasy* led her to ask for a sequel, which had not been part of my original plan. It was so much fun to revisit my characters.

This is a work of historical fiction, and I have a master's degree in history, which makes me a bit of a fanatic. It led me to happily obsess for many, many hours over books about World War II, the "Far East" as it was then called, and the early CIA. This book is underpinned with many facts, and I tried my best for historical accuracy in broad strokes, but fiction necessitates some liberties. There are also facts that can never be known, particularly in the history of the secret service. The death of King Ananda by a bullet through the head was never solved, and the story that he was playing with a gun in bed is thin indeed. The early CIA was active in Southeast Asia during the years after the war, while pursuing better-known plots to overthrow governments in Guatemala and Iran; elsewhere, agents planned assassinations of Fidel Castro in Cuba and Patrice Lumumba in Congo. Following the grand actions of World War II, meddling in the highest levels of state in countries deemed at risk of Communism was an acceptable tactic. As well, the Americans really did recruit Nazis as secret agents against the Soviets, though they were not to my knowledge employed in Southeast Asia. However, the US chose Thailand as its base against Communism in Asia. Bill Donovan, the former head of the entire American secret service during World War II, was appointed ambassador there in 1953. Perhaps "ambassador" should be in quotation marks. He was well acquainted with the region, having struggled to demobilize his irregular OSS agents on the Burma border right after the war, because they "preferred to concentrate on the heroin trade" (*The Old Boys: The American Elite and the Origins of the CIA* by Burton Hersh). The early CIA supported Chief Phao Sriyanond of the Thai national police and armed his men. When Chief Phao's officers strangled, burnt, and buried five political figures in 1952, he said: "There is nothing under the sun that the Thai police cannot do" (*A History of Thailand* by Chris Baker and Pasuk Phongpaichit).

Other books on these topics that I found interesting or useful include: *The Secret Army: Chiang Kai-Shek and the Drug Warlords of the Golden Triangle* by Richard Michael Gibson and Wen H. Chen; *Siam Becomes Thailand: A Story of Intrigue* by Judith A. Stowe; *The Railway Man: A POW's Searing Account of War, Brutality, and Forgiveness* by Eric Lomax; *A Life for Every Sleeper: A Pictorial Record of the Burma-Thailand Railway* by Hugh V. Clarke; *Behind Japanese Lines: With the OSS in Burma* by Richard Dunlop; *Far Eastern File: The Intelligence War in the Far East, 1930–1945* by Peter Elphick; *OSS Special Weapons and Equipment: Spy Devices of WWII* by H. Keith Melton; *The Overseas Targets: War Report of the OSS (Office of Strategic Services)* by Kermit Roosevelt; *Spymistress: The Life of Vera Atkins, the Greatest*

Female Secret Agent of World War II by William Stevenson; *Code Warriors: NSA's Codebreakers and the Secret Intelligence War against the Soviet Union* by Stephen Budiansky; *Perilous Missions: Civil Air Transport and CIA Covert Operations in Asia* by William M. Leary; *Counterspy: Memoirs of a Counterintelligence Officer in World War II and the Cold War* by Richard W. Cutler; *The Very Best Men: The Daring Early Years of the CIA* by Evan Thomas; *Legacy of Ashes: The History of the CIA* by Tim Weiner; and *The Nazis Next Door: How America Became a Safe Haven for Hitler's Men* by Eric Lichtblau.

I found the recruitment of Nazis by the American secret service to be particularly chilling and wanted to raise awareness of it, as it seems largely forgotten. Frank Wisner—an OSS spymaster in Europe during World War II who became the CIA's head of covert action—recruited Gustav Hilger, a Nazi behind the SS Einsatzgruppen, the mobile killing squads that exterminated Roma and Jews (Thomas). A CIA officer apparently having moral qualms revealed in 1953: "We will pick up any man who will help us defeat the Soviets, any man regardless of what his Nazi record was" (Lichtblau).

On a more minute level of historical fandom, where possible I have used spellings common in that era, which have changed considerably. As an example, the grand palace's Gate of Supreme Victory used to be spelled Vises Jaisri in a 1930s guidebook, while the modern tourist brochure from my own visit to the palace spells it Visechaisri Gate. Street and canal names have also evolved, while Nakom Paton has been spelled in every possible variant. Siam was sometimes called Thailand in the period between 1932 and 1948, when the name because permanent. For simplicity's sake, I continued to use Siam in my book, on the assumption that most ordinary people would keep the ancient name out of habit and the fact that the Allies rejected the 1939 renaming by the Japanese puppet government.

Much gratitude and many hugs to those who have read my manuscript drafts over the years and provided creative feedback, including both friends who are professional writers or those just literary at heart. You know who you are, and please hit me up for a beer or three. My wordsmith mom stepped in when needed, while grants from the BC Arts Council and Access Copyright helped me soldier on. To my editorial gurus—at St. Martin's, Nettie Finn, and at Douglas & McIntyre, Caroline Skelton and Anna Comfort O'Keeffe—thank you for pushing me to be the best I could be. Any mistakes or follies are my own.

Most of all, my thanks to all the readers who still love to read.